Willa
of
Dark Hollow

Willa of

DARK HOLLOW

ROBERT BEATTY

DISNEY · HYPERION
LOS ANGELES NEW YORK

First Hardcover Edition, May 2021
First Paperback Edition, May 2022
1 3 5 7 9 10 8 6 4 2
FAC-025438-22091

Printed in the United States of America

This book is set in 12-pt Adobe Garamond Pro, Liam, Qilin/Fontspring; Minister Std/Monotype
Designed by Phil T. Buchanon

Library of Congress Control Number for Hardcover Edition: 2020936849
ISBN 978-1-368-00948-5

Visit www.DisneyBooks.com

The Great Smoky Mountains

1901

The world is neither flat nor round.

It’s *mountains.*

Willa pivoted toward the sound. The sharp, popping cracks of fracturing wood rolled like thunder through the forest air. Then came the rain-like noise of a thousand snapping branches and tearing leaves crashing down. When the massive trunk finally struck the ground, the earth shook beneath her bare feet. A gust of wind swept through the forest and blew through Willa's long bark-and-moss-colored hair. And as the realization of what had just happened sank into her mind, her chest filled with pain. The human loggers had cut down the great hemlock tree that lived at the bend of the river.

She stood frozen like a young deer.

It was a tree she had sat beside on sunlit mornings, watching the river flow past its roots, a tree she and her twin sister had curled up in on misty nights, gazing up through its outstretched branches toward the Great Smoky Mountain and the moon above. The trees of the forest had shrouded and sheltered her all her life. They had consoled her when her sister was killed. They were her earth and her soil, her sunlight and her song.

But now she heard the axmen chopping and sawing and shouting to each other, their harsh, barking words circling through the treetops like quarreling ravens. The quills on the back of her neck went up and a burst of heat flashed through her body. She knew she should flee this killing ground or blend her green skin into the leaves of the undergrowth and disappear from the coming human eyes. She must run from their tromping feet and escape their cutting blades.

But how could she run away when her friends were dying? How could she just leave them?

She had to stop the loggers, but she had no sharp claws or long teeth. She had no weapons or ability to fight. She didn't *hurt* living creatures, she *helped* them.

The human loggers had jagged metal saws, axes, knives, guns, animals in chains, vast metal contraptions for dragging murdered trees from the forest, and black, steaming beasts that rolled on long gleaming tracks. She was a lone thirteen-year-old Faeran girl without a clan. How could she fight the men of iron?

The crash of another tree broke like a wave through the forest, the wind of it brushing her cheek.

Her heart pounded in her chest.

She knew she couldn't protect the trees the way they had protected her. She couldn't shroud them or shelter them or hide them from the world.

But she couldn't just abandon them, either.

She took a few uncertain steps, her legs trembling. Her eyes watered with burning tears.

And then she ran toward the sound of the falling trees.

Willa plunged into a dense thicket of briars, whispering to the spiky plants as she pushed through them so their sharp, talon-like thorns would turn aside and glide across her bare skin and her woven-reed tunic without doing her any harm.

Beyond the thicket, she dashed through a stand of tall pines, nothing but soft, wet needles squishing beneath her feet.

The odor of burning brush touched her nostrils and she curled her lip in revulsion. The smoke drifting through the forest stung her eyes, and the stench of spilled sap filled the air.

She crept forward through the leafy underbrush, quieting her breathing. The skin of her face and arms tingled as it changed to the color of the leaves and branches around her. Thin green vines grew along her limbs and torso, enshrouding her, as if they knew she was more like them than like the loggers.

She finally stopped at the edge of a rocky ravine, crouched down, and looked across to the other side.

The oaks, chestnuts, and tulip trees—all the trunks of her dead friends—lay flat across the ground in long, helpless stretches, their limbs broken, their beautiful leaves ripped and crushed, and the skin of their bark gouged and torn. She knew she had to be quiet, but she couldn't help crying out at the sight of the slaughter. A surge of bile heaved up from her gut and burned as she swallowed it back down. The human loggers had felled many of the trees and were hacking at them now with axes and mauls, pulleys and chains, cutting them apart piece by piece.

All around the edges of the logging site, men stood with rifles in hand, gazing out into the forest. They looked like local hunters of some kind, with heavy beards, raccoon-skin hats, and knives at their sides. But they weren't hunting. They appeared to be guarding the loggers. Over the last year, she'd seen more and more logging crews coming into the mountains, but she had never seen these guards before. Something must have happened. Were they frightened of the wolves and other wild beasts they imagined haunted the ancient forest they were killing?

She had once thought of the long metal rifles as *fire-sticks*—vile, mysterious weapons that killed animals from a distance—but since then she had learned so much, about humans and her own kind, about guns and trees, about greed and love, and about herself as well.

As she gazed across the ravine, she could see the great hemlock tree she had come for. Her heart sank when she saw that her old friend—once towering to the sky with its mighty branches—was now lying across the forest floor like a toppled giant.

The massive tree had crushed many of the trees around it when it came down, no longer their ally and protector, but their destroyer. More than a dozen men were standing on its severed stump.

Her grandmother had told her that this tree had sprouted from the ground and splayed its first needles to the sun more than five hundred years ago, and it had been a beloved friend of the Faeran people living in the hidden coves of these mountains ever since. Now these men cheered and congratulated each other for bringing down such a gargantuan prize.

The logging crew had cut down many smaller trees, too—beeches and maples—and the carcasses were being pulled by mules over mile-long slides toward the logging train farther down the mountain. Young cherry trees and birches had fallen victim as well, the thin saplings, green and fine, slashed and trampled and dragged to their death. Willa clenched her teeth and pulled air in through her nose to try to calm herself. But it was to no avail. She had seen it before: the humans would leave nothing but dead, bare ground.

As she looked toward the hemlock, she realized that even though the humans had cut it down, her friend was still alive, its sap still circulating through its trunk and limbs, its leaves still pulling in sunlight and breathing out air. The trees around it would continue to provide nourishment to the stump through their interconnected roots, trying to keep their wounded brother alive, for trees do not just *compete* for sunlight and water, they *cooperate*, hold each other aloft, protect each other from the wind, and share nutrients among them, the strong giving to the weak. Lying on the forest floor, a fallen tree would take months, sometimes years, to die, and even then it wouldn't be truly dead. Lichen and mushrooms and tiny flowers would grow from its sides. The small beginnings of new trees would sprout from it. Beetles and millipedes and other tiny creatures would live beneath its aging bark. And foxes would make dens in the hollows of its bones. A tree in the forest didn't die in the normal sense of the word—it changed shape into a thousand other lives.

But none of that was going to happen now. The humans were stripping the bark from the felled hemlock's trunk. They did not value the wood of hemlock trees. But they craved the acid of its tanbark, which they used to turn the skin of dead animals into the clothing they wore. When they were done tearing the bark from her friend, they would cut the trunk and limbs into sections, drag them away, and slice them into thousands of long, rectangular pieces to be sold as junk wood.

Willa wanted to help the tree, to heal its wounds, to stop the sap from pouring from its ancient soul, to bring it back up into the sky as she had done for so many of the plants in the forest. But the loggers were everywhere, surrounding it, attacking it. And even if she could somehow get through them, the great hemlock was just far too large for her to heal or raise. It would have taken a hundred Faeran woodwitches to do such a thing. And as far as she knew, she and her grandmother, who had died the year before, had been the last.

She watched helplessly from the forest at the edge of the ravine, trying to figure out what she could do. She knew she shouldn't be here. The humans, the machines, the guns, the falling trees . . . it was far too dangerous. Nathaniel and Hialeah, her adopted father and sister, were going to be angry if they found out she had gotten this close to the loggers.

But as long as she remained in the forest, she could change the color of her skin and hair and eyes to match her surroundings, and the humans would never see her.

As the men cut into the trunk of another tree and then shouted as it crashed to the ground, an aching pain filled Willa's chest and her eyes blurred with tears. She could barely see. She was becoming so intently focused on the horror of what the loggers were doing across the ravine that she stopped paying attention to what was around her.

And that was a mistake.

She jolted in surprise when she heard a loud, moaning roar and heavy, pounding footfalls just behind her. She spun around. It was a bear, just a few strides away. Rushing straight at her.

The bear charged toward her with its biting teeth and tearing claws. She shrank into a crouch, raising her arms to protect her head. But at the last second, the bear abruptly turned and ran the other way. Willa blinked in confusion, wondering what had happened. But then the bear pivoted and came right back at her. It swung up onto its hind legs, standing tall, immense, but facing away from her now, and then it dropped again, pounding its front paws against the ground, blowing air through its mouth and clacking its teeth. The bear wasn't attacking her. It was pacing back and forth along the edge of the cliff and looking down into the ravine.

Willa scuttled forward and peered over the edge.

Her heart lurched when she saw a small black bear cub trapped at the bottom of the ravine, where a fast stream was gushing down the mountain. The little bear was scraping at the rock wall with his paws, frantically trying to climb to his mother. Willa watched as he tried and tried again, clawing and whimpering. He was just a tiny thing. He couldn't even get started.

He climbed a few lengths of his body and then slid down again, bawling to his mother high above.

"Come on, little guy, you can do it . . ." Willa whispered to herself.

The cub managed to scrabble onto a small boulder, getting himself a little higher.

"Good . . ." Willa said, encouraging him.

From there the cub began making his way slowly up the sheer face of the rock wall, hooking his claws into the cracks and crevices of the stone and pulling himself up. The higher he got, the more confident he became, his little legs pumping as he climbed faster and faster.

"Please don't fall . . ." Willa said beneath her breath, her heart beating fast as she watched him. She couldn't believe it, but he was doing it. The little guy just kept going, scaling the wall, straight up toward his mother. He climbed past jutting rocks and large boulders. *He's going to make it!*

But then, right at the top of the cliff, just a few feet from his mother, he reached an area of loose gravel and it crumbled beneath him. He scraped rapidly with his claws, but there was nothing for them to hang on to. The cub began sliding back down the wall, his four legs splayed out as he desperately tried to hold on, howling for his mother as he fell. He hit a rock and tumbled, down, down, down, all the way through the boulders and jagged stone, until his little black body hit the bottom of the ravine and went into the water. Willa gasped. The cub just lay there, half in the water, half on the rocks. Completely unmoving.

His mother snorted and paced. She lunged her massive shoulders over the edge and tried to go down to him, but the gravel immediately shifted around her feet, forcing her back. Another step and she'd fall to her death.

As Willa watched the tiny black lump in the bottom of the ravine, she breathed one, two, three times. *Get up, little bear, get up!* Four, five, six . . .

Finally, the lump moved. Willa's chest swelled. The little bear got himself up onto his feet and shook himself off. Then he gazed up at the top of the cliff and cried for his mother. She grunted in return, urging him to try again.

Willa looked across the ravine. The loggers were still hacking and chopping away. The guards with the guns had not yet heard the bears, but she knew they soon would.

She took several slow, deep breaths . . . in and out . . . in and out . . . trying to think it through.

Never go near the logging sites, Willa, her father had warned her many times. *They're too dangerous, especially for you.*

Willa knew he was right. The world was changing and she couldn't stop it. There was nothing she could do to protect the trees from the loggers. But as she gazed out from the foliage, she thought that maybe she could help the mother bear and her little cub. Maybe she could do this one good thing.

She stepped out from the cover of the trees. And then she darted past the mother bear, turned around, and slid feetfirst over the edge of the cliff.

She plummeted down the steep wall of the ravine, her hands dragging across the craggy rock as she tried to slow her fall. The gorge was as deep as a tree was high. By the time she made it to the bottom, she was panting for breath and her palms and fingers were bleeding.

Her skin tingled as she reflexively blended into the gray and brown rocks around her. She thought that becoming one with her surroundings would calm her, let her catch her breath, but then her ear twitched. She immediately looked up at the other side of the ravine, expecting to see the loggers or some other kind of danger. Her senses were seldom wrong. She scanned the cliff. But strangely, no one was there.

She made her way through the boulders toward the cub. The little bear gazed at her with his small, brown, pleading eyes. He whined louder and louder as she got closer, desperate for her to reach him. If she had been a human, he would have run from her in terror. But he did not fear her. She wasn't his mother, but he knew she'd come to help him.

"Dela dua mar, eeluin," she whispered in the Faeran language. *Time to go, little one.*

Just as she was about to reach out and take hold of the cub, she felt a prickling sensation in the quills on the back of her neck. She quickly turned and looked at the wall of the ravine. Goose bumps flashed cold up her arms. Something was there, even if she couldn't see it. She was sure of it. As she traced her eyes across the rocks, she couldn't make out anything unusual, but one thing was clear: she and the cub needed to get out of this place as quickly as possible.

She bent down and lifted the cub onto her shoulders. *"Telic meh una, eeluin." We're going to have to climb, little one.*

Knowing exactly what to do, the cub clung to her back and wrapped his legs around her torso. Willa winced as the baby bear's claws dug into her sides. She could barely breathe, but at least she knew he wouldn't fall off.

Willa heard the sound of shifting gravel behind her. She immediately spun around, ready for an attack. But no one was there. She frowned, studying the rocks. She could have sworn someone had been sneaking up behind her. But she didn't have time to search.

She turned back to the rock wall and began to climb. Her fingers gripped the crevices, and her toes found small ledges to push against, but the weight of the cub on her back was making the ascent far more difficult than she had expected. She reached a handhold above her head and tried to pull herself up to it, but her fingers were slippery with blood and she lost her grip. Her gut dropped as her hands flailed for something to grab on to. And then, suddenly, something was pushing her from below. Actual *hands* were shoving her upward. And then a shoulder was supporting her.

"I've gotcha," a girl's voice said.

"Wha . . . Who are you?" Willa sputtered as she looked down, but couldn't see who was helping her.

"Just climb!" the girl said, pushing.

Knowing it was her only chance, Willa reached up again, clamped her fingers onto a crevice, and hoisted herself. Then she grabbed the crack above that and reached for the next. Hand over hand she climbed, one hold after another, the clinging cub whimpering as they went higher and higher.

"You've got it now!" came the voice from the bottom of the ravine.

Willa looked down and saw the pale face of a human girl gazing up at her. She appeared to be about twelve or thirteen, and her long hair was the color of wheat.

"You can do it!" the girl called up to her, nodding encouragingly. "But you've got to hurry—they're coming!"

Willa didn't want to turn away from the girl. But she felt her arm muscles shaking, her fingers slipping from their holds.

Willa reached up to the next crack, and then the next one. She climbed past the largest of the boulders and the jagged stones. She was almost to the top. When she spotted a cluster of small yellow flowers hanging over the edge of the cliff, she gasped with hope. She just had to reach those flowers! But then a ledge of rock beneath her right foot broke away and she slipped. Half climbing, half running, she scrambled up the wall of the ravine, no choice but to ascend as fast as she could, her hands and feet throwing gravel behind her. The little bear squealed in terror. The roaring mother slapped at the ground above. With one last, desperate leap, Willa flung herself up and grabbed hold of the momma bear's massive paw, clenching her fingers around the thick, curving claws. The huge bear's flailing motion dragged her upward. Willa's arm scraped across a rock, tearing her skin.

Her face was jammed into the earth, and she got a mouthful of dirt. But still she held on. The instant she felt the woody vines of jessamine underneath her hands at the top of the cliff, she panted out, *"Florena!"* The vines twisted around her wrists and fingers, grabbing hold of her. She got a knee up over the edge of the cliff, and then a leg. Gasping for air, she finally clambered onto the level ground and collapsed, the vines retreating and the cub tumbling away from her.

Willa quickly wiggled back over to the edge and looked down into the ravine. The wheat-haired girl, whoever she was, was gone.

The mother bear and the little cub came together, pushing and rubbing against each other, making the deep, rhythmic pulsing sound that Willa knew meant they were extremely happy to be reunited. As the mother bear sat down and pulled the cub into a sweeping embrace, she caught Willa as well, and held her and the cub against her body while nuzzling them both with her massive snout. Willa's skin turned as black and textured as the bear's fur and she disappeared into the mother bear's chest. The heat of the bear's body and the heavy, musky smell engulfed her. The thick fur pressed against her mouth and nose almost smothered her, but Willa didn't care. She was just relieved that she'd been able to help them.

"Look over there!" a man shouted from across the ravine.

Startled, Willa hunkered down. The loggers and the guards were gathering on the other side, some of them pointing in her direction.

"It's a bear!" one of the loggers shouted.

"Lordy, look at that thing," said another. "It's gotta be three hundred pounds!"

Understanding the danger of the humans, the mother bear began to hurry away, grunting for her cub to keep close. Willa ran with them, her head low as she blended into their black fur.

A stout, commanding man on a dark brown horse rode up to the other men across the ravine. "Don't just stand there gawping at it," he demanded. "It'll feed the whole camp. Shoot it!"

The guards raised their rifles to their shoulders and fired.

Willa screamed as she wrapped her body around the cub and the gunshots split the sky.

The bullets hit in rapid succession.

The little cub in Willa's arms convulsed, whimpering and clinging to her.

The mother bear stopped running and slumped to the ground with a guttural groan, the air pushed from her lungs by her own weight. Willa was dragged down with her. The cub scrambled from Willa's arms and burrowed into the thick black fur of his mother's chest.

The mother bear grunted to her cub and tried to pull him closer with a sweep of her paw, but it was no use. She was too weak. Willa watched helplessly as the bear struggled to turn her giant head and move her once-powerful back legs to get her cub to safety, but the injured animal was unable to rise from the ground.

Willa breathed faster and faster, her chest tightening. It felt like she was suffocating. She pressed her trembling hands to the bullet holes, trying to keep the blood inside the mother bear. *"Neah da eesha,"* she whispered. *Just hold on.* But the warm liquid oozed between her fingers. She couldn't stop it from coming.

"The bear's still moving!" one of the men shouted as he pointed across the ravine.

"No, there's a cub next to it!" said another.

"But do you see that? There's something else there, too . . ." another man said, his voice sharp with fear.

Willa crouched closer to the mother bear's body, her hands black and red as she pressed them to the bear's wounds. *"Neah da eesha,"* she whispered again, but the mother bear's head was lying on its side now, and she was taking long, labored breaths, as if it was all in the world she could do.

The little cub pressed his snout to his mother's muzzle as he made soft, pleading sounds, begging her to wake up. Willa could see that he desperately wanted to run from this terrible place and escape the humans, but he wouldn't leave her.

"We need to get the meat," the foreman said as he pulled the reins around and pivoted his horse. "Get over there and finish the job."

The three guards slung their rifles over their shoulders and clambered down into the ravine.

Willa's chest seized with panic. *"Un dae uusa!"* she urged the mother bear, pushing against her body, trying to get her to her feet. *We need to go!*

But it was impossible.

The three humans, who had now reached the bottom of

the ravine, were wearing leather coats made from the skins of animals they had killed. One wore a coonskin cap on his head. The other had what looked like a necklace of bear claws. And all three of them carried knives on their leather belts.

As they scaled the wall of the ravine toward her and the bears, Willa could smell the stench of their bodies and the sharp tinge of gunpowder. They climbed hand over hand up the cliff, just as she had moments before.

Willa's lungs were heaving. Her heart was in her throat. The little bear grunted and squealed as he pushed at his mother's head.

"Un dae uusa!" Willa urged the mother bear again.

The bear opened her deep brown eyes and just gazed at her.

There were no sounds between them. But Willa could see the look in her eyes. She knew what the mother bear wanted her to do.

Willa didn't think she *could* do it. But she swallowed, and then nodded, touching the mother bear's snout gently with her hand. *"Un daca,"* she whispered. *I promise, I will.*

Willa turned toward the three grim-faced humans as they climbed up over the edge of the cliff like snarling predators. They drew their long, sharp metal knives and came toward her and the bears.

Having no choice now, Willa knew what she must do.

Willa leaped to her feet.

"Watch out!" One of the startled hunters gasped as he stumbled back in surprise. The second hunter slashed the air with his knife as if she were an attacking animal. But Willa snatched up the squalling cub and darted into the forest.

"What in tarnation was that?" asked the third hunter in wide-eyed confusion about what they had all just seen: something half bear, half leafy bush, but then a glimpse of arms and legs, almost human, and then just a blur of black and green.

Willa raced through the stand of pines, her heart hammering as she carried the little bear away. She had promised the dying mother that she would protect the cub, and that's exactly what she intended to do.

As she ran, tears welled in her eyes, but she clenched her teeth and kept on going. She knew that somewhere behind her the hunters were finishing their work, that the mother bear was passing away, and that the Great Mountain would absorb her blood and bones back into the earth to bring life to the trees around her.

Willa delved deep into a remote area of the forest, breathing so hard that her lungs ached. Seeing her opportunity for escape, she plunged into the green wall of a laurel slick and climbed. No human could pass through these impenetrable thickets of rhododendron, but the plants allowed her to slip through them. The cub in her arms cried and struggled, his claws digging into her, his snout pressing hot against her neck. He was trying to get away from her, desperate to return to his mother. What he didn't realize was that there was nothing but men and metal behind them now, loggers with their tree-chopping axes and hunters with their bear-killing guns and skinning knives. She hated them all, but she couldn't fight them. She hadn't been able to protect either the great hemlock or the mother bear. She just clung to the cub like she'd promised and kept running.

She climbed a high ridge, went down into the shadowed, forested glen on the other side, and then up again toward the top of the Great Mountain, putting as much difficult terrain between her and the humans as she could so they wouldn't be able to follow her.

Her arms and shoulders ached from carrying the cub. When she finally slowed to a walk and set him down, she expected him to cling to her, lost and scared. But as soon as his feet touched the ground, he immediately pulled free of her and ran away, calling out for his mother in a whimpering howl.

Willa snapped her quills in frustration. He was going to end up right back in the hands of the hunters.

She pulled in a long, deep breath. She didn't *want* to go back to that place, with all its death and destruction. And she knew she *shouldn't* go. But once again it felt as if she had no choice but to do what she knew she had to do.

She ran to catch him.

"*Charka,*" Willa said beneath her breath as she chased the little cub. The grunting sound his mother had used to call him reminded Willa of the Faeran word *charka,* which meant *determined,* so that was the name she gave him as she ran.

She knew that Charka didn't fully understand or accept that his mother had passed away, but she was sure he remembered the terrible fear he had felt when he saw his mother lying on the ground, and the frightening scent of the humans, and the terror of their menacing faces as they came at him with their knives. Still the brave little cub was running back to his momma, to help her, to *save* her, to reunite with the only love and protection he had ever known.

Willa chased Charka through a dense thicket of twisting branches that seemed determined to slow her down until she asked them to kindly let her through. She had expected Charka to go downhill, back in the direction of his mother near the logging site, but for some reason he was rushing *up* the mountain. Had the shock of losing his mother bewildered the little bear's mind? Or was he just plain lost? Either way, she had to catch him.

She followed him so far up through the narrow gorges of the mountain that she was getting closer and closer to the burned-out ruins of the lair where she and the rest of the Faeran people had once lived. Trekking along the northern slope, just below where the lair had been, she passed through a shaded stand of black-and-white-trunked birch trees with heart-shaped leaves. The ground was covered with a thick carpet of dark green moss so cold that it felt as if there must be frost in the earth beneath it. Her grandmother had told her that places like this were the relics of an ancient past when massive sheets of ice had come down from the north until they were stopped by the Great Mountain and its surrounding brothers and sisters. The trees, the Faeran, the animals, and all manner of forest life had hidden in these highest places for hundreds of years, and when the ice receded, they spread back out into the rest of the mountainous world.

When she finally caught up with Charka, the little bear had slowed to a walk. He was looking back and forth at the dense canopy of the trees. Willa thought he must be worried about why the forest had suddenly become so dark. Whatever had caused him to finally slow down, she sighed in relief, happy that she hadn't lost him.

But then she saw what he was peering at.

Thousands of small glowing lights—green and white and blue—were floating above their heads in the branches of the trees. They looked almost like fireflies, but she knew that was impossible. It was too cold here, and it was *daytime*. And unlike any group of fireflies she had ever seen light up the evening forests and meadows of other places, there wasn't just a single species or color here. It was as if she and Charka were witnessing a great gathering of many types of fireflies—the green kind that came out in the spring in the lower valleys, and the rare whitish kind that sometimes emerged high on the slope of the Great Mountain in the late summer, and even the low, hovering blue ghost fireflies that haunted the hidden coves. They were all here, floating in the shadows beneath the canopy of the trees, as if time and place had no meaning to them anymore.

Willa looked around, trying to understand what kind of place this was. It was hard to tell because of the crowdedness of the trees, but they appeared to be in a hollow, a shallow depression in the mountainous terrain. There was a dark and eerie beauty to it all, but her palms went cold and sweaty. The trees of the hollow were short and squat with twisted trunks and low-hanging crooked limbs, so lifeless and still that it seemed as if there had never been a breeze or living being here. And the bark of the trees wasn't brown and craggy like she was used to, but black and smooth and wet. The tangle of branches overhead was so thick that no sunlight at all touched the damp, oily ground. And when she peered into a small forest stream, it was so shaded that the fish had no eyes and the scuttling crawdads were the color of bones, like creatures that lived in caves.

What is all this? Willa wondered again, the fine hair on her arms tingling. Over the years of her life, she'd been all up and down the slope of this mountain, and this dark place had not been here before. It seemed impossible, but this place was *new.*

She caught the vague form of a disturbingly familiar shape out of the corner of her eye. As she turned, Willa pulled in a long, uncertain breath. In a rocky crevice far above her, the skeleton of a massive, ancient tree hung upside down, wedged there by the flow of a river a thousand years before. Her people had called it the Watcher. The bare, weatherworn frame of a tree had once marked the entrance to Dead Hollow, the lair where the Faeran had lived. But it, too, had changed. Its whitish gray trunk was now scorched and black. Dead Hollow had burned to the ground the year before and it had been abandoned ever since, nothing left there but the gray ashes of the whispering past.

The place she was standing now was just below where the lair had been, as if the remnants of her home had toppled down the mountain and landed here. Or as if it had *grown* here, oozing from the earth like a bizarre, fast-growing fungus. Dead Hollow had become Dark Hollow.

Willa turned in a slow circle as she tried to comprehend all that she was seeing.

She took a few steps forward, uncertain. Charka followed her closely, making a nervous chattering sound with his jaw.

Willa squinted through the darkness. She could see that there were ferns growing beneath the black trees. And among the ferns lay many sets of deer antlers, as if bucks had done battle here for a hundred years.

She took a few more steps, wondering what peculiar thing she was going to see next. Cast across the ground were what looked like the horned skulls of hundreds of bison—massive forest beasts that had been killed off by the humans long before she was born, and that she only knew from her grandmother's stories and the paintings on the cave walls in the old Faeran lair.

Bison bones? None of this had been here before.

As Willa moved forward, she heard a crackling sound, like the breaking of many tiny sticks, and she felt small, sharp fragments beneath her feet. When she looked down, she saw that she and Charka were standing in an area of wet, blackened soil strewn with the bone-white skeletons of thousands of raven wings and small birds, bobcats and otters, and bizarre creatures she didn't recognize.

"Come on," Willa said to Charka, pulling him along by the shoulder, anxious to get out of this strange, shadowed place. Of all the spots he could have gone, what had brought him here?

As she quickly led him away from the carpet of bones and into the ferns, she noticed that there were many flowers blooming here, but their petals were an unusual mix of dark purple and deep maroon, and the leaves were a shade of blackish green she had never seen before. The center of the blossoms seemed to glow with reddish light. And the leaves and petals appeared to be covered in a clear, shiny coating as if they were frozen in time. An iridescent blue butterfly—a type she had only seen in the sunlit meadows of early spring—flitted through the darkness above the ferns.

It was a place of impossibilities.

Then something scurried across the ground in front of her. She and Charka jumped, startled by the sudden movement. It took her a moment to realize that it was nothing more than a chipmunk. But then she noticed that its fur wasn't brown, but whitish-gray. And when the rodent stopped and its tiny head looked up at her, its eyes were smoldering with what looked like black smoke.

Startled, Willa quickly turned and went in the opposite direction. Charka followed her closely, his shoulder pressed against her leg.

As they hurried through the blackened trees, she began to see grotesque growths of orange and yellow slime mold all over their trunks and roots. Then she saw something even more disturbing.

At various spots on the forest floor, there were patches of mushrooms in the shapes of fallen human or Faeran bodies, as if the travelers before her had collapsed to the ground and the fungi had consumed their decaying bodies and thrived. The place smelled of sickly rot. Had the stench overwhelmed the previous travelers? Or were the previous travelers the source of the stench?

The idea that a human or Faeran could become something else, something so *changed*, sent a shiver down Willa's spine. She looked up, hoping to see the top of the Great Mountain, to find some reassurance in its ever-presence, but all she could see was the looming shape of the Watcher against the black-barked trees that blocked out the sky.

Charka grunted and ran ahead of her. Willa thought he must be terribly frightened of this place—and she couldn't blame him—but she soon realized it was far more than that. He stopped and turned and gazed around at the forest, his eyes watering as if he had just sensed something of miraculous importance. He snuffled the ground repeatedly, and then raised his head and sniffed the air, turning this way and that. It was as if he thought his mother was here, nearby, with them. He rose onto his hind legs and bawled for her, then went back down on all fours and scrabbled frantically at the dirt with his claws as if he could dig his way to her. He crashed into a thicket of fetter-bush and then rushed out again. Willa ran forward to help him before he hurt himself. But just at that moment, Charka stopped dead still.

Everything went quiet.

The air around them changed.

Charka was standing on his hind legs and staring at some-thing in the undergrowth.

Willa's pulse began to thump. But before she could figure out what the cub was looking at, she felt the earth beneath her feet start to seep and tremble. The gnarled roots of the trees around her seemed to be vibrating, making the skin all over her body itch. The smell of rotting wood emanated from the ground. Her throat went cold. It was summer, but she could see her breath in the air.

She heard a gritty, scraping noise as something disturbed the soil in front of her. The earth swelled beneath her feet and she stumbled back, pulling Charka with her. The dirt and gravel rose into a mound, broke apart, and fell away. Up through the ground emerged the head and body of a twisting snakelike creature. Unlike any natural animal she had ever seen, it was a foot thick and at least ten feet long. And its slimy, dark gray skin appeared to be smoking, as if it were disintegrating before her eyes, like some sort of phantasm in a nightmare. It slid across the ground in a rapid, sidewinding fashion between the trunks of the trees, making a raspy, crackling sound. And it was coming right for them.

"Watch out, Charka!" Willa shouted as she pulled the terrified cub back from the snake's path. A second snake, thinner and faster, burst through the ferns behind them, its long, serpentine body winding across the forest floor.

Willa yanked Charka to a small, blackened tree and they scrambled up the trunk. Charka cowered and whimpered, clutching her leg as they huddled together, shrinking from the snakes.

"Don't move . . ." she whispered, trying to hold him tight, but her entire body was shaking uncontrollably.

The two of them watched, their eyes wide, as the snakes slid past the base of the tree.

The dark gray skin of the beasts seemed to be wet with slime, and the stench was horrible.

As the snakes slithered into the ferns on the other side of the tree, Willa stayed right where she was, still trembling, waiting like a little rabbit after a hawk flies by, too spooked to move.

The smell and the icy cold air finally began to recede.

Willa kept watching, terrified that the creatures would turn back toward her and Charka and attack. But the snakes, or whatever they were, moved farther and farther away and finally disappeared into the underbrush in the distance.

"I think they're gone," Willa whispered.

Charka grunted, telling her he was all right.

But what had they just seen? The creatures had gone in the same direction Charka had been running moments before, back toward his mother. But why? What were they?

After climbing down the tree, Willa set Charka on the ground and hugged him. He clung to her, trembling, clearly as shaken as she was, and when he looked up at her, she could see the uncertainty in his eyes.

"Come on, we're getting out of here," she said, and he stayed right with her.

When they found their way up to higher ground, back among the green, living, sunlit trees, she felt relief pour through her.

Charka paused and looked over his shoulder toward the dark hollow behind them, staring at it for a long time. When he finally turned away and gazed up at Willa, she could see that something had changed in his eyes, as if something in that place had finally made him realize that his mother was truly gone and the girl standing beside him was his only remaining companion.

"De lia, eeluin, harn da una," she said softly as she gathered him into her arms. *Don't worry, little one, you're coming home with me.*

As Willa followed the faint trace of an old fox path through what seemed like a very natural and normal part of the forest, she felt her tension unwinding. She and Charka had put Dark Hollow hours behind them, and she was more than just relieved; she felt lucky to be alive.

The cub trundled along beside her, speeding up when she sped up, and slowing down when she slowed down. He was a quick and limber little guy, but so young and small that he was clumsy sometimes, tripping over his own paws or falling over a branch, and then running forward to catch up with her again.

Willa took in everything around her as she walked—the movement of the squirrels foraging in the undergrowth, the song of a flycatcher singing in the branches above her head, and the leaves of the trees sweeping gently back and forth, as if in time to the steady thrum of the afternoon cicadas. As she and

Charka trekked past moss-covered rocks and babbling streams, she was just glad to be heading home.

Home. The word had come to mean something so different to her over the last year.

The lives of the Faeran had once been beautifully intertwined with the forest, but by the time Willa was born, her clan had become rife with violence, hunger, and decay—the last remnants of a desperate and dying people. She and her twin sister, Alliw, had been raised by their parents in the old ways of the Faeran. But when Willa was six years old, the guards of the padaran—the new leader of the clan—killed her mother, father, and sister in a single night. In the six years that followed, Willa's grandmother had cared for her and taught her the ancient lore of the woodwitches. Willa ended up becoming the very thing that the padaran most despised: a guardian of the old ways.

Sometimes Willa wondered about the things that had happened in the past and all the choices she had made. And as she walked down the path toward home with Charka, it all started welling up again, like black mud oozing from an old creek bottom.

She knew her grandmother had taught her the old Faeran ways out of love for both her and her people, but sometimes Willa wondered if her grandmother had always intended for her to one day rise up against the padaran and destroy him. Had she *planned* for Willa to do the things she did? Had the choices Willa made been her own, or had they come from the seeds that had been planted long before? She wondered at what point a young Faeran was supposed to stop living out the choices of her parents and grandparents and start making her own. Was there a certain age? When she was twelve? Thirteen? Or did the choices just begin to flow into each other, like one river blending into another?

Earlier that day, when the mother bear and the little cub had needed her help, did she have any choice but to help them? She knew it wasn't the decision her adopted father would have wanted her to make—and he definitely wasn't going to be happy about it. But had it truly been her own decision, or had it come from the way her parents and her grandmother had raised her?

Willa and Charka came to the rushing white water of a tumbling, boulder-strewn river. A faint human-made path ran along its bank. One way led miles downstream, past the homes of a few other mountain families and toward a distant town she'd never been to. The other led upstream, farther up the mountain, into the largest of the trees, and toward her home. That was the path she followed.

The year before, when Willa had risen up against the padaran, it had led not only to his death, but also to the murder of her beloved grandmother, the burning of the lair in which the Faeran people had lived for generations, and the collapse of the entire clan. The last few hundred of them had been left to fend for themselves, like bees scattered to the wind without a hive. And the members of her clan blamed *her* for the destruction of all that they had known and depended on. Could she have chosen *not* to throw the spear and save the wolf that day? Could she have decided *not* to go back and release the human children from the padaran's prisons? Had all those been *her* choices? Or were all the branches of the tree of her life already growing by the time she had the roots she needed to stand aloft?

As she and Charka traveled, she looked out through the forest toward the layers of misty blue mountains cascading in the distance. She caught a glimpse of the Great Smoky Mountain far above her, with its gentle rounded top and its vast body sloping down into the world. Throughout all the turmoil of her life, it felt as if the Great Mountain had always been with her, watching over her.

When she and Charka came to her favorite grove of beautiful oak trees, she said to them, *"Ena dua un, dunum far." It's good to see you, my friends.*

Finally, she stepped out of the forest into an open area of green grass. A man-made lair—what the humans called a *house*—stood before them.

The house had a slanted, shake-shingled roof and windows across the front, and steps that led up to a wide, railed porch. And beside the house grew a large walnut tree that reached above the roof and into the sky.

After her grandmother was killed, Willa had been lost in anguish, wandering without hope until the day she encountered a man working in this yard, tears streaming down his face. She had finally found a home for her broken heart with this human whose heart had been broken even worse than her own. His name was Nathaniel. She and this man had started out as enemies, but once they had become friends and allies, once they had become *father* and *daughter*, nothing could pull them apart.

They were all choices she had made, one after the other, but as she walked now through the evening wood and stepped into the yard in front of the house, it felt as if, strange as it all was, there was no other path she could have followed except the path of her own heart.

Nathaniel was just coming out through the front door, putting his wide-brimmed slouch hat on his head and gripping his hiking stick in his hand. He appeared to be going out to tend to their orchards before it got too dark. He was a tall, rugged-looking man, with the hint of a beard and mustache. He wore a long-sleeved white shirt with a brown vest, along with plain trousers and a leather belt. Stopping in mid-stride, he paused there on the porch, as if he sensed something. As he lifted his head, his face became slowly visible beneath the brim of his hat. When his soft blue eyes landed on her, he smiled as only Nathaniel could smile, and it warmed her soul.

Hialeah, her fifteen-year-old adopted sister, came out onto the porch right behind him, nearly as straight and tall as he was, but with the beautiful long black hair of her Cherokee mother, who had been slain the year before. Remembering that she had quarreled with Hialeah earlier that morning, Willa felt a pang of guilt. They had argued about who had—or had *not*—helped their father gather the chicken eggs the previous day. Sharp and crooked words had followed like splintered sticks and Willa had stormed off into the forest. It seemed so foolish now. Seeing her sister standing there on the porch looking at her, all Willa wanted to do was run to her and hug her.

Through all the destruction of the tree-cutting men of iron and the shattered Faeran clan, through all the death and conflict that had been the soil of her life, she had found a kind of sunlight that she had never expected: a home among humans.

"Why did you bring home a bear?" Hialeah asked, frowning as she looked at Willa and her new companion. "Last week there was a pack of wolves wandering around our woods looking for you in the middle of the night, and now you have a bear?"

"Let's talk about this calmly, girls," Nathaniel said, stepping between them.

Willa liked that her father looked at her sister before he looked at her. She definitely thought Hialeah deserved the look more than she did. But then he turned and Willa felt the full weight of his eyes on her, too.

"I'm being calm," she said.

"So, who's this little guy?" he asked, gesturing toward the cub peering out at him from behind her leg.

"This is Charka."

Nathaniel reached out his open hand, but Charka quickly scuttled around to the other side of her legs for protection.

"And why is he here?" Nathaniel asked, clearly trying to keep his voice even and fair.

"He's my friend," Willa replied.

"You can't keep him, if that's what you're thinking," Hialeah said firmly as she walked toward them.

"Why not?" Willa asked, looking up at her.

"Bears don't belong in the house," Hialeah said.

"Neither do I!" Willa snapped right back at her.

"Willa, no." Her father's voice was like a boulder coming to a stop at the bottom of a hill. He considered them both, and then turned to Willa. "I'm afraid Hialeah's right," he said softly, "Bears don't belong in the house. Even little cute ones."

"Little cute bears grow up to be big mean bears," Hialeah said.

"I swore to his mother that I would take care of him," Willa told her father.

Nathaniel's eyes widened in surprise. "You swore to his mother? And where *is* his mother?" he asked, peering into the forest in all directions.

"Shot dead by the loggers," Willa said.

"You saw the loggers?" Nathaniel asked in alarm, his voice taking a dark, angry turn as his gaze snapped back to her.

"Yes," Willa admitted softly, knowing she had awoken a bear of another kind.

"Tell me you didn't get too close," her father demanded. "Tell me you kept your distance. I've warned you before, Willa. When you see the loggers, you've got to run away."

"You can't go rescuing bears from the logging sites," Hialeah said, emboldened by the fact that she and her father were on the same side. Willa knew that she liked being right.

"But the bears needed my help."

Nathaniel nodded, seeming to understand. "Where did you see the loggers?"

"Down by the Elkmont Camp."

"The Elkmont Camp!" he exclaimed, throwing up his hands in exasperation. "Of all the places, Willa, what were you doing down there? I told you to stay away! That's one of their main camps."

"I was angry," she said, glancing up at Hialeah but not saying anything more.

"And what, you wanted to become angrier, so you went and watched the loggers?" Hialeah said. "That doesn't make any sense."

"I told you to never go near the loggers," Nathaniel said so softly that it pulled at Willa's heart. She could hear the confusion and disappointment in his tone. Her heart beat hard in her chest. She'd been caught out, and she knew it. What could she say to him to make him understand?

A year ago, his wife, Ahyoka, had been killed by attackers in the night. The murderers had been Faeran, guards of the padaran. A few months later, another tragedy began to unfold. Inali, Nathaniel's five-year-old son and Willa's adoptive brother, came down with a high fever. Poor little Inali tossed and turned in his bed. The sickness lasted for days. Nathaniel brought a human doctor to the house, and Willa searched the forest desperately for medicinal plants, but nothing worked—the fever wouldn't break. And then one night, with his father, older brother, and two sisters all around him, Inali went quiet. Willa remembered sitting there in the darkness with the others and hearing Inali's last breath as he passed away.

Over the past year, Willa had seen Nathaniel become deeply protective of his family and his land. All he wanted was for them to be left alone and in peace. And it was the loggers who angered him and frightened him the most. They wanted his land along the river, not just so they could cut down its beautiful, giant trees, but because it was the only route where they could lay their steel tracks and reach the valuable trees on the higher slopes of the mountain. To protect him from the loggers, Nathaniel had sent his ten-year-old son, Iska, to live with the boy's cousins in the Qualla Boundary, a region owned and controlled by the Cherokee, on the other side of the Great Mountain. He had tried to send Hialeah as well, but she had stubbornly refused to leave her father.

"Why did you go down into the Elkmont area?" Nathaniel pressed Willa. "Why *there*?"

"Because my friends live there," she said, knowing it wouldn't be a good enough answer.

"Your friends?" he asked, still frowning and angry. "What friends?"

"She means the trees," Hialeah said, staring coldly at Willa.

"You don't care about anything, do you?" Willa glared back at her.

"Willa, now stop," Nathaniel said. "Just go to the river and simmer down."

"How come *I'm* the one who has to go to the river?" Willa retorted. "I didn't do anything wrong!"

"Neither did I!" Hialeah said fiercely.

Nathaniel closed his eyes as he took in a breath and let it out again.

"Willa, you *like* sitting by the river," he said, clearly trying to keep his tone even. "Don't act like it's a punishment when you know it's not."

Willa stepped back, rubbing her eye with the back of her hand. "I'm sorry, Father."

Nathaniel looked at her and Hialeah together. "Both of you need to listen. There's no point arguing about how many baskets of apples we're going to pick or who has to scrape the honey frames this week, or what we're going to do with a bear cub. We're a family. We'll figure it out. But we need to stay focused on the real problems we face. Those loggers down there have been doing everything they can to get us off our land, to push us out of the way, but we're not giving up. This is our land and we're keeping it. Do you understand? But there's going to be a point when they come at us hard. We've been training for it: the lookout in the tree, the path out back, the hiding spot, the gun by the front door—we've gone through it all. When they come, they might do it in a way we don't expect, but whatever happens, we're in this together. We don't bicker. We don't fight. We stick together no matter what. Got it?"

As Willa felt the heat of shame rising to her cheeks, she lowered her head and nodded. She knew her father was right.

She raised her eyes and looked at her sister. Hialeah was already gazing back at her, her expression softer.

Willa knew that her sister had been struggling with something for a long time, something that she never talked about but was always there between them, beneath the surface, like black mold on the roots between two trees.

"I'm sorry, Willa," Hialeah said. "I just didn't know where you'd gone this morning."

Hialeah's words caught her off guard. When Willa had stormed off earlier that morning, she purposefully hadn't told Hialeah where she was going. It was meant to hurt her, to worry her, and it had worked too well.

"I'm sorry, too," Willa said softly. "I shouldn't have left without you."

"You shouldn't have gone at all," Nathaniel corrected her.

Willa paused and swallowed. "I'll try to stay away from the loggers the best I can," she promised him.

"Good," Nathaniel said, nodding as he looked at the two of them.

After a moment, he turned his attention back to Charka, now trembling behind Willa's leg, frightened by the tone of their voices. "Tomorrow we'll see if we can find a proper home for Charka, somewhere with other bears so he'll learn how to roam and find food and protect himself. That's his only chance of survival."

"I think I know where we can take him," Willa said, trying to show that she understood.

"Very good," Nathaniel said. "But for tonight, we'll have our supper out here on the porch so he can eat with us. I've got some leftover potato hash that I'm pretty sure he'll like."

"Thank you," Willa said.

"I'll start bringing out the table and chairs," Hialeah said.

When Willa looked at her, Hialeah gave her a small, nearly imperceptible smile, and Willa gave her one in return. Tiff or no tiff, they were still sisters.

Later that night, after supper, Willa and Hialeah cleaned the dishes in the kitchen sink while Nathaniel fed the last of the potato hash to Charka outside. Willa noticed that her father's trekking boots, which he'd left lying next to the bench by the door with his rifle, were terribly muddy, like he'd been out slogging through the riverbank that day.

"Did Father go out hunting while I was gone?" Willa asked, but she knew it was unlikely, for he normally hunted in the early morning.

"He was gone all day, but I don't know where," Hialeah said, her voice unusually steady, like she was purposefully trying to keep it that way.

Willa felt a pang of guilt when she realized that both she and Nathaniel had left the house that morning without telling Hialeah where they were going. Her sister must have been worrying all day. But Willa sensed that there was something more, something that had been lingering between them that she couldn't put her finger on.

"Hialeah," she said very softly as they worked, "what's been bothering you?"

"Nothing."

But Willa knew that wasn't true.

Sometimes when Hialeah looked at her there was a harshness in her eyes, a darkness, almost like she hated her. But Willa knew that wasn't true, either.

"Are you still mad at me from this morning?" Willa asked, pressing her.

"No," Hialeah said, but the way she said it, the curtness of it, made it clear that there was *something.*

"Tell me," Willa said, touching her arm. "What's bothering you?"

Hialeah turned and looked at her with her deep brown eyes.

"There's nothing bothering me," she said firmly. "I'm all right."

That phrase, Willa thought, *I'm all right.* That's what people said when they weren't all right. No, her sister wasn't angry, but she was hurting.

By the time they had cleaned up and done their other chores, it was late. Nathaniel and Hialeah said good night and went upstairs to their bedrooms to sleep. Willa loved being with Nathaniel and Hialeah, but she did not sleep inside. She had tried several times to share a room with Hialeah, which they were both excited about doing at first, but Willa could never get used to the stillness of the air and the deadness of the wooden walls.

Instead, she went outside and climbed into the walnut tree in front of the house. Charka followed right behind her, using his sharp claws to climb as quickly and easily as she did. The two of them curled up together in the crook of several branches, just above Hialeah's bedroom.

Willa smiled when she heard the sound of Hialeah opening the window. She and her sister weren't sleeping in the same room, but they were as physically close as they could be, the quarrel they'd gotten into earlier well behind them now.

"Good night, Willa," Hialeah said softly.

"Good night, Hialeah, I love you," Willa said in return.

"I love you, too."

She wasn't sure, but Willa felt like she had heard a trace of regret in her sister's voice. But regret of what? It was almost as if Hialeah was ashamed of how angry she'd been earlier. But there was something else, too, as if they were two trees and their roots were reaching toward each other beneath the ground, but an ancient vein of rock in the earth was coming between them.

Charka snuggled his warm, furry body up to Willa's and nuzzled his snout beneath her chin. She could feel his long nose breathing gently on her neck, and his paws holding on to her sides, as if she was still carrying him through the forest. As the little bear slowly fell into an exhausted sleep, Willa stared up at the moon and stars rising above the silhouette of the mountains. It was a warm summer night. The katydids were pulsing, the tree frogs trilling, and the whip-poor-wills whistling their names. It was on nights like this that memories of Alliw came floating into her mind, memories of sleeping curled up with her sister in the crook of the great hemlock tree by the river, the very tree that the loggers had cut down that morning. It had been seven years since Alliw had passed away, and now the tree had, too. All that remained of those nights were her recollections, and even those were drifting further and further away. When she thought about her Faeran sister and the great hemlock by the river, it felt as if soon the river itself would stop flowing and disappear.

She didn't know why, but there hadn't been any Faeran babies born for many years. Willa was thirteen years old and had been one of the last. When Faeran babies *were* being born, they were always born as twins and given names that were the reverse of one another. Willa and Alliw. The left and right. The dark and the light. She and Alliw had been inseparable, together in all things. One of her fondest memories was the two of them swimming with a bevy of little otter pups in a stream, dipping and diving, splashing and playing. When Willa was the water of the river, Alliw became the stones—the dark and the light, the left and the right, their camouflage all the more effective when they were together. Sometimes Willa wondered if that's why her sister had died. It had been one of those rare times when they weren't together, blending with each other into their surroundings. The padaran's guards had been able to see her.

Sometimes now, when Willa heard the sound of a river or the gentle buzz of the insects on a moonlit night, it felt as if half of her was there and half of her was missing.

But as Charka groaned and snuggled closer, and Hialeah slept quietly in the bed just through the open window, Willa looked up at the Great Mountain, thankful for what the world had given her.

The warmth of the rising sun graced her cheek. The light coming through her closed eyelids turned her sleeping world a rosy pink. And the flutter of a warbler's wing in the branches around her whispered across her ear.

She did not open her eyes, but tilted her head away from the sun and nestled into the leaves of the tree in which she was sleeping. The branches held her, cradled her, and would never let her fall.

When Charka moved beside her, she opened her eyes, remembering that she wasn't alone.

The sun had just come up over the top of the mountain.

Below her, she heard the creak of the front door opening and closing, and then saw Hialeah heading toward the small meadow, ringed by forest trees, that lay a short distance from the house. Silver and gold rays of morning sunlight slanted through the mist floating across the meadow. The lush, dew-covered grasses and purple-fringed orchids seemed to glow with the light.

From her perch in the tree, Willa watched Hialeah walk to the far end of the meadow and stand in front of two mounds of earth marked with small, white-painted wooden crosses. A few months before, on Decoration Day, she, Hialeah, and Nathaniel had all gone to the graves, added more dirt where some had washed away, planted yellow flowers they had gathered from the forest, and placed a double ring of stones around the two mounds. And then, gathered around the last resting place of their loved ones, they ate a wonderful picnic, sang the old songs, and told the stories of the lost. It was the first Decoration Day Willa had ever experienced, and she remembered how close it had made her feel to everyone in the family, both the living and the dead.

One of the crosses was for their brother, Inali. The other was for Hialeah's mother. Willa had never met Ahyoka, but she knew that she had been the solid earth, the nourishing water, and the glistening sunlight of Hialeah's life. Hialeah came out here to her grave every morning, rain or shine. Over the months, Willa had never seen Hialeah cry, but many times she had seen her pause midway through a sentence, unable to finish it. Or she'd bring a hand to her eye and turn away. They were brief, jagged moments, like rocks beneath a current, when the loss of her mother was more than Hialeah could bear. And then she would compose herself and press on with whatever she had been doing, her face steady and stern.

As Willa watched her praying in front of the graves now, she wondered, when Hialeah looked at her—and saw her green skin and her bark-brown hair and her leaf-colored eyes—was it possible that she didn't just see *her*, she didn't just see *Willa*, but she also saw the people who had murdered her mother? Was this the vein of rock that kept them from reaching each other? If it was, then how could she break through it? Willa could change the color of her skin and eyes, and she could tell Hialeah stories of the Faeran heroes who had lived long before the murderous wretches who had killed her mother. But what could she do to truly mend a wounded mind?

Willa imagined that Hialeah was praying to her father's god and to her mother's god, to the English and the Cherokee. But Willa knew that deep down, Hialeah was having to find her own path, just like she was, alone in the world in many ways, finding her own god to heal her soul.

A few minutes later, as Hialeah walked back to the house to begin her chores, she passed under Willa's tree.

"I know you're watching me," Hialeah said without looking up.

"I didn't want to bother you," Willa said softly.

"Come on down from there and help me make breakfast," Hialeah said. "Father's gonna be up soon."

When Willa started climbing down the branches of the tree, Charka woke up, cried out because she was leaving him, and scampered after her. She was just about to reassure him that she wasn't going anywhere without him when several birds cried *jay! jay! jay!* in the distance. She reflexively froze and blended into the leaves. When blue jays called out, it meant danger was approaching.

"What are you seeing, my friends?" she whispered in Faeran as she looked out in the direction of the jays.

And then she heard it.

The normal whispers of the nearby river had turned angry.

Her muscles tightened.

It was the sound of the rushing water hitting the knees of trespassers wading across the shallow part of the river. Then came the thudding of many heavy boots as the intruders climbed the rocks onto the shore. As they made their way through the grove of oak trees toward the house, she smelled their human bodies, the oil and sawdust on their clothes, and the blood of trees on their hands.

Six dark figures came toward the house, all spread out and slinking low, moving quietly from one trunk to the next, and gripping weapons in their hands.

They had come with killing in mind.

Willa immediately thought about the gun and ammunition that Nathaniel kept hanging on the wall just inside the front door, and she knew he slept with a loaded rifle on the bed beside him.

"Hialeah!" Willa shouted in a raspy whisper down to her sister below. "They're here! They're coming! Run out the back door and hide like Father told us!"

Hialeah understood immediately. "Stay safe!" she whispered up to Willa, and ducked into the house.

"Charka, you stay where you are," Willa told the little bear. "Stay in the tree."

She wanted to hunker down and hide with him, but she had to warn her father. Willa turned toward the house. Remembering what the flying squirrels had taught her years before, she flung herself through the air. She couldn't fly, not even close, but she could leap and she could cling. She hit the side of the house hard, her body slamming into the wood siding, which nearly knocked the wind out of her, but she made it to the windowsill. She scrambled in through the opening, toppled to the floor, got to her feet, and ran for her father's room.

"Father, wake up, they're here!" she said as she shook his shoulder. "They're here!"

"What?" he said groggily as he woke. He reached for his gun and looked around them. "What's happening, Willa?" He quickly got out of bed. As usual, he was fully dressed, ready for whatever came.

"Six men with guns just crossed the river and are coming slowly toward the house," she said. He had trained her in exactly how to speak to him—the number of men, the weapons, the direction and character of movement.

"Where's your sister?"

"I told her to run out the back door."

"Good girl," Nathaniel said, quickly nodding. "Now hide, Willa, just disappear. No matter what you see, don't come out. If something happens to me, I want you to protect Hialeah and get away from here. Promise me."

Willa nodded, her heart hammering in her chest. But she hated how it all seemed so disturbingly similar to what the mother bear had asked her to do, to take her cub and flee.

"Un daca," she told him, but then realized her mistake. "I'm sorry. I mean, I will, *I promise.* But please don't die, Father, please!"

"Don't worry, I don't plan on it," he said, holding her by the shoulders. "Now, hide, Willa. Hide!" And then he grabbed his rifle and raced out of the room.

Willa sprinted down the hallway, dashed through Hialeah's bedroom, and leaped out the window. She flew through the air and landed spread-eagled in the boughs of the tree, then grabbed hold of the swaying, bending branches and scurried up like a squirrel. The instant she got to a steady spot, she crouched and blended into the leaves.

Worried that her panting would give her away, Willa quieted her breath and slowed the beating of her heart. The ability to consciously control the innermost parts of her body was a wood-witching skill that her grandmother had taught her well.

And then she relaxed her muscles, loosening her arms and legs. Remembering the trick that a tree snake had shown her the year before, she textured herself just the right shade of green, and swayed gently in the breeze, becoming indistinguishable from the branches and leaves around her.

She watched the six men creeping through the forest toward the house, their long metal guns gripped in their hands. She could see by their slow, careful movements that they were trying to be quiet, but she could hear their heavy breathing, the rustle of their clothes, and the twigs breaking beneath their feet.

When she recognized one of the men, she clenched her teeth. It was the foreman of the logging crew, the man who had been on the horse. He was on foot now, but she would never forget him. He was the one who had given the order to shoot the mother bear. Older than the rest, he had a close-shaven beard and short, iron-gray hair. He wore a long, practical travel coat and his calves were clad in dark, knee-high leather snake-boots to protect against copperheads and rattlers in the underbrush. He was crouched with the others, his rifle in his hands. The men around him looked like loggers from his crew.

The fourth man had taken cover lying down behind a log a short distance away, the long barrel of his rifle peeking over the edge of it, and the tail of his raccoon-skin hat hanging down his back. *It's one of the guards, the hunters,* Willa thought, remembering the sight of them crawling up over the edge of the ravine.

The two remaining intruders were different. She couldn't tell what they were. But one of them wore a pistol at his side and a piece of shiny metal on his chest.

As the men got closer to the edge of the forest, they hunkered down behind the trunks of the trees and looked across the grass toward the house. Willa snarled at the thought of these tree-killers using the *trees* to protect themselves.

"Steadman!" the pistol-carrying man called out. He had a thick white mustache and a pudgy face, and the brim of his hat was bent up on the sides. "Come on outta there with your hands in the air!"

There was no reply from the direction of the house. Nothing but stillness.

"We gotta get in there fast, Sheriff!" snarled one of the loggers, spitting tobacco chew from the side of his mouth. "Otherwise he'll sneak out the back like a rat."

"Nathaniel Steadman!" the white-mustachioed man shouted. "It's Sheriff Blount. And I've got Deputy Grant here, and four men from the Sutton Lumber Company. We don't want no kinda trouble! But we're coming up to the house!"

The sheriff looked over at the deputy. He was a younger, thinner man, but there was a severe kind of certainty in his expression, as if nothing in the world was going to prevent him from doing what they'd come to do.

From her position high in the tree, Willa turned and scanned the forest behind the house. She spotted Hialeah running through the trees, her long black hair flowing behind her. Feeling a surge of hope, Willa thought, *Run, Hialeah, run!* But where was Nathaniel? Why wasn't he running with her?

As Willa turned back toward the attackers, she noticed something in the foliage behind them. She thought it must be a seventh man she hadn't seen yet. Or maybe it was an animal. But then Willa's eyes widened in disbelief. It was the wheat-haired girl! The girl she'd seen in the ravine the day before was now hiding in a thicket right behind the men, watching them and the house beyond. Willa's brow furrowed in confusion. What did she have to do with all of this?

The hunter lying behind the log seemed to spot something and he readied his weapon. He was a lean, sinewy man with dark hair and steady, keen eyes that reminded her of a sharp-shinned hawk, the kind of eyes that had seen plenty of things die.

Willa heard the creak of the front door as it slowly swung open.

"He's coming out, Sheriff!" the deputy whispered.

The tobacco-spitting logger who had urged the sheriff to rush in just moments before threw himself to the ground and cowered, gripping his double-barreled shotgun to his chest, as if he was expecting a hail of bullets to come flying his way. The other men quickly crouched behind the trunks of the trees and aimed their rifles at the front of the house.

Willa's heart lurched. They must be aiming at Nathaniel! But why was he coming out? Why wasn't he running out the back with Hialeah? He could get away!

Her chest tightened when she saw him run forward and position himself behind the stone well as he pointed his rifle in the direction of the intruders.

"What are you doing here, Sheriff?" he shouted, his voice darker and angrier than Willa had ever heard it.

The tobacco-spitting logger leaped wildly to his feet and yelled, "You know why we're here, you son of a—"

"Get down and shut up, Luther!" the foreman of the loggers barked as he pulled him down.

Luther was a tall, gangly man who looked to be about the same age as her father. He wore a thick leather belt, a hatchet at his side, and a beat-up old hat. His trousers were torn and stained with sap, and his suspenders were fraying. As he got to his feet, he pulled back his long, ratty brown hair and wiped the tobacco juice from the corner of his mouth with the back of his hand, scowling at the foreman who'd yanked him down. Luther had a narrow, bony face, like he'd been raised more on moonshine than food, and he had an old jagged scar across his cheek. When he peered at the foreman, there was menace in his eyes.

"You know we gotta get him," he urged the foreman. "I'm tellin' ya, we gotta get him!" But Willa noticed that as he said these brave-sounding words, Luther kept himself low and hidden behind the base of a large tree and left it to the foreman to keep watch on the house.

Nathaniel's voice rose from the direction of the well. "I'm asking you again, Sheriff, why are you here?"

"I reckon Luther Higgs got it about right for a change," the sheriff called back to Nathaniel. "You already know why we've come."

"I sure don't," Nathaniel said, "and I'm running out of patience. So make yourself plain."

As the sheriff crept over to a thicker tree trunk, Willa could see that he was a slow-moving, heavyset man. It didn't look like he was none too anxious to start a gunfight with Nathaniel Steadman.

"We're here to ask you some questions about a crime that has taken place," the sheriff said.

"The only crimes I'm aware of are people cutting timber without a permit, destroying private lands, and dynamiting rivers. You mean those crimes?"

"You can rot in a pit, Steadman!" Luther shouted from behind the oak tree that he and the foreman were using for cover. "Them ain't crimes you're talkin' 'bout! Every man's got a God-given right to make a livin'. Nothin' you can do to stop that, you mountain-man freak!"

"What's this all about, Sheriff?" Nathaniel said, ignoring Luther in a way that made Willa think he'd been trying to ignore this man for years. "I don't know anything about any kind of crime."

"Two men working for the Sutton Lumber Company were killed yesterday," the sheriff said. "One of them was Luther's brother, a man I believe you know."

Willa blinked in shock.

Some of the loggers had been killed?

But she had just been there!

She saw Nathaniel's face go gray. His expression didn't look like surprise, exactly, but a kind of dread, as if he'd realized things had just gotten a whole lot worse.

Willa squinted into the forest toward where the wheat-haired girl had been, but she was gone now. The girl was the only person Willa had seen at the logging site other than the loggers, and she'd been hiding in the rocks. Willa couldn't help but wonder if she might have something to do with the murder of the two men. Or maybe she had at least seen something from the shadows. Willa scanned to the left and the right, looking for her in the undergrowth. Had she crept closer? Had she run away? Whoever she was, she seemed to have disappeared.

"But what's all that got to do with me, Sheriff?" Nathaniel asked, his voice steady and sober now.

"You know you've made it more than clear how you feel about the Sutton Lumber Company," the sheriff said.

"And you know better than most that for a rational man there's a long distance between desire and action."

"Don't let him get away with anything this time, Sheriff," Luther urged him. "He's a good talker. He tricks people! We gotta string him up! We gotta hang him!"

"Just shut up and let the sheriff do his job," the foreman told Luther, holding him down so he couldn't jump up again. It was obvious that the foreman was used to having his orders followed by his men, and he'd had just about enough of Luther Higgs.

"Listen to what I'm saying, Nathaniel," the sheriff called out. "Two loggers on the Elkmont crew were murdered yesterday. That's a fact."

"How do you know they were murdered?" Nathaniel asked. "Maybe it was an accident. How did they die? Did anybody see it happen?"

The sheriff glanced over at the deputy and shook his head, seeming to signal that it was getting pretty clear that their suspect wasn't going to come willingly. The deputy nodded to the sheriff, encouraging him to press on. "Put the question to him. Get him on the record."

"Nathaniel," the sheriff said, "I need you to tell me, for the record, where you were yesterday."

"I was working in my orchards," Nathaniel said.

"Can anybody but your kinfolk vouch for that?" the sheriff asked, peering out from behind the tree trunk as if he wanted to actually see Nathaniel Steadman's face when he answered the question.

Willa remembered the mud she'd seen on her father's boots. But the orchards weren't near the river.

"I told you, I was working in my orchards," Nathaniel said. "You have my word of honor. I was nowhere near the logging site."

"Well, I'll be, will you look at that!" Luther shouted to the others as he pointed his long, bony finger.

Charka came trundling across the open grass straight toward Nathaniel, whining for more of the potato hash he'd been fed the night before.

Willa gasped. *Oh no, Charka, not now!* In her panic, she'd forgotten all about him. But what could she do? How could she stop him?

"That's the cub!" Luther hollered, jumping up and down excitedly as he pointed. "That's the cub! There it is!"

The sheriff looked over at the foreman. "What's he blathering on about now?"

"We shot a sow bear yesterday at the logging site," the foreman said, his voice filled with the even tone of authority. "And that cub was there."

"And now it's here." The third logger spoke for the first time. He was filthy with sap and sawdust, a limb-chopper like Luther, and he had an unsettling quietness to his voice. "That's the cub we saw . . ." he said eerily. "And now it's here with Steadman. . . ."

"I saw it, too," the hunter agreed.

"It proves that Steadman was there!" Luther shouted. "He said he wasn't at the logging site, but he was! That's the cub. Steadman's a liar! This proves it!"

Willa's teeth clenched in anger at the accusation. She wanted Nathaniel to shout back at them, *My Faeran daughter was there, not me!*

But he didn't.

He didn't say a word.

It took three beats of her heart to remember that these men had no idea the Faeran race even existed. They thought he had one daughter, not two, and it was clear her father was determined to keep it that way.

In a burst of blustering motion, Luther pulled away from the foreman, came out from behind the oak tree, and raised his shotgun, aiming it straight at the cub. Willa sprang through the branches and was about to leap from the tree when Nathaniel lunged out, snatched the little bear, and pulled him behind the protection of the well with him.

"Fine, Steadman," Luther said, aiming his gun directly at Nathaniel. "I'll shoot you instead!"

"Don't be an idiot!" the foreman shouted, pulling Luther back by the collar like a rabid dog. "You're going to get your head blown off."

"But he's the one! He killed my brother!" Luther cursed and grumbled.

The sheriff shouted back at Nathaniel, his voice filled with new firmness, as if he hadn't been certain of the suspect's guilt until these last few moments. "You just told us, on your word of honor, that you weren't anywhere near the logging site."

"I wasn't at the logging site," Nathaniel said again, his voice as taut as a wire as he aimed his rifle at the sheriff. "I think you and these other men need to get off my land now."

"That's not gonna happen, and you know it," the sheriff said. "I gotta bring you in."

"I didn't murder anyone!" Nathaniel said fiercely.

"That will be decided in a court of law in front of a jury of your peers," the sheriff said.

"The whole town already knows he's guilty!" Luther shouted.

"Look, Nathaniel," the sheriff said. "One way or another, you ain't got much choice in this. Either you're comin' with us or we're gonna have some kind of reckoning here."

"I didn't start this!" Nathaniel shouted.

A sinister whisper came from the hunter lying behind the log as he peered through the sights of his rifle. "I've got a good shot, Boss. I can take him out. Just give me the word and he's dead."

Willa watched it all, her heart pounding in her chest.

But then the sheriff stepped out from behind the cover of the tree. "Steadman, I don't want to be killin' you here in front of your own house—that's no kind of end for a man. And I figure you don't want to be killin' us, either."

"No, I don't," Nathaniel agreed. "So get off my land!"

"Listen to what I have to stay, and I'll make you a deal," the sheriff said. "I know what you're worried about. I give you my word that if you come peacefully with us, I'll make sure nothing happens to your daughter or your land. You understand? I won't allow anyone to come up here while you're gone. Your daughter and your home will be safe."

Nathaniel stared at the sheriff, seeming to consider his words.

After several seconds, he glanced back at the house. It was as if he was making absolutely sure that Hialeah had escaped out the back.

And then, to Willa's amazement, he looked up into the tree where she herself was hiding. She could see his bright blue eyes searching for her. At first she thought he must be checking to make sure she was safe, just as he had done with Hialeah. But then she realized that he already knew she was safe. He was looking for her just to see her one last time. And to tell her silently that he loved her. She wanted to reach out to him, to hold him, or at least change her colors so she was visible to him for just an instant. But she didn't. Because she knew, in this particular moment, that was the last thing he wanted.

And then Nathaniel slowly turned to the sheriff and the other men.

"I promise you no one will touch your daughter or your land," the sheriff repeated.

"I'm not going in any handcuffs, if that's what you're thinking," Nathaniel said. "I'll go of my own accord, as a free man."

"No handcuffs," the sheriff agreed. "We'll all just walk on down to Gatlinburg and get this mess sorted out."

Nathaniel seemed to be studying the sheriff. Finally, he nodded his head and said, "All right, we'll take a walk."

He pulled in a long, defeated breath, and ejected the cartridges from his weapon.

The six men immediately surged forward. The hunter snatched the gun from his hands. Luther Higgs and the deputy grabbed his arms, nearly pulling him off his feet.

"Come on, ya murderer," Luther snarled as he shoved him forward. Now that Nathaniel Steadman had given in and was surrounded by the other men, Luther was suddenly filled with confidence and bravery.

Willa shuddered at the violent way they were treating her father, but she didn't know what she could do. How could she help him?

"So, you got your man, Sheriff," the foreman said, walking up to him.

"Yeah, we got him," the sheriff said, clearly relieved that it hadn't ended in gunfire. "Thanks for your help. The deputy and I will take him down to Gatlinburg."

"Me and my men are heading back to the Elkmont site," the foreman said. "Mr. Sutton has given me quotas to fill—a full trainload every day, come hell or high water—and for me at least, today is already shot."

"If it's all right, sir," said Luther, "I'll go with the sheriff and make sure this rat gets what he deserves."

The foreman frowned and looked at the sheriff.

"We may need him," the sheriff said.

The foreman turned back to Luther. "Listen here. You do

what you need to do for the sheriff, then hightail it back up to the site. There's work to be done! We need every man we got on those saws, you hear me?"

"I will, Boss, I will," Luther said.

With that the men split into two separate parties. The foreman, the hunter, and the other logger went in one direction. The sheriff, the deputy, and Luther took Nathaniel in the other.

As she watched them drag her father away, Willa just tried to breathe steady and strong. Her whole body was shaking, and her eyes were watering. She kept thinking he would turn and run, or he would fight them, or he'd scream out, but as they held him by the arms and pushed him through the woods, there was nothing he could do but go with them.

The sounds of their boots tromping on the ground and their shoulders brushing against the leaves gradually receded into the distance.

And then her father was gone.

Still trembling, Willa climbed down the tree.

Charka came running over to her, oblivious to the trouble he'd caused.

She walked out into the middle of the grass where her father had been standing moments before.

But he was gone. He was truly gone.

She stared after him, seeing nothing but the empty trees.

What was she going to do?

When she finally turned and looked toward the house, she was startled to see Hialeah standing on the front porch, her face as stern and serious as Willa had ever seen it. There was a long knife sheathed at her side, a bag of ammunition slung over her shoulder, and a rifle clenched in her hands.

"What did you do, Willa?" Hialeah said.

"Wh-what? When? What do you mean?" Willa stammered.

"Yesterday, at the logging site, what did you do?" she demanded.

"I didn't do anything!" Willa said, her voice shaking. "I just tried to save a bear!"

"You got Father arrested, that's what you did!"

"I didn't!" Willa cried in frustration.

Gripping the rifle, Hialeah stormed down the steps and strode across the grass in the direction the men had gone.

"Leave the bear here," she said as she walked straight past Willa toward the trees. "We're going after them. We're going to get Father back."

"But he didn't want to fight them," Willa said as she turned toward her. "He knows he's innocent. He didn't do anything wrong."

Hialeah threw herself around and glared into her face. "You don't think it's possible that Father could have killed those two loggers yesterday?"

"Wha-what are you talking about?" Willa said, her voice tightening.

"You need to grow up, Willa!"

"I don't think—"

"He hates the loggers!" Hialeah said, cutting her off. "They probably attacked him and he had to defend himself. Or he was protecting our land."

"But he said he didn't kill them."

"I don't care what he said or what he did. We're going after them and we're going to get him back!" Hialeah whirled back around and continued down the path the men had taken through the forest. "Come on, Willa!" she shouted without looking back.

Willa's hackles went up. It riled her that her sister wasn't asking her what she thought they should do. She was demanding blind obedience.

"You've got to stop, Hialeah," Willa said when she caught up with her sister. "This isn't what Father would want. Someone's going to get hurt."

But Hialeah charged ahead. "When they get to the Sugarland Gap, we'll take them from above."

"Hialeah, no!" Willa said, trying to grab her arm. "We can't kill those men."

"We're not going to lose Father," she snarled, yanking her arm away and continuing down the trail at an even faster pace.

"Just stop, Hialeah!" Willa shouted.

Finally, Hialeah turned and looked at her.

"What?" she demanded.

"I agree that we need to save Father, but shooting the sheriff and the deputy would just make things worse, not better. You go after Father. Follow him. Protect him. Make sure those men don't hurt him. And if you can, get the help of the other mountain families. Father is respected. They'll want to help him, especially if it's related to the Sutton Lumber Company."

Hialeah stared at her, her eyes storming, but she was listening.

"What about you?" Hialeah said finally. "What are you going to do?"

"I'll follow the loggers. They came here to make sure Father was arrested, but I think something is going on, something they're not talking about."

Hialeah nodded. She knew the plan made sense. "You be careful, Willa," she said, sounding like a big sister again. "Those loggers are dangerous men. They'll kill you if they catch you. Especially that foreman—you watch out for him! And the hunter. They're not going to let anything get in their way."

"And you be careful, too," Willa said. "Protect our father."

"I will," Hialeah said fiercely.

She gave Willa a quick hug and then turned and ran.

As Hialeah disappeared into the woods, Willa felt her stomach sink. Her father was gone. Now her sister was gone as well.

She turned and looked over at Charka. He was staring at her with worry in his eyes. She knew he didn't understand English, but he seemed to grasp the gravity of what was happening.

"Come on, Charka," she said in the Faeran language, and then headed after the loggers. "We've got a mystery to solve."

13

Willa followed the three loggers at a safe distance as they walked along the human-made path that led northwest through the forest, back toward the Elkmont logging site.

Hoping to glean some clue about what had happened the day the two men were murdered, she crept close enough to overhear the loggers talking. They spoke of food and cutting trees, of tools and weapons, and the other things that consumed their lives, but nothing that could help her father. It was as if they didn't even realize or care that they had destroyed a man's life and the lives of his children. Either that or they thought they had done good work in helping to bring a murderer to justice and they didn't need to speak of it further.

All through the day, a gusty wind blew down from the summits of the surrounding mountains, riling up the treetops and making a muffled, roaring sound through the forest. As Charka walked beside her, he gazed up into the blowing trees, his eyes wary. He seemed to be sensing something, but she wasn't sure what it was.

The noise of the wind in the trees allowed her and Charka to get even closer to the humans as they walked down the trail. It also made it more difficult to hear their conversation, but she did manage to make out that they planned to camp for the night in Raven's Gap, where they'd be out of the wind.

"Come on," she whispered to Charka. "We'll get ahead of them and find a good spot to hide."

A short time later, she and the cub reached the gorge that the local families called Raven's Gap. A stony trail with rock walls on both sides, it was one of the only passes through this part of the mountains.

She did not follow the human path but climbed up through the trees to the top edge of the gorge. Once there, she lay on the ground on her stomach, the rock hard and sharp beneath her elbows. From this vantage point she could look down and have a close but safe view of the humans. She concealed herself in the mountain laurel, her skin blending into the green leaves and delicate white and pink flowers.

Staying close to her, Charka crouched, seeming to know that he had to stay as low and quiet as he could. He could not change the color of his fur, but when he stayed still he was surprisingly good at remaining hidden.

At the far end of the gorge, she heard the voices of the men as they approached, talking to one another as they trekked down the path.

"Stay down," she whispered to Charka. "They're coming."

The hunter with the hawkish eyes and extra-long rifle led the way. The foreman and other logger followed in single file.

Willa hated these loggers, even the sight of them. *These are the men who are responsible for what happened to my father,* she kept thinking. *These are the men.*

The thought of the sheriff and Luther Higgs dragging her father off to Gatlinburg filled her with dread. And what about her sister? What was Hialeah going to be able to do against those forces?

As the humans entered the gorge, they slowed their walking and began to look around. Their eyes scanned the place where she and Charka were hiding in the laurel, but they did not linger.

"We'll make camp here," the foreman said, throwing down his pack and rifle.

"I'll get a fire started," the hunter said.

"No, I'll work on that," the foreman said. "You get us some fresh meat for supper."

The hunter nodded and turned to go into the woods.

"Erect the tents right along here," the foreman told the remaining logger, the one who never said much. The limbchopper slung his pack off his shoulder and went to work.

As she watched the men beginning to set up their camp, Willa smelled something. Not the humans, but something else. It was a strong odor of dead, decaying wood.

Charka whimpered and began looking frantically all around them, making far too much noise in the mountain laurel.

A slithering sound came from the trees. The quills on the back of Willa's neck went up. She leaped to her feet and turned to face the attackers.

The ferns thrashed back and forth as a long, dark gray shape moved rapidly toward them across the forest floor.

Charka squirmed wildly, scrambling to escape Willa's hold.

"Watch out!" she shouted, trying to pull him out of the way, but the little bear flung himself backward, away from the attacking creature. Squealing in terror, he tumbled over the edge of the cliff. Willa lunged forward, reaching for him. But in an instant, he was gone.

Three of the beasts burst out of the underbrush, winding like giant snakes right toward her. The creatures were as thick as tree branches, but they made a terrible hissing sound and moved with startling speed.

As the fastest and thinnest of the three came at her, she leaped out of its way. It slithered past, inches from her leg.

Gasping for breath, she pressed her back against a tree to keep away from it. Her nostrils went frigid with the sharpness of ice, and the air coming into her lungs felt astonishingly cold.

As the second and third creature came at her, she sprang into the branches of the tree. The largest of the beasts brushed under her dangling foot, jolting her with a freezing pain that shot through her bones. Her lips went dry and the skin of her face and arms felt as if it had been pulled taut. Even the slightest touch of one of the creatures seemed to have drained much of the water from her body.

She clung to the branch and looked below her, expecting to see them circling the trunk with their long, winding bodies. But they weren't. All three of them slipped over the edge of the cliff and disappeared down into the gorge.

Willa dropped out of the tree and ran to the ledge.

Where was Charka? What had happened to him?

She peered one way and then the other. But he wasn't lying dead or wounded at the bottom of the gorge. He wasn't there at all. He had disappeared.

The fiendish beasts were now serpentining at high speed toward the humans.

Then she spotted something else. The wheat-haired girl was crouched behind some boulders and peeking out, watching the creatures as they attacked the men. Willa's chest seized. She couldn't believe it. What was the girl doing? Had she summoned these beasts? Was she controlling and directing them?

The hunter lifted his rifle and fired repeatedly at the monster charging at him. *Bang! Bang! Bang!* the gunfire rang out, reverberating off the stone walls. The bullets appeared to hit the beast, one thud after another, but they didn't stop it or even slow it down. The hunter kept firing, as if certain there wasn't a problem in the world his gun couldn't solve. But he was wrong. The creature slammed into his legs. The man grunted from the force of it and dropped his rifle as he crumpled to the ground, screaming in agonizing pain. His skin turned gray as if the water and nutrients were being sucked from his body.

The wheat-haired girl came running out from behind the rocks, shouting as she charged at the other two men. *It's her,* Willa thought. *What is she doing?*

The second creature snaked rapidly in the direction of the logger who had been putting up the tents. He'd been a quiet man, but now he was screaming louder than she'd ever heard a man scream. As the beast fell upon him, he tripped backward in white-eyed terror, shouting, "Help me! Help me! Somebody help me!" The slimy creature crashed into him. The man shrieked as it wrapped around his body and tore him to the ground.

The third and largest of the snakelike beasts, so dark that it was almost black, hurtled toward the foreman. He ran into the rocks in an attempt to escape the oncoming attacker, but now the other two fiends had left their initial victims and were moving his way. All three creatures were slithering their long, winding bodies in his direction. And the wheat-haired girl was charging at him as well. He didn't stand a chance.

Through all the chaos, Willa scanned the gorge for Charka. She knew he'd fallen over the cliff, but where had the little bear ended up? Had he scampered away and hidden in the rocks before she'd spotted him? Had the wheat-haired girl or the slimy beasts already gotten to him?

It was only then that she heard the whimpering.

15

The sound was coming from just below her. When she looked down the side of the cliff, she saw Charka's frightened face looking up at her from only a few feet away, his trembling body clinging by his long, curved claws to the jagged rock. She didn't know how she had missed seeing him before.

"Charka!" she gasped, dropping to her knees and reaching down to him.

The little bear slowly raised a shaking paw toward her. She grabbed hold of it with two hands. Using all her strength, she managed to slowly pull him up to the top of the cliff. "I've got you," she said as she dragged him onto level ground and embraced him.

He grunted frantically in return, as if he was explaining everything he'd been through.

"We're all right," she said as she held him. Looking down into the gorge, she saw that everything had gone quiet and still. It was difficult to be certain, but the creatures and the wheat-haired girl did indeed appear to be gone.

She turned and checked the forest behind her. Nothing but trees.

Willa wondered again how the creatures and the girl were connected. She was pretty sure the girl had helped her climb out of the ravine by the logging site, but now . . . What was she doing? Why was she skulking through the forest with these dark, shadowy beasts?

With Charka clinging to her back, Willa carefully climbed down the sheer wall and into the gorge.

As they got closer to the where the creatures had attacked the men, one of the veins in Willa's neck began to pulse, and her legs tightened.

"Stay back," she whispered to Charka, touching his shoulder with her hand.

She did not want to see what lay ahead of her, but she moved slowly forward alone, one step at a time.

The first human she came to—the hunter—was on the ground, curled up into a ball. As she got closer, she could see the side of his withered face. Something that looked like black, spidery roots had grown up his neck and over his cheeks.

Willa gasped and pulled back. What *was* that? Some kind of fungus? She was afraid to get any closer. She put her hand against the trunk of a tree to keep her balance, inhaling and exhaling three times before she was able to continue.

The second human—the logger who had screamed so loudly when the beasts attacked—lay on the ground a few steps away, his body just as motionless.

What had those creatures done to these poor men?

She glanced back toward Charka to make sure he was all right. He hadn't moved from the spot where she'd told him to wait. He was lying on the ground, head on his paws as he watched her with frightened eyes. He didn't like being here any more than she did.

As she continued slowly forward, she expected to find the body of the last of the three humans—the foreman who had been in charge of the others. Multiple creatures had barreled straight at him.

But as she proceeded down the path, she didn't see anything. She scanned the boulders. She searched the underbrush. But his body wasn't there, either.

It wasn't until she walked farther and looked over a second ledge that she saw the human lying in the rocks below the main path. His long coat was torn and dirtied, crumpled around his shoulders from his fall, and his leg looked badly wounded. But his dark gray eyes were blinking and fresh blood was trickling down his forehead.

At first Willa thought the man must have fought off the creatures, but then she realized that, in his frantic rush to escape, he had actually tripped backward over the ledge and fallen to the rocks below, out of their path.

She stared down at the human, not sure what she should do. If she simply stood still and blended into the rocks, he would never see her. And if she turned away and went back into the woods, he would never know she had been there.

If he were a deer or wolf, she would not hesitate to help him. But he was *human*. And not just any human, but a logger, a murderer of trees and a killer of bears—the kind of man she most despised.

How could she help such a man as this?

She watched as he slowly raised his head, wincing in pain even from that small movement.

He sucked in a breath and then put his bloody, shaking hand flat against the ground, groaning as he pushed himself into a partially upright position. He looked around, clearly trying to understand what had happened to him and the others.

Finally making a decision, Willa slowly stepped forward, shifted her skin to an even green, and showed herself to the human.

His eyes widened like he was seeing a ghost.

"My name is Willa," she said.

Blinking in confusion, the man wiped the blood and grime from his forehead with the palm of his hand. It looked like he thought he was hallucinating.

"I am Nathaniel Steadman's daughter."

The man's brow furrowed in confusion. "So you're Cherokee. . . ."

"No," she said, but didn't add anything else. *That's him,* she kept thinking, not quite able to absorb the fact that she was standing so close, and actually *talking* to, the man who had overseen the killing of thousands of ancient trees. This was the man who had personally given the order to cut down the great hemlock by the river, and to shoot Charka's mother so that his crew could eat the meat.

"Then . . . then what are you?" the man asked, struggling to find the words. She knew that her green skin and bright emerald eyes and the dark brown stripes and dots that ran along her cheeks were not things he had ever seen before, but she did not answer his question.

"What is your name?" she asked.

"Jim McClaren," he said. "I'm the foreman of the Elkmont crew. Are my men all right?"

Willa wasn't sure what to tell him. He must have seen what happened with his own eyes. But his mind wasn't letting him believe what he knew must be true.

She decided she had to say it bluntly. "Your men are dead."

The blow seemed to hit him in the face and he turned away. Growling in intense pain, he grabbed the edge of a nearby rock and dragged himself up to his feet by sheer will.

Pulling his wounded leg behind him, he climbed up from the ledge that had saved his life. He limped over to the bodies of his men and stared down at them.

"What were those things?" he asked, his voice filled with a ragged, haunting soberness.

"I don't know," she said softly.

"They were like . . . like some sort of snake . . . but ice-cold. I've never felt anything like that in my life. It was like death itself."

Willa didn't want to agree with anything this human had to

say, but he was right. "I felt that, too," she said. "No matter what you do, don't let them touch you."

"So you think they're coming back. . . ." He fearfully scanned the forest around them.

"You need to get out of here, Jim McClaren," she said.

He gestured toward the hunter. "Jared is . . . he was our guide up into these parts."

"What does that mean?"

"It means that I don't know the best way through these mountains, especially on a bad leg."

Willa exhaled loudly through her nose, surprised that a man who had spent so much of his life cutting down the forest couldn't find his way through it.

"These men . . ." he said, still staring at the bodies on the ground. "I need to . . . tell their kin that they won't be coming home."

"Where do you live?" she asked begrudgingly.

"Cades Cove," he said as he looked at her.

The human paused, studying her as if she were a peculiar kind of puzzle that he couldn't quite solve. He was clearly a man who was used to being in charge, used to being in control of whatever situation he was in, and his mind was working to get there again. "If you're Steadman's girl, then you must know your way around these mountains pretty well . . ." he said in a half statement, half question.

Willa knew what he was asking her. But the last thing she wanted to do was help a logger. She kept thinking about the damage this human had done. And about the damage he was going to do. How could she aid a man such as him? The very thought of it churned her stomach.

"I need you to guide me back to Cades Cove," he said, laying his request flat out in front of her. "I need to get home and find a doctor for my leg."

She pursed her lips and looked away, gazing out into the trees, not sure how to reply.

"I'm saying I would appreciate your help," he said.

Willa didn't want his appreciation. She didn't want *anything* from this man or anyone like him.

But then she had an idea.

"You're in charge of the Elkmont crew . . ." she said to him, half statement, half question, just like he had spoken to her a few moments before, but now there was edge in the tone of her voice. "And you had my father arrested . . ."

"The sheriff arrested your father on suspicion of murder," he said.

"He didn't murder anyone," Willa said. "And you know it."

"No, I *don't* know it, and neither do you—unless you were there to see it."

"Did you find the bodies of the murdered men? Had they been shot? What exactly did you see?"

"Are you going to help me out of here or not, girl?" McClaren said, raising his voice. Willa could tell that he wasn't used to being talked to like that, not by his men, not by anyone.

She wanted to leave this badly wounded man lost and bleeding in the forest to die. But there was another option. . . .

Willa narrowed her eyes at him. "Can you speak for the

company you work for and where it cuts in these mountains?"

"Where the Elkmont crew cuts is my decision," he said flatly. "What about it?"

"I will get you home," she said. "But first you must make me two promises in return."

"I'm not used to making deals with little girls," he said angrily.

"And I'm not used to saving the life of a man who slaughters trees by the thousands."

"So you really are Steadman's daughter . . ." he said. "What are your conditions?"

"First, you will tell the authorities the truth about what you saw or didn't see at the Elkmont Camp the day those men were killed."

"I can make that promise," he said, nodding. "What's your second demand?"

"You and your machines and logging crews must never come near my father's land."

Jim McClaren stared at her, clearly understanding the gravity of what she was asking.

"You have no right to ask me to make such a promise in the condition I'm in," he said.

"And you have no right to cut trees on my father's land. We exchange these promises or we don't—it's up to you. If you wish, I can disappear, and you can find your own way home."

McClaren exhaled a long breath as he looked down at his men and then around at the walls of the gorge. Then he turned back to her.

"I'll agree not to do any full-scale logging on your father's property, but I need to cut a right-of-way along the river so we can lay the tracks for the railroad. We need to get to the forests above his land. There's prime trees up there."

"No," she said, staring at him. "There won't be any railroad on my father's land, and you won't cut a single tree. You'll stay clear of the east side of the river entirely, upstream and downstream."

"Nathaniel Steadman doesn't own that river," McClaren demanded, getting increasingly angry.

"And neither do you," Willa replied. "Make this agreement or I'll leave you here to bleed. Good luck with the wolves tonight."

Jim McClaren scowled. When he spat on the ground, the sputum was shot red with blood.

It was clear that he didn't want to make the promise she was demanding, but he was obviously in considerable pain. He could barely stand, let alone walk a long distance over difficult terrain. He needed to get home by the shortest, easiest path possible.

"Fine," he growled. "I'll do it."

"Give me your word of honor," she demanded, using the phrase she had heard her father use.

"You're straining my patience, girl," McClaren said, glaring at her. "I give you my word."

"Good," Willa said. "Now let's go."

A few hours later, Willa watched Jim McClaren limp down the path in front of her. He wasn't out of shape, but he was a large man with heavy-booted feet, and he was dragging a wounded leg. He breathed louder than a full-grown boar bear, and he smelled far worse. He never looked up at the forest around him or paused to listen to its whispering voices. He trudged along, one step after another, wincing as if every movement caused him pain.

He's persistent, if nothing else, she thought begrudgingly.

She and Charka and the human followed the winding, up-and-down forest path. McClaren sometimes stopped, his body bending as he leaned against a tree to catch his breath. She could see that he was suffering. And part of her didn't care. She kept thinking about the enormous pain he had caused . . . all the destruction . . . the wanton murder of the trees, the shooting of the mother bear . . . There were so many things the loggers had done that she despised. And as she walked along this trail, she kept thinking about her father being dragged in the opposite direction—all because the loggers had accused him of something he hadn't done. She imagined her sister following him and the other men at a distance, watching over him the best she could.

Willa heard something in the distance behind her and stopped. She turned and listened, scanning the forest and sniffing the air. She kept expecting to see the ferns thrashing, or hear a slithering sound, or smell the odor of rotting decay, but there was nothing other than the breathing of the forest, the soft padding of Charka's paws, and the ponderous steps of the human.

"That cub seems to go everywhere with you," Jim McClaren said, not even noticing that she had paused to listen.

A while later, as they continued on down the path, she grew tired of watching him limp along, slow and plodding. The sooner she got him home, the sooner she could be rid of him.

"Stop here," she said.

McClaren obeyed and rested against a tree, too exhausted to do anything else.

Willa strained her ears to listen once more.

The forest was filled with the flute-like song of a wood thrush and the sound of trees swaying in the breeze. Whatever had been following them must have stopped or changed its course.

"Sit on the ground here and wait for me," she ordered him.

"Where are you going?" he asked, his voice hoarse and weak.

"To get something for your wound," she said. "It won't take long. Just wait here."

With those words, she split off into the forest, Charka trundling after her.

She searched a glen of weeping, leafy ferns among a gathering of ancient oak trees, and then hunted in between the delicate blue wildflowers growing on a sun-dappled slope. When she spotted white blossoms in the distance, she moved toward them, sensing that she was getting close. Growing in the boggy earth beside a gentle creek, she found the small plants with striped leaves she was looking for.

"*There* you are," she whispered as she squatted down and picked some of the leaves from the elusive little plants.

A memory began flowing through her mind. She and her grandmother were kneeling beside Alliw, who had hurt her arm falling from a rock. Willa remembered her grandmother holding her hands, showing her how to apply the crushed leaves to her sister's bleeding arm.

"There you are," Willa whispered again, but this time to the elusive little memory she had long forgotten.

The recollections of her sister were getting fewer and farther between. She had lived six years of her life with Alliw, but now seven without her. Would there come a time when she wouldn't be able to remember her at all? Did that mean Alliw would disappear? The thought of it made her sadder than she had been in a long time.

She rubbed her face, trying to clear her mind. Ever since leaving the gorge, her lips had been dry and her head ached like she hadn't been drinking enough water. She and Charka leaned down and drank from the stream.

When she returned to the human, he was sitting on the ground, his back against the trunk of a tree, his eyes closed. His skin was paler, grayer than it had been before. He looked so still that she almost thought he was dead, but then his eyes slowly opened.

"I'm not doing too good," McClaren said in a ragged voice, looking down at the blood oozing from his leg.

Kneeling beside him, she put the leaves into her mouth and began chewing them.

"I thought maybe you got lost out there," he said.

"I need to apply this to your leg, but I have to warn you, it's going to hurt."

"What is it?"

"It will help stop the bleeding," she said as she pressed the wet mash into his wound with her fingers.

He growled and pulled away sharply. "Enough!"

"I told you it would hurt—now stay still," she said as she worked the leaves into the gash like her grandmother had taught her. "We need to start moving faster. Something's following us."

"What is it? Is it those creatures?" he said, the color draining from his face entirely as he tried to get up, but she pushed him back down.

"I don't know what it is," she said as she tried to finish her work. "But quick now, tear off two pieces of your shirt."

McClaren winced as she used one of the scraps to wipe blood from his wound.

"Stay here," she said, and then she ran into the woods, leaped over a small gully, and tossed the bloody rag into a thicket.

"What's going on?" McClaren said as she came back to him.

Ignoring him, she grabbed a handful of dirt, blew into it, and cast it onto the path behind them, an old woodwitch spell that her grandmother had taught her.

"What's that for?"

"If we're lucky, it will throw off the scent," she said as she helped him onto his feet.

"The scent of what?" he asked.

"You," she said. "Now come on, we've got to go."

"What's back there? What's after us?" He looked over his shoulder as he followed her down the path.

Using his rifle as a crutch, he moved more quickly now.

"I can feel that stuff numbing my leg," he said as he limped along.

"That means it's working," Willa said, glancing behind them.

"What did you put on me?" he said, the spirit in his voice stronger now. "Some kind of herb or something?"

"I don't know the name of it in English."

"Then in what language *do* you know its name?"

It seemed so wrong, so *dangerous*, for a man such as him to know the word *Faeran*, so she didn't answer.

"You said you weren't Cherokee. So what are you?"

"I'm the forest you're destroying," she said, wanting to shut him up. It was bad enough allowing a human like him to see her, but it was even worse talking to him. She walked faster to put more distance between them.

"I'm not destroying the forest," McClaren said emphatically, limping after her as if the anger rising between them was giving him fuel.

"I saw you with the Elkmont crew yesterday," she snarled at him.

"What about it?" he asked, ire rising in his voice as he struggled to keep up with her.

"I saw you and your men cutting those trees."

"We were doing our job," he said.

She turned sharply, right in front of him, bringing him to an abrupt stop. "You are a murderer and you should be ashamed of yourself," she said, glad that she was finally able to say it to his face. And then she turned back around and continued on down the path at a quicker pace.

"A murderer?" he said incredulously, limping after her. "What are you talking about? I haven't murdered anyone!"

"Don't try to deny it. I saw you do it. You killed the bear."

"You can't murder a bear—that's ridiculous," he said. "You need to watch what you say, throwing around accusations like that."

"I mean the bear, the trees, the birds. I mean *everything.* You're murdering it all!"

"Just hold on a minute," he said, reaching out to grab her and turn her toward him. But she reflexively stepped out of his reach and disappeared into a tree.

"What the—" he gasped in alarm.

"Do not try to touch me!" she hissed at him, invisible from within the forest.

"I can't even *see* you!" he said, peering into the vegetation. "Where did you go? How are you doing that?" His earlier anger had transformed into pure astonishment.

"I'm here," she said, stepping away from the trees and shifting back into a shade of green that he could differentiate from the other greens of the forest. "Just be quiet." Looking down the path behind them, she squatted down and held on to Charka. "I need to listen."

The human seemed to understand what she was doing, but he was still making too much noise. "Quit shuffling your feet," she ordered him.

Once again, she turned and tried to listen.

"Now stop breathing . . ." she whispered.

She cupped her hands behind her earlobes to amplify the sounds of the forest behind them. The setting sun had dropped below the ridge line, so the tree frogs were beginning their evening chorus, and the buzzing of cicadas had given way to a symphony of crickets and katydids. But through all the other noises, she heard something else: the faint padding of footsteps making their way across the forest floor.

"Someone's following us," Willa said, her lungs starting to pull in more air. She had a feeling it was the wheat-haired girl and her gray slithering snakes. It was going to be difficult to fight them in the darkness.

McClaren leaned against a tree, raised his rifle, and pointed it down the path.

Pulling Charka toward her, Willa crouched and blended into the ferns.

There was no mistaking it now. Whatever it was, it wasn't stalking them anymore. It was running full tilt straight toward them.

Willa listened again.

A few seconds before, she thought she had heard a person running behind them. But that sound was gone now, as if whoever it was had stopped or veered off in a different direction. In its place, she heard the soft, wave-like noise of many fast, four-footed creatures, the muffled push of furred paws against the leaf-covered ground, and the faint click of claws against the stones. *They're coming this way.*

Pulling in a quick breath, Willa looked down at the wound on Jim McClaren's leg. The healing herbs she had applied had slowed the bleeding, and he'd definitely been moving more quickly, but that wasn't enough. A small trickle of blood was dripping down his leg and onto the ground. Their pursuers were tracking him, sensing his weakness, mile after mile.

"What is it? What's wrong?" McClaren asked, clearly alarmed by the look on her face.

But before she could answer, Charka cried out in dismay. Sniffing at the air, he turned and tried to run. Willa grabbed him and held him tight. There was only one predator in the forest relentless enough to follow them this far, so it was no time for anyone to go off on their own.

"It's a pack of wolves," she said to McClaren.

"Wolves!" McClaren said, eyes wide as he gripped his rifle and scanned the forest.

Willa knew that her attempt to cast their scent had failed. She could hear the wolves moving through the forest now, fanning out left and right, surrounding them.

Charka grunted frantically, huffing air through his nose.

"Get up the tree!" she said in the old language, touching a young pine. Charka shinnied rapidly up its trunk and into its branches.

"I don't see them . . ." McClaren whispered as he peered into the darkness.

"They're getting closer . . ." Willa said.

Their pursuers had stopped running and were now creeping through the ferns toward them, so close that she could hear their breathing.

"Just stay calm . . ." she whispered to McClaren.

The wolves slowly emerged from the misty undergrowth, two and three at a time, until she and Charka and the human were surrounded by their yellow eyes glowing in the moonlight.

All the members of the pack stalked closer, moving as one, their bodies crouched low and their shoulders hunched, growling as they came.

"If you've got a weapon, girl, get it out!" the man said, his voice shaking. He aimed his rifle this way and that, trying to figure out how he was going to fight off so many predators. "Look at them all! There must be thirty of them! But I've only got a dozen cartridges!"

The wolves pressed in, staring intently at McClaren, baring their teeth and snarling.

As he raised his rifle to shoot the closest one, Willa put her hand on the long, killing barrel and said, "No." The cold metal surface of the gun felt so alien to her, almost like it would burn her Faeran skin.

"We've got to kill them off as fast as we can!" McClaren shouted, trying to pull the rifle away from her.

"No!" she said again. "Put your gun down and I will get you through this. It's our only chance."

McClaren gripped his rifle, ready to fire, but his arms were shaking as he gazed around at the snapping, biting wolves. They were everywhere. There was no doubt in Willa's mind that he wanted to shoot them—out of fear, out of anger—he wanted to kill them all.

"I can stop the wolves!" Willa said to Jim McClaren. "But you have to put down the gun. . . ."

"I hope you know what you're doing," he grumbled, and then, finally, he lowered his weapon. Slowly.

Willa did not hold back. She stepped forward, right toward the wolves, so that they could all see her, and she could see them.

She looked into their eyes to make sure they knew her spirit and her intention. And then she pulled in a steady, even breath and began to speak to them.

"Ena dua un, dunum far." It's good to see you, my friends.

To her surprise, the wolves ignored her Faeran words. They continued growling and moving closer, just as they had been before, tightening their circle, snapping their teeth, their eyes locked on the weak and bleeding human. They seemed to sense instinctively that he was not just their prey but also their enemy, and that his wounds made him vulnerable.

Willa tried to stay steady and calm, but her heart began thumping in her chest. What was wrong with these wolves? Why weren't they listening to her?

But then, as she looked into their faces more carefully and noticed their tucked ears, their lowered tails, and the haggard positions of their bodies, she realized that it wasn't just the intensity of a predator's stare that she saw in their eyes.

It was hunger.

Desperate, all-consuming *hunger.*

Their fur was ragged and their bodies were thin. Many of these animals were starving. One of them was suffering from a bullet wound to his shoulder.

The wolves stalked toward the wounded, bleeding man. With the smell of his blood in their nostrils, they were ready to attack the moment their leader gave them the signal. They were ready to bite and snarl, lunge and tear. They were ready to *eat*.

But one of the wolves, a large and powerful female with beautiful silver-gray fur and striking amber eyes, stared at Willa in a different way. She was not snarling. She was not stalking. She was just gazing at Willa.

"Luthien . . ." Willa said gently, the warmth of her heart filling the sound of her friend's name.

The wolf dropped her head a little, and then stepped slowly toward her.

Willa knelt down and wrapped her arms around her. "I've been so worried about you and the pack," she said in the old language.

Luthien rubbed her shoulder against her in reply, and then nuzzled her with her snout. Willa leaned into her, their foreheads gently touching as she stroked the fur of Luthien's neck. It felt so good to see her old friend again.

The other wolves stopped growling as they realized that the pack wasn't going to attack.

Willa could see several wolves that she knew. But it appeared that many were stragglers from other packs that had been decimated by human attacks. These lone, wandering, starving creatures had joined with Luthien, their last hope of survival.

"I'm afraid I have a favor to ask you," Willa said. "This human is not my friend, but I am bound by a promise to get him home. I'm sorry that I must ask you and your pack to go hungry a while longer. I must ask that you find your prey elsewhere tonight."

As Willa spoke, she touched Luthien with her hands and her face, for it was through touch that wolves gave true meaning to the sounds and motions of their language. When Willa was done talking, Luthien gazed at her, and then she slowly pushed her large furred head against Willa's chest.

Willa rested her head on the she-wolf's shoulder, thanking her.

A moment later, Luthien pulled gradually away and started to retreat into the undergrowth. When Luthien paused and gazed at the other members of the pack, they followed her, and together they disappeared into the misty haze of the forest.

"The wolves have decided to leave us alone," Willa said to the human.

"Just because we can't see them doesn't mean they're not out there, circling, waiting for the best moment to attack us and kill us!" McClaren said, still gripping his rifle as if his life depended on it.

"The wolves won't be bothering us again," she said calmly. She didn't want to argue with him. "Now you should rest."

"I don't understand," he said, exasperation in his voice. "Just what are you? Those wolves acted like they knew you."

"More importantly, I know them," she said quietly.

"What was that language you used?" he pressed her. "What did you say to them?"

"The wolves were hungry, but I asked them to leave you alone tonight."

"What do you mean *tonight*?"

"I promised I would get you home, Jim McClaren. And that I will do. But I will not bind the wolves to a promise longer than my own."

"So, in other words, if I'm walking through the woods on some other night, then it's all right with you if they kill me."

She held his gaze for several seconds, but she did not reply to his words. "Your rest is over," she said and continued down the path.

Charka grunted, scuttled down the tree, and chased after her.

"This little cub acts like you're his mother or something," McClaren said as he caught up with them.

"No, I'm not his mother," she said wearily. "You ordered your men to shoot his mother and cut her body into pieces."

"So you *were* there!" he said. "You're that thing we saw!"

"Yes, I was there, and I saw you kill the bear."

"What of it? Killing that bear was completely justified. It was a danger to the men."

"No," Willa said. "She wasn't."

"The men need to eat," he insisted, "and they have a right to protect their families from dangerous animals."

Willa stopped in the path and turned toward him.

"So do the wolves," she said.

As Willa walked down the path with Charka and Jim McClaren toward Cades Cove, a memory of her sister and her grandmother slipped into her mind. The three of them were huddled together, hidden beneath the lowest boughs of a pine tree and whispering as they watched a group of wolves outside their den. Three pups wrestled among themselves and with the two adults, growling and pouncing, their mouths open and biting, but only in play.

"The wolves are a family, loving and caring for one another, depending on one another," her grandmother had told Willa and her sister. "But unlike the Faeran, wolves are hunters. They track down and kill other animals for food."

"They don't *look* scary," Alliw said as they watched the wolves.

"When the white-skinned humans arrived in these forests," her grandmother continued, "they started shooting, trapping, and poisoning the wolves in great numbers. They will not stop until they exterminate all of them and make this world like the one they came from."

"But why do they want to kill the wolves?" Alliw cried in dismay.

"They're frightened of them," her grandmother said. "And they believe them to be competition for the deer and elk that the humans need to survive, for they, too, are hunters."

"But do the wolves kill *all* the deer?" Willa asked.

"As deer become scarcer, the wolves naturally have fewer pups, which keeps their numbers in balance," her grandmother replied. "I will tell you a little story. Our friends the Cherokee are hunters just like the white-skinned humans and the wolves. The Cherokee have seen that in those areas where there are no wolves, the deer become too numerous and eat all the plants, and without the plants, the deer starve in great numbers, and without the deer, the Cherokee suffer. The plants, the birds, the deer, the wolves, the Cherokee . . . they're all connected, each one keeping the world from breaking. Do you understand?"

Willa nodded along with Alliw, and then she asked, "But what do *we* do? I mean the Faeran. What part do we play?"

Her grandmother's eyes softened as she gazed at her. "We are the voices of the trees, Willa, and the words of the wolves. We are the force that carries the birds in the sky and the magic that turns the sunlight into life. We are the parts that are missing, the invisible, the *in-between*. When we live and when we die, we are the soul of the forest, in whatever form it must take."

Willa's memories of her sister and her grandmother seemed so long ago to her now, like it hadn't just been a different time, but a different world altogether.

As she, Charka, and McClaren continued down the path through the quiet, moonlit forest, the cub trundled beside her, eating berries and grubs and whatever else she could find for him along the way.

But the human trudged along. He stumbled frequently, unable to see the foot-snagging roots and rocks in the darkness. Much of the trail was steep and twisty, and trickling with streams that were difficult for him to cross.

Willa moved quickly and easily, often looking behind her and listening, not for wolves, but for the other thing she had heard. The two-footed thing. Had the wheat-haired girl been tracking them and then the wolves interfered?

"Thank you for what you did back there," Jim McClaren said as he carefully picked his way down the path on his wounded leg. "Those wolves looked hungry."

Willa didn't say anything in return. She only hoped that Luthien and the pack were able to find other food.

She knew that wolves seldom attacked human beings. But the recent logging in the area had frightened away many of the deer and other prey. The wolves were starving and desperate. Sometimes she thought she understood all the damage the loggers were doing to the forest by cutting down thousands of trees, but other times it shocked her to see all the interconnections that were being torn apart.

"Why do you do it?" she asked McClaren as they walked. "Why do you kill the trees?"

His brow furrowed and his mouth tightened. "Why do I . . ." He didn't seem to understand her question. "Do you mean why am I a logger?"

"Yes, why?"

"When I was young, I signed on with a logging crew to make some money, working as a bushwhacker at first, then a sawyer, and then a boom operator. I worked my way up. Now I run my own crew. Eighty-five men. And it's the same with them. It's a job, a livelihood like any other. And mind you, we're not the only ones. The Sutton Lumber Company and other logging outfits are coming in here and cutting these trees one way or another. Might as well be us folks in the Cove making some of the money. We need to feed our families just like everybody else. I've got a bushelful of children at home."

"But you're cutting down the world," Willa said.

He scowled. "I don't even know what that means. The country needs the wood, and we're providing it."

"You're destroying the forest!"

"You keep saying that, but Sutton isn't destroying the forest. Most of the employees live here, same as you. We're not going to do anything we think is harmful to the place we live. There's plenty of forest, more than we could ever cut."

"But what is this company you work for? What does it want?"

"The logging company is owned by a Northerner named Mr. W. B. Sutton."

"Why has he come to our mountains?"

"Years ago, when Mr. Sutton was young, he worked for a logging company up in Pennsylvania, but when all the forests in his home state were cleared, he found himself out of a job. He and some of the other loggers went west in search of new timberlands. At that time, Ohio and Michigan were entirely covered in forests. It was said that a squirrel could travel from one side of Ohio to the other without ever touching the ground. So they brought in their trains, fired up their steam-powered loaders, and went to work. It took them about forty years to clear-cut it all, nothing left now but empty fields. Most folks think that the lumber industry in the East is done now, all the forests gone, but when old Mr. Sutton heard about our southern mountains, he got a gleam in his eye. The mountain slopes here are so steep that loggers have never been able to reach them. But with the help of the new gear-wheeled locomotives that Sutton used up north, we're now able to harvest the trees and haul the wood down to the mill. I can tell you that many people doubted Mr. Sutton's plan, but he was right. We're doing it. It's working. And now many more logging companies are going to follow."

"You sound like you admire him," Willa said, curling her lip in disgust.

"Of course I do. He's a bold man with a bold vision, and I respect that. He built his sawmill and railroad yard here just last year, and now he's laying the spurs of the railroad all up and down these mountain ridges. The railroad's the key. There's a whole new town down there now, about fifteen miles from Cades Cove, that has grown up around the mill. They call it Sutton Town. That's no accident. People love him. He's changing everything around here, bringing some real progress to these parts."

Willa could hear the adoration in McClaren's voice, but she listened to his story in horror. She didn't recognize much of what he was saying—like the names of places and machines—but she understood enough.

"Do you not see?" she asked, looking at him in astonishment.

"See what?" he asked in return. "A lot of people might have doubted Mr. Sutton at first, but nobody resents him around here. People appreciate a good, cash-paying job."

"Maybe in Cades Cove and Sutton and Gatlinburg nobody resents him, but there's a lot more to 'around here' than those places," she said, gesturing in the direction of the Great Mountain and her father's home.

"All right, let's take your pa as an example," McClaren said. "Most people in the cove reckon your pa knows these woods better than just about anybody. But he's struggling up there with his grist mill, his orchards, and his bees. It's no way to make a real living. He's been offered a job with the lumber company, and not just crew work, either. He'd be scouting and prospecting, mapping out where the best stands of good-quality lumber are and the most efficient way to get to them. That job is his for the taking, anytime he wants it. It'd be a load off his mind, income he can count on instead of always trying to make his own way. He's got mouths to feed just like I do."

Willa had not been aware of any of this and a question formed in her mind. "When you made him this offer, how did he reply?"

"I won't repeat his particular phrasing," he said, "but it was a no. He's just being stubborn and ornery for the sake of it."

Willa smiled, imagining her father's response.

"And you should say no, too, Mr. McClaren," she said.

"I'm not going to say no to a good paying job for me and my men."

"But don't you see?"

"You keep saying that, girl. See what? I see plenty of trees in these mountains—that much is obvious if you just look around—and I don't see any harm in taking a few of them."

"But what about those places you mentioned?"

"What places?"

"You just told me about them. Michigan, Ohio, and all those other places. What about your sons and daughters?"

"What about them?" he asked. "That's the whole point. Like I said, I've got mouths to feed."

"But now that all of Ohio's forests have been cut down, do people still live there, or is it a wasteland like one of your stump-riddled cutting sites?"

"Of course people live in Ohio!" he said. "Before you start getting all high-and-mighty about me cutting a few trees, you need to get some learnin' in ya, girl! What's your father been teaching you up there? Of course there are people in Ohio! Why do you think they cleared all that land? For houses! Houses made of wood!"

"It's true that I don't understand what you're saying about Ohio," she admitted glumly. "But without the trees, where do the animals live? The bears? The wolves? The mountain lions? The otters?"

"Those animals don't live in Ohio anymore," he said. "But I can tell you this: the farming is good."

He said it so flatly, so confidently, that it seemed as if it was obvious in his mind and should be obvious in hers as well, that this one statement he was making was more important than everything she knew and valued.

The farming is good.

Willa thought about that for a long time as they made their way down the mountain. She truly didn't understand.

19

A few hours later, as the sun was rising, Willa and McClaren caught their first glimpse through the trees of the place the humans called Cades Cove.

It was a beautiful, oval-shaped valley, several miles long, with waving fields of corn, wheat, barley, and rye, surrounded by deep green forest and rising mountains on all sides. Log cabins and small white clapboard houses dotted the countryside, their chimneys laying fine gray traces into the dark blue sky above. Skirts, trousers, and other human clothing hung on long lines in the yards and fluttered in the breeze. A small herd of pigs and cows was grazing in one of the pastures, and a farmer in a wagon was rolling along one of the valley's dirt roads. Deep down, Willa had to admit that it seemed to be a kind and tranquil place.

"There it is," McClaren said, a bit of cheer finally in his voice. "We made it."

Willa turned to him. "I've kept my promise. Now you need to do the same."

"I always remember my promises," he said, limping down the path.

"Jim McClaren," she said quietly.

He stopped and looked at her.

"I have to help my father," she said.

"I know you do," he said gently. "I would expect nothing less."

"I need to ask you something, and I need an honest answer. You owe me that much."

"Ask your question."

"Did you actually see—I mean with your own eyes—my father at the Elkmont Camp the day those men died?"

"No, I didn't," he said, holding her gaze. "Luther and some of the other men reported the incident to me."

"The same Luther who is with the sheriff and my father right now?"

"That's right."

"What do I need to do to make sure the sheriff lets my father go?"

"The surest way to help him is to prove that someone else murdered those men."

"Is it possible that Luther himself did it?"

"It's possible," Jim McClaren said grimly. "But Luther Higgs never struck me as the killin' type."

"And my father does?" she asked in surprise. "You were willing to believe what Luther and the other men told you."

"Your father has always struck me as the kind of man who would pull a trigger if a trigger needed pulling," Jim McClaren said.

Hearing those words, and the tone in McClaren's voice, sent a chill down Willa's spine.

"It doesn't help his case that he's considered one of the best rifle shots around," McClaren added.

"Do you think it's possible that those snake creatures we saw killed those men?"

"I don't know . . ." McClaren said. "But it would be difficult to prove such a thing. I saw those creatures with my own eyes, but I still don't know what they were or what words I could use to describe them to other people."

"You will have to tell them something," Willa said.

The man swiped his hand down his face. "Yes," he said with a heavy sigh.

"And you *will* keep the promises you made to me," Willa said firmly.

"I always keep my promises, Willa Steadman," he said again, and he started hobbling away once more.

Standing in the forest, with Charka at her side, Willa watched the man named Jim McClaren make his way down into the valley.

She knew the wound to his leg would soon heal, but as he and his men killed the forest around them, she wondered what would become of him, his wife, and his children, who would live in a treeless world.

20

Prove that someone else murdered those men.

That's what Jim McClaren had told her.

A pang of loneliness reverberated through her. Her father and Hialeah seemed so far away now, days of walking, but she could still see their faces and hear their voices. What were they doing to her father? Had her sister had to use the gun? Somehow, she had to solve the mystery of who or what had murdered the loggers at the Elkmont Camp that day, and she needed to do it quickly.

Had it been the wheat-haired girl and her slithering gray snakes? Were Nathaniel and Hialeah in danger from those same creatures even now? Willa had seen wolves and bears and even panthers in these woods, but she'd never encountered anything like those strange, deadly beasts with their unearthly coldness. She shivered at the recollection.

Or maybe there was a far more mundane explanation, like that Luther Higgs had committed the murders. But why would he kill his own brother? None of it made any sense.

Her grandmother had taught her many things, but she hadn't told any stories about strange yellow-haired girls or weird snakelike creatures. Willa wondered if anyone from her Faeran clan had ever seen beasts like that before. Maybe one of the elders knew what they were or could solve the mystery in some other way. Regardless of whether the Faeran helped her or not, she had to warn them.

She knew the members of her old clan would not be pleased to see her. To them, she was the one who had started the series of events that destroyed their lair and shattered the clan. But if there was something she could do to help them now, she had to try.

She and Charka trekked up through the thick stands of spruce and fir trees that grew on the slopes of the Great Mountain. The cub was whining for food, begging her to stop and search for more grubs. Yet she pressed on, knowing that somewhere out there her father and sister needed her to do her part.

She climbed through thickets of blackberry brambles and pushed her way through the hobblebush. But when they finally came to the area where she'd last seen her Faeran clan, no one was there.

She got down on her hands and knees and studied the grasses and ferns, but none of them were disturbed or matted. Her Faeran kin not only weren't there, they hadn't been there for a long time.

She sniffed the ground, trying to pick up a scent, but there was nothing. Thinking that she was searching for a new kind of food, Charka joined in excitedly, pushing his snout against the dirt over and over.

Frustrated, Willa sat on a rock and tried to think. Where would the Faeran have gone?

The last time she had seen them, in the fall of the previous year, they'd been wandering the forest, frightened and discouraged, arguing among themselves about what to do. Her friend Gillen had been trying to get them all to work together, to strive toward common goals like the Faeran of old. She wondered if they had been able to build a new lair so they could survive the winter. Or had the clan disintegrated?

She looked up into the sky as six or seven of the local ravens flew overhead, cawing to one another with their croaking voices. An idea sprang into her mind.

"I need your help, my friends!" she called up to them in the old language.

The large black birds tilted their wings and rolled, seeming to almost fall through the air, and then with a final flare of their feathers, they landed in the trees, cocking their heads and looking at her with curiosity.

"I'm trying to find the others of my kind," she explained, knowing that ravens insisted on quick answers when they discovered a visitor in their territory.

Most of the animals of the forest understood the old language instinctively when it was spoken to them. If they responded, it was not in the Faeran words but in their own natural forms of communication—the sounds, movements, and behaviors of their own kind—and these were up to each Faeran to learn. She knew wolf, bear, otter, fox, bobcat, and many others. But of all the inhabitants of the forest, the ravens were the true masters of sound and meaning. They were the poets of the sky.

The ravens in the trees above thrummed low, gurgling sounds deep in their throats, and they clicked and clacked with raspy pops and shrill whistles, arguing among themselves, not about whether they were going to help her—there seemed to be no question among them about that—but exactly where they had last seen the Faeran clan.

Willa knew ravens were aware of nearly everything that happened in their territory. Yet it appeared they had reached a seemingly impossible consensus: the Faeran clan had simply disappeared.

All agreed save one—a particularly young raven, rattling and cawing, bobbing his head as he shuffled madly back and forth across a branch, insisting that he had indeed seen the Faeran, and he knew where they were.

Suddenly, the whole flock of ravens burst into the air and flew through the trees like a black driven rain.

Excited, Willa ran after them as fast as she could, trying desperately to keep up as she shouted for Charka to follow.

As she climbed, gasping for breath, up through the rocky terrain, she saw that the young raven had led the others to a narrow, tree-shaded gulch tucked between two spurs of the mountain.

The boisterous flock circled overhead, tipping and diving as they called out to her.

"Thank you, my friends!" she shouted up to them, waving.

Still cawing and croaking and whistling to each other, the ravens whirled in the air and flew on toward their favorite lookout—a tall, gnarly spruce in the distance that towered above the other trees growing from the ragged edge of the mountain.

When the ravens were gone, Willa peered into the gulch. The walls were far too steep and too thick with rhododendron bushes for her to walk into it. She was going to have to climb down.

"You stay here, Charka," she said, and the little bear curled up to wait for her.

She lowered herself over the edge and descended hand over hand, using the rhododendron branches like the rungs of a ladder. Beneath the canopy of the large waxy leaves, the sunlit day turned into a green-shaded underworld. The sound of the wind and the distant ravens gave way to quiet and the faint trickle of water. The ground beneath her feet became colder. And her nose filled with the odor of wet rock and earth. It was just the kind of place that a Faeran clan would hide.

When she got to the bottom of the gulch, she peered around, hoping to see her people gathering food from the forest, taking care of one another, and telling the stories of old. The Faeran were a collective people. They stuck together. But the truth was, after the padaran died and the lair burned, with neither a strong leader nor a shared home to unite them, the clan had suffered many struggles. And she knew her hopes of what she would find now were but memories of her early life.

She searched one side of the gulch and then the other, but no one was there.

And then she saw it.

The thing the ravens had brought her to.

It looked like nothing more than a black crevice, a shadow leading to an even deeper shadow.

It's a cave, she thought, remembering that the ravens had told her the Faeran had disappeared.

Her heart started to pound. Her lungs suddenly wanted more air.

She stared at the opening for a long time, unable to move toward it or away from it. She didn't want to get near the cave. She didn't want to see what was inside. But she knew she must.

She climbed hand over hand up through the rocks to reach the mouth of the cave, her skin beginning to crawl. And then she peeked into the darkness.

A grayish-white hand became visible.

Startled, she pulled back.

The fingers were curled inward and they had long, sharp nails. She thought it was a corpse at first, but then she saw that the hand was trembling.

She grimaced as she slowly tilted her head and looked up into the shadows.

Dozens of mottled, grayish-white bodies clung to the inner walls of the dripping cave. And then she began to see the faces. All the eyes of the Faeran clan were staring at her.

21

Willa jerked back from the entrance of the cave. Something came scuttling out of it like a giant crayfish. As it rose up onto two spindly legs, Willa saw that it was an old Faeran woman with slimy, dark gray skin and extremely long, scraggly white hair that fell down to her ribs.

"It's you!" the old woman spat, her mouth twisting in revulsion as she charged at Willa.

The quills on the back of Willa's neck snapped straight up. "Keep away from me!" she warned, thrusting out her hands to fend off the woman.

"We don't want your kind here, woodwitch!" the old woman rasped, pointing a wretched, bony finger into Willa's face.

"It's the witch who burned down the lair!" another Faeran shouted as he crawled from the cave. Willa recognized him right away. His name was Tanic. He had lost his two sons in the uprising against the padaran. Tanic's body was far larger and stronger than the bony old woman's, but his skin was just as splotchy gray and slimy, and his huge eyes bulged with hatred as he spotted Willa.

And then another Faeran came out of the cave, and another. The entire clan surrounded her like angry hornets disturbed from their nest. They were all hissing and jeering, pushing at her. Willa's cheeks burned as she ducked and winced, but she held her ground.

"Stop it!" someone called out. "Leave her alone!"

Willa looked up to see her friend Gillen elbowing her way through the swarm. Gillen grabbed her by the arm and yanked her away from the snarling attackers.

"I'll talk to her—just stay back!" Gillen shouted at the surrounding mob, the muscles in her neck and shoulders tightening as she pushed them aside.

Gillen had dark green spotted skin, but she had never learned to blend, so she didn't change color. Her face had an angular, forceful look, and she had steady eyes that gave her a determined appearance. The others begrudgingly listened to her, withdrawing from her barking commands.

"We don't have much time," Gillen said to Willa as she quickly pulled her through the undergrowth. "I can only hold them off for so long."

Gillen stopped beneath the gnarled branches of an old tree that had grown out of the cracks of the surrounding rock.

"What are you doing here, Willa?" she demanded, still holding her by the arm. Gillen wasn't that much older, but there had always been something about her that demanded attention. "Why did you come?"

"T-to help," Willa stammered, uncertain now. She just had to get straight to it. "Listen, Gillen. There are creatures killing people in the forest. Everyone in the clan is in danger."

"What are you talking about?" Gillen said, narrowed her eyes at her. "What creatures?"

"They look like gray snakes, but they're giant, and they move under the earth," Willa said. "They can kill with just a touch. I saw them attack three humans right before my eyes."

"Kill with just a touch . . ." Gillen said.

"I came here to find out if any of the elders have ever seen or heard of anything like this before. But what's going on, Gillen? Have the creatures already come? Why is everyone in the cave?"

"It was the only place where we could find shelter," Gillen said, her voice ragged with discouragement. "But there's no food."

"I can find food for you," Willa said, letting a trace of hope trickle into her voice as she grasped Gillen's hand and tried to pull her toward the sunlight. "Come on, the forest is full of it. I'll show you where to find it."

"It's not just me this time, Willa," Gillen said bluntly, holding firm. "It's *everyone*! The clan is starving!"

"You need to get out of that cave," Willa argued. "Can't you see how gray everyone looks? You all need light to live. You need water from the streams. Go out into the forest!"

"The forest can't help us," Gillen said, shaking her head.

Willa looked at her in alarm. She had never heard such

obscene and depressing words come from her friend's mouth. "You can eat berries, shoots, nuts, mushrooms, leaves—there's so much! But do it soon—you have to stock up for winter."

"You're a fool, Willa," Gillen said. "Without a lair, we're never going to survive another winter!"

As she and Gillen were talking, Willa saw the other members of the clan moving slowly toward them, their heads ducking one by one below the low-hanging branches of the old trees. Their gray bodies were hunched, and their faces scowling with bitterness as they came. Many had their hands clenched into fists. Others were carrying sharpened sticks as weapons, a remnant of the padaran's ways.

Willa felt her lungs pulling in more air, the muscles in her legs bunching, readying her to run. She tried to stay brave, tried to convince herself that these were her people and they wouldn't hurt her.

"They're coming back . . ." she said to Gillen.

As Gillen turned to face them, the Faeran quickly surrounded them.

"Woodwitch!" the bony old woman shouted, pressing her face so close that Willa could see the spittle that flew from the woman's curling lips.

As Willa tried to back away, she noticed that there were younger Faeran at the rear of the crowd. They weren't shouting or hissing. They were just watching what the elders were doing, dismay clouding their faces. And then she noticed something else—the face of one of the boys was covered with brown splotches laced with jagged black streaks.

"Sacram is suffering from oak wilt," Willa said to Gillen. "We need to help him."

"Leave the boy alone!" the bony old woman snarled, shoving Willa back with her clawlike hand. "You've done enough! Our people are none of your concern now!"

"Can't you see that he's sick?" Willa insisted. "Look at him! I can help him!"

Gillen turned over her own hand and showed Willa the dark gray streaks spreading up the underside of her arm like the decaying veins of a dead leaf. "A quarter of the clan has already died from it, Willa. And many more have the disease."

"Please let me help you, Gillen, at least with this. Please," Willa begged her, trying to ignore the mob of Faeran pressing in on them and speak directly to her old friend.

The large, bulgy-eyed Tanic pushed through the crowd and thundered toward her. "You're the one who started the uprising!" he shouted. "You have no right to be part of this clan!"

Willa retreated from him quickly, only to slam straight into the crowd of angry Faeran pressing in behind her. Their hands grasped at her. Their shoulders jammed against her. And their teeth gnashed in her ears.

"Murderer!" one of them hissed.

"Burner!" snarled another as he gripped her arms.

"Clan-breaker!" the bony old woman rasped, shoving her crooked finger under Willa's chin and pushing back her head.

Willa stumbled back, desperate to escape. As she tripped over the roots of a small tree, she reached out and grabbed its trunk to keep from falling.

The moment she touched the tree, she felt its power. Its alliance. It was as if in that moment, this small, seemingly insignificant little tree living in the shade of a rocky gulch was reminding her of one thing: who she truly was.

If they wanted a woodwitch, then a woodwitch she would be!

"Eera-de thaolin!"

The tree reached down and lifted her up in one swift motion, pulling her out of the reach of the grasping claws of the surrounding mob.

As her Faeran clan gasped and cowered in fear, she blended into the leaves, quickly climbed through the upper branches over their heads, and disappeared from sight.

Willa climbed out of the gulch and shifted into a color that Charka could see. The little bear made a thumping noise deep in his throat that sounded like someone knocking on a hollow log. He was happy to see her. But she didn't stop. She gathered him into her arms and kept going until she was sure the seething mob of the Faeran clan was well behind them. She only set him down again when she had crossed over the next ridge.

She knew the Faeran were never going to let her back into the clan—they despised her—but they were *her* people, the last of her kind, and she couldn't let them die. Traveling down the slope of the mountain, she crossed through the cool, shaded stands of spruce and firs, and then, farther down, through the beech trees, yellow birch, and mountain maple, until she reached the dryer, warmer, more exposed western slopes that were filled with tall pines and mighty oaks.

She finally came to a particularly large and sturdy oak tree, its grayish-brown bark set with deep, craggy grooves, its trunk wider than she could stretch her arms, and its thick branches soaring in the sky. She found a peacefulness in its age and its size, in its ancientness.

"Hello, my friend, it's good to meet you," she said in the old language. "My name is Willa and I need your help."

She climbed into the upper branches of the tree and carefully examined its leaves. They were green and strong, wet with life. Her grandmother had taught her that the Faeran and the oak trees were so closely related that the wilt disease afflicted both alike. It was caused by a fungus carried by sap beetles and other insects. And just as the stronger trees of a forest nourished and sustained the weaker ones through their interlocking roots, the only way for a Faeran to survive the wilt was by eating the wet leaves of a healthy oak tree. Nathaniel had taught her that humans were sometimes afflicted by a disease called scurvy, which was, in a similar way, caused by a lack of certain kinds of fruits and vegetables in their diet.

"Thank you," she whispered to the tree as she gathered leaves from its branches. "My people really need these."

When she had collected what she thought was enough, she descended. Charka came running over, whimpering and pleading, thinking she had found something good for him to eat.

"I'm sorry, little one, these aren't for you," she said as she headed back up the mountain. "We'll get some food for you soon, once we do what we need to do."

When they arrived at the gulch, she asked Charka to hide and wait for her once more, and then she climbed down inside.

She did not reveal herself to the Faeran but watched the members of the clan from a short distance away.

Gillen appeared to be organizing some of them into small groups. Willa recognized the boy named Sacram, the one who was suffering from oak wilt, and his twin brother, Marcas, who appeared to be afflicted in nearly the same way, but on the opposite side of his face.

The two boys were carrying sticks they had sharpened into spear-like weapons. Willa frowned and pressed her lips together. The Faeran of old did not use weapons of any kind—only the padaran and his guards had. What were Sacram and Marcas doing?

Knowing she only had one chance, Willa walked straight toward them.

Sacram's eyes widened at the sight of her abruptly appearing out of the forest. Marcas flinched and raised his spear to protect himself from attack, then realized it was her and lowered the weapon.

Gillen strode toward her. "What are you doing back here, Willa? I told you to stay away, for your own good."

"Just eat these," Willa said, handing her the oak leaves she had collected. "They come from a very old and healthy tree, only the topmost leaves. That's the key."

Gillen paused and looked at her, taken aback by what she had done.

"I told you not to . . ." Gillen scolded her softly.

"I did it anyways," Willa said with a smile. "You know I'm no good at listening to my leader."

Smiling, Gillen reluctantly took the leaves from her hand. She put two of them in her mouth, and then handed the rest to the boys.

"Eat these," she ordered them bluntly.

Glancing nervously at Willa as they stepped forward, the boys obediently accepted the leaves from Gillen, but then they hesitated.

"Eat them right now!" Gillen ordered them fiercely.

Obviously scared of her, Sacram and Marcas quickly stuffed the leaves into their mouths.

"They're just fresh oak leaves," Willa assured them gently. "It will help cure the wilt. It won't take long and you'll feel a lot better."

"Thank you," Sacram said, nodding at her as he chewed. It felt surprisingly good to hear his voice, much lower now than she had remembered, and to see his eyes looking at her.

The eyes of many of the other Faeran had turned dull gray over the years, along with their skin color, but Sacram's eyes were hazel and filled not just with the sense that he wanted to survive, but that he wanted to *understand*.

When the boys had finished chewing and swallowing the leaves, Gillen said, "Good. Now go. Be back before morning."

Sacram and Marcas nodded, gripped their spears, and headed off into the forest. This was a command they understood.

An unsettled feeling crept into Willa's stomach.

She turned and looked at Gillen. "Where are you sending them?"

Gillen gazed at her for several seconds, hesitating.

"Where, Gillen?" Willa pressed her.

"Down into Cades Cove," Gillen said finally.

Willa couldn't believe what she was hearing. "Why are they going there?"

Gillen lowered her eyes. "We need food and supplies."

"Please don't tell me . . ."

"I've re-formed the jaetters, Willa," Gillen blurted out.

The *jaetters* were the bands of young hunter-thieves that the padaran had created to sneak into the homes of the humans and steal from them. Both Willa and Gillen had been trained as jaetters from a young age, and they both knew it was wrong and dangerous.

"We've got to survive," Gillen grumbled, "just like the padaran taught us."

The words burned in Willa's ears. They had risen up against the padaran! They had stopped the jaetters! What had it all been for? For this? For huddling in a cave? For more of the young hunter-thieves to go stealing in the night?

"The padaran is dead," Willa said, trying to keep her voice flat and firm. "We need to find a better way to survive than what the padaran taught us—the stealing, the hurting each other, the trapping and killing animals. I want to help you."

Gillen hesitated, tilting her eyes to the ground as she began to speak. "Most of the members of this clan believe you are the one who caused all this," she said quietly.

"But what do *you* believe?" Willa said, her voice shaking.

Gillen raised her eyes and looked at her. "You *did* cause all this, Willa."

"You know that we had to stand up against the padaran. We *had* to," Willa said. "But I did not murder him. He died in the fire."

"Everyone believes that you started the fire."

"I didn't!" Willa insisted, relieved to finally be able to say it to someone. "I would never do that. The padaran lit those torches to block the corridor to his rooms, and one of them caught the wall on fire."

Willa warily eyed the Faeran gathering in the trees and undergrowth a short distance away. Some of them had spotted her talking to Gillen and were now moving toward her.

"They are filled with fear," Gillen said.

Willa tried to meet her friend's gaze, but Gillen would not lift her eyes to hers.

"We must give them direction and hope," Willa urged her. "It's the only way for our people to survive."

"I've been trying, but I can't do it," Gillen said, still averting her eyes.

"You *can* do it," Willa said. "And you *have* to do it."

"You called me the leader, but I'm not," Gillen said. "Most of them don't listen to me. They don't believe in me. I'm not like the padaran was."

"No," Willa said, grabbing her by the shoulders. "Look at me, Gillen. You are *not* like the padaran. Don't even try to be. Find another way to lead—your *own* way."

Finally, Gillen raised her eyes and truly looked at her. "The old ways of your grandmother and the woodwitches are gone, Willa," Gillen said, her voice blunt and sober. "Everything has changed. We can't go back to that."

"Then we need to create a different way to live, combining the good of the old and the good of the new. But not the padaran's way. Please."

Gillen looked over at the Faeran coming toward them. "They don't want to change," she said. "The only time I can get them to listen is when I tell them what they want to hear. Some of them are trying to leave the clan, to strike out on their own. Until we can find some kind of lair, something to hold us together, there's no hope for us."

The Faeran began hissing and clacking their teeth as they encircled her and Gillen.

"You better go," Gillen said softly.

"Get them to eat the oak leaves to ward off the wilt," Willa urged her friend even as she moved away from her. "Just start with that, and when it begins to work, they'll see that they can trust you, and they will listen to you more and more."

"I will," Gillen said. "Now go!"

The Faeran had surrounded them and were now closing in.

"And watch out for the creatures I told you about," Willa said. "Whatever you do, don't let them touch you!"

"No one's going to touch us, traitor!" the bony old white-haired woman shrieked as she lunged forward and tried to grab Willa's arm. "Especially *you*!"

Willa darted out of her reach.

The bulgy-eyed Tanic shoved forward and tried to knock Willa to the ground, but she rolled into the ferns, blended into their leaves, and disappeared.

"Just leave her alone!" Gillen shouted at Tanic and the other Faeran as they scoured the underbrush for her.

As Willa reunited with Charka and put the Faeran far behind her, she couldn't help but wonder, was all of this the result of the decisions she had made? Was all of this the world she had created? There was so much she had wanted to ask her Faeran kin, and so much she had wanted to tell them. But there was no hope of that now. They *hated* her.

Nothing, Willa thought in discouragement as she and Charka walked away. She had learned nothing from her Faeran kin that would help her solve the mystery of the murderous, snakelike creatures, other than the fact that they had not yet attacked her people.

I'm trying, Father, she thought, wondering where he was and what the other humans were doing to him. Somehow, some way, she had to help him.

Walking beside her, Charka began to whimper pleadingly.

"I know you're hungry," Willa said, stroking the fur on the little bear's head. "Let's find some food."

The acorns, chestnuts, and walnuts that she was sure Charka would love were not yet ripe. She did manage to find some shoots and buds for the two of them to eat, and Charka gobbled them out of her hand and licked her fingers with his thick wet tongue.

But for every one shoot she nibbled, he devoured twenty. He was small, but he was voracious. She picked some wild cherries, red and plump, that made him chortle with delight. And after more searching, she discovered a batch of grubs under an old rotted log. He ate them in an instant and looked up at her for more.

Willa knew that ever since he'd been born, young Charka had been traveling with his momma, learning where to find food and how to avoid danger. And it was becoming clear that he needed to be eating almost constantly, not just so that he could grow into an adult, but also to fatten himself up for his long winter sleep. Without a momma to teach him the skills he needed, there was no way the little cub would survive.

As they were foraging, she and Charka came to a grove of gigantic trees, worn and weathered but tall and strong, with thick, powerful bases that had withstood the tribulations of time. As Willa gazed up into the mighty limbs, she realized that each one of these giants had to be hundreds of years old and filled with stories of their own. And as she walked among them, listening to their whispers, she began to feel safe in a way that she hadn't in a long time. No snakelike creatures slithering across the ground. No obstinate, leg-dragging human. No hissing, sneering Faeran. Just her friends, the quiet, gentle trees.

But as she walked through the peaceful, protective shade of her companions, something began to happen. The softness of the dappled sunlight was turning harsh and overly bright. The graceful breeze of the forest was shifting into something more akin to a callous wind. Even the smells of the air had changed.

She and Charka were standing on the edge of the unimaginable.

The rest of the forest was gone.

In front of them stretched a wide, barren clearing for as far as they could see. There was nothing left but saw-cut stumps. No trees. No ferns. No flowers. No vines. No bears or wolves or foxes or otters or birds of any kind. No gentle running streams. Just the trampled, dead, treeless world left behind by a crew of loggers.

Losing all the strength in her body and her soul, Willa fell to her knees, her heart *breaking*. She began to cry, pulling in rough, sobbing breaths, and rubbing the back of her hand across her nose.

She didn't want to cry. She wanted to fight. She wanted to stop this! But how? How could she fight the men of iron? How could she battle the machines? The weapons? The sheer number of them invading the forest?

The world wasn't just dying. It was being killed.

Tree by tree, animal by animal, river by river. It was all being killed.

She turned and looked toward the rounded peak of the Great Mountain in the distance.

"I don't understand," she said. "You must stop this. For all our sakes, for *your* sake, you must stop this."

But the mountain did not reply, not with a glint of light, or curling mist, or birds flying high.

The Great Mountain sat in silence.

It wasn't that it didn't understand what she was asking. She knew it did.

And it wasn't saying that it couldn't do what she wanted.

There was just no answer at all.

It was as if it was saying: *This is you. This is yours. This is your problem to solve.*

But the truth was, she didn't know what to do. She didn't know how to save the entirety of the world from itself. All she could do was try to save the ones she loved, like her father, and she was running out of time. She sensed that the shadowy snake-like creatures were part of what had happened at the Elkmont site the day the two loggers were killed, but she had to learn more. She had to do better. Somewhere out there, her father and Hialeah were counting on her.

She tried to remember the first time she and Charka had encountered the beasts slithering through the forest. Just thinking about it, a dark and heavy dread oozed into her body. Her mouth grew dry and her heart began to pump with greater force. Taking a long, deep breath, she turned and looked way up the slope of the mountain toward the old, burned-out lair of her people and the eerie domain that had begun to grow beside it.

Was Dark Hollow the answer?

Was that where these creatures were coming from?

She tried to think of alternatives, of other answers. Anything but that strange and terrible place.

But finally she realized she could avoid it no longer.

"I've got to go back," she said.

When she gazed down at Charka standing beside her, he looked up at her, his eyes filled with love, with loyalty, with the certainty that wherever she went, he was going to follow. But after everything that had happened and all he'd been through, she didn't have the heart to take him back to that haunting place. It was just too dangerous. As much as she hated the idea, she needed to find him a new home, someplace where he could learn all he needed to learn, and be among other bears.

If he were an orphaned wolf pup, she would have howled for Luthien. She didn't know any momma bears. . . . But she did know where she might be able to find one.

"Atagahi," she said, using the Cherokee name.

The Cherokee had been telling stories around their campfires for years about the healing lake of the bears. She had never met a human who had actually seen it with his or her own eyes, but she had been to the lake herself, and she had felt its magic work on her. Whether she could find the elusive body of water on her own was the question. But she had to make sure her new friend was safe. Only then would she continue on to Dark Hollow.

"Come on, Charka," she said. "We've got a ways to go."

Hours later, when they finally reached the rocky high ground that Willa had been pushing toward, she and Charka stood on a weathered gray crag and looked out across the world. The misty blue-green mountains cascaded into the distance, layer after layer, until they faded into the sky. *The world is neither flat nor round,* she thought. *It's mountains.* The bluish-white mist rising from the forests sank into the low areas between the peaks and ridges of the mountains, creating the appearance of hundreds of cloud-filled lakes. If she hadn't been here once before, she would have never known that one of those pockets of mist held a great secret. Even now, it was difficult to be sure. So many things from her past seemed like nothing but dreams. Had Luthien and the other wolves truly brought her to this lake? Had she truly had a twin sister she used to laugh with and play with years ago? Had the Faeran people truly once lived in harmony and grace with their forest world?

Was the world dying or was it but a dream that it had ever lived?

Willa started down the rocky slope in the direction of where she thought the lake was hidden.

As she and Charka descended into the valley, they came to a dense wall of mist. She knew from the stories—and from her own experience—that there was no way to find *Atagahi* unless you were a bear or followed a bear's path to reach it.

"You need to lead the way, Charka," she said in the old language, gently moving the little cub in front of her. "Follow your nose to the smell of the water and other bears. You're going to love it here! There's going to be lots of bears, swimming and wallowing in the lake."

Charka put his nose to the ground and began to follow the trail, leading them through a white fog so dense that they couldn't see anything around them. Willa walked slowly forward with her hands out in front of her, frightened that she was going to run into something. But she knew she had to trust Charka, and she had to trust the mist.

The first time she had come, she had heard the whistle of wings as ducks flew overhead, but she didn't hear them now. As she and Charka made their way through the cloud, there was nothing but a muffled silence.

Finally, the mist began to clear. At first all Willa could see was a diffuse, shimmering gold light ahead. But as she moved forward, a panoramic view opened before her: a perfectly calm lake surrounded by rolling green mountains, with the orange light of the setting sun reflecting across the water. She pulled in a long, deep breath, swept away by the beauty of what she was seeing.

The last time she was here, the lake had been full of bears wallowing in the warm, healing waters. But now there were no other bears in sight. The shore was deserted.

Charka looked around in bewilderment, seeming to know that something was wrong. This wasn't how it was supposed to be.

As the disappointment seeped slowly into Willa's body, she heard something farther down the shore. She looked over and saw a large white bear in the distance, sitting near a jagged rock at the edge of the lake.

Willa frowned. What was he doing way down there?

"Come on, Charka, I want you to meet someone," she said, and they walked together toward the bear.

Black bears normally had shiny, jet-black fur, but the great leader of the bears, who had been the protector of this hidden lake for longer than anyone could remember, had lived so many years that his fur had turned pure white.

As she approached the bear, Willa noticed that he looked much changed from the last time she had seen him. His face was more weathered, and his eyes were filled not just with weariness, but actual *loneliness*.

She hesitated and slowed to nearly a standstill, a current of confusion and sympathy passing through her. But beneath it all she felt a pang of true fear. What had happened to him?

When the white bear saw her coming toward him, he lifted his snout and sniffed the air, as if to double-check that what he was seeing was in fact true, for it is mainly through their noses that bears understand the world. And then he stood up on his hind legs to his full height and faced her. His paws were huge and his shoulders were mountains all unto themselves. His claws were longer than her hand and the span of his jaws far, far bigger than her head. But she could see in his behavior and his face that he remembered her and she had nothing to fear from the massive creature. Still, her heart beat hard in her chest.

"Greetings, great leader of the bears. I come in peace with my new young friend," she said, gesturing to Charka.

As the white bear gazed at the cub, his eyes softened. He seemed more than pleased to see the arrival of the little one, as if he had lost hope that he would ever see such a thing again.

Charka stared up at the giant white bear in awe and amazement, his eyes as steady as he could hold them, but his tiny body quivering in trepidation.

When the white bear turned and looked at her, Willa held his gaze. The first time she'd met him, she had felt so scared and intimidated that she'd barely been able to lift her head. This time, she peered right into his eyes and let him peer into hers. And it was clear that much had happened since they'd seen each other. She could see it in the way he looked at her, the tenderness and sadness of it. Willa knew he had stories to tell that would break her heart.

"What has happened?" she asked him in the old language. "Where are all the other bears?"

As the white bear regarded her, she fell into his deep, all-seeing eyes, and she knew what he was thinking.

"It's the humans . . ." she whispered, feeling the weight of it in her chest. "The logging, the killing of the forest. The bears are fleeing and dying."

And she could see by the slow movement of the bear's head, and the way he turned his eyes down along the empty shore of the lake, that she was right.

"But surely the lake is safe," Willa said. "It's shrouded in mist. The humans will never find it."

As the bear went down onto all fours and walked along the shore, she began to understand.

The magic of this place was tied to the lake, and the lake was tied to the mist and the rain, and the mist was tied to the forest, and the forest to the trees.

"The trees . . ." she whispered, a great darkness coming over her, tears welling in her eyes.

And when she looked at the great bear again, as he lumbered slowly down the length of the shore, his shoulders shifting first to one side and then the other, she began to see the aching sorrow in him. He was the leader of the bears, but all the bears were leaving. He was alone. And alone he had no purpose. He was an ancient, magical beast who had lived here and watched over these forests for five hundred years. He was the world's eyes, and its heart, and its wisdom. But now his time was coming to an end.

"No," she said, refusing to accept it. *"No!"*

She ran forward and caught up with him. She walked beside

him along the lake, close at his shoulder now, so close that she could feel the brush of his fur against her and the tremor of the earth each time he put down a paw.

Once again, she found herself thinking that she could not save the world, but she could help one good and loyal friend.

"I have a favor to ask you," she said to the white bear. She glanced over her shoulder back at Charka, who was following along behind them. "His mother was killed by the loggers. I've been trying to take care of him the best I can, but he's very young. If I continue, I'm worried that he'll turn into a Faeran instead of a bear. I don't know how to teach him all the skills he needs to become who he needs to become."

The white bear slowed to a stop and turned toward Charka.

Startled by the gaze of the great bear, Charka immediately fell over. He hunkered down and quivered in fear. But the white bear walked toward him and nuzzled the little cub with his snout, pushing him gently this way and that. Then he put his paw on him and scooped him across the ground. Soon the two of them were playing and growling, with Charka rolling on his back, swatting up at the paw of the larger bear.

Already the white bear was teaching him the language of their kind and a bond was forming.

When Willa looked at the white bear and the white bear looked back at her, she knew that he had accepted Charka into his care.

She knelt down and said good-bye to her little friend, hugging him and kissing him.

"You're going to stay here for a while," she explained. "The great bear will take good care of you, and you'll take care of him."

Charka cried and whimpered as she said good-bye, pawing at her, trying to keep her there.

"I'll come visit as often as I can," she promised. "But you must listen for my call from outside the walls of mist, for without you, my little friend, I will not be able to find my way back in."

As she walked away from the lake, up through the mist toward the high ground, she rubbed her eyes and wiped her nose, and she forced herself to keep walking. She knew that leaving Charka behind was the right thing to do. She had found him a home and a father. But as she reached the rocky ridge line far above and looked out across the mountains with the valleys of mist in between, she felt a sharp stab of melancholy in her heart. It made her even more desperate to see her father and sister again.

Pulling in a determined breath, she turned and set her direction toward Dark Hollow.

25

Willa crept through the darkness, her skin tingling as she blended into the ferns around her. Many of the plants bent their fronds toward her and touched her, while others wrapped around her, concealing and protecting her.

She breathed slow and steady as she raised her head just enough to peer over the top.

A short distance ahead of her, the forest appeared to be glowing. The faint, almost imperceptible light rose in intensity and then faded, rose and then faded, over and over again.

That's it, she thought. *I'm here.*

She waited and watched, studying the glow from a distance.

She listened for sounds of hissing or slithering.

She sniffed the air.

But she didn't see or smell anything other than the ferns and trees.

There did not appear to be an immediate danger.

She glanced up. No stars or planets were visible in the black sky above, just strands of gray, misty clouds drifting across the moon.

Finally, she slowly rose to a standing position and moved cautiously forward through the undergrowth until she was walking beneath the glowing canopy of Dark Hollow's low-hanging trees.

She saw now that the glow was coming from thousands of fireflies. They were not flying or hovering as they had been before, but clinging, quiet and still, to the blackened leaves and branches. And thousands of large, green, glowing luna moths covered the trunks of the trees, their whispering antennae swaying back and forth, their wings slowly pumping in perfect unison, but none of the luna moths taking to the air. The soft, susurrant sound of the moths' wings was everywhere, all around her, a slow, rhythmic pulse. It was as if the entirety of Dark Hollow was breathing in long, deep, gentle breaths.

"It's sleeping . . ." she whispered to herself as she gazed around at the hollow in amazement.

She was careful to say the words very softly so she wouldn't wake the hollow—especially the moths, which her grandmother had taught her had very good hearing. "It may not look like moths and butterflies have ears," her grandmother had told her, "but don't let that fool you. They listen using veins in their wings, which funnel sound down into tiny ears hidden at the sides of their bodies. If you ask them to do something for you, they may ignore you, pretend they can't hear you, for they aren't always the most cooperative of friends, but they can hear just fine."

As Willa pressed on through the eerie, glowing darkness of the hollow, she tried to focus her mind. *Just get what you came for,* she told herself fiercely, like she used to when she was a jaetter sneaking through the lairs of the humans.

Tonight, she had one purpose: to find clues as to what might have happened to the men who had been killed at the logging camp. Had they fallen victim to the snakelike creatures? Was she right in her suspicion that those creatures had originated in Dark Hollow? She kept thinking that if she could just explain to the humans exactly what had happened, then they'd have to let her father go.

She walked past what looked like glowing slugs on the ground.

And then a sparkling ruby-red and emerald-green hummingbird buzzed past her, hovered over a blackened rose, snatched a glowing gnat from one of its leaves, and sped off. Willa knew that roses didn't grow this high in the mountains, gnats didn't glow, and hummingbirds normally didn't come out at night, but here apparently they did.

Yet, for all the strange and disturbing things she was seeing, she saw no sign of the shadowy creatures or anything else that could help her father.

When she caught some movement out of the corner of her eye and looked up, she spotted six or seven flying squirrels clinging to a tree trunk. As she walked past them, the squirrels did not glide through the air or scurry along a branch to escape her.

And they were not asleep like many of the other creatures in the hollow. They just stared at her with large, bulbous eyes that glowed an eerie silvery black. She swallowed hard, certain that these weren't natural, living animals.

Willa kept walking, determined to reach the other side of the hollow, to make a map of it in her mind, to understand it in any way she could.

And then she came into an area of black-scorched stone that she slowly realized she recognized.

She stopped and gazed at everything around her, trying to find her bearings. Her lips went dry.

So much had changed that it was nearly unrecognizable, but she was sure now.

This was the place where she had lived for the first twelve years of her life.

Willa's feet sloughed through a thick layer of dark gray ash as she walked through the burned-out ruins of what had once been the great lair of her people.

The walls were gone and the rock of the mountainside had been blackened by the fire. A few bats were fleeting across the moon, which was peeking through the clouds above, but there was no other movement or sound, not even a breeze. The air was perfectly still, as if even the sky had perished on the night of the fire.

Her grandmother had told her that the walls of the lair had once been living, tightly intertwined green plants woven together by the magic of the Faeran woodwitches of old. But Willa had never seen it that way. When she was growing up, the walls were made of nothing but brown, dead, dry sticks. When the fire came, it was fast and all-consuming. The lair had once included hundreds of dens in which Faeran families had lived and a magnificent great hall where her people had come together. In the lair of the past, there was no *I*, only *we*. But tonight, a year after the fire, the hallowed chambers of her people were silent and empty. She was truly alone.

When she came to the center of the ruins, she stopped.

Back when she had lived here with her family, they'd had a miniature tree that they watered and nurtured in a small circle of sunlight that filtered down into their den. The Little Tree had been no taller than Willa's knee, but it had the perfect shape and appearance of a full-grown tree, with dozens of tiny branches and thousands of even tinier leaves. Willa had grown up with the Little Tree. She had spoken with it, cried with it. And when the fire came, she had taken it with her. After the fire had burned all there was to burn, she had returned to the center of the ruins, dug down into the ash, and replanted the tree. She had worried that it would get lonely in this gray, desolate place, so small and on its own, and so she had knelt in front of the Little Tree and sung to it, infusing her voice with the woodland magic that her grandmother had taught her. Before her eyes, the Little Tree had begun to grow, rising to a towering height, its trunk thick and strong, with a magnificent spread of branches, and its leaves a hundred shades of green.

And now she stood before the Little Tree once again, its branches reaching into the midnight sky far above her head, its canopy spreading across the heavens in all its splendid glory.

"It's good to see you, my old friend," she said. And as she looked up at the tree, an overwhelming feeling of warmth and safety flooded into her chest and through her limbs, like she was embracing her grandmother again, or listening to her mother's whispering songs, or playing with her sister so long ago.

As if in reply, the highest boughs of the tree began to sway in the breeze coming down from the peak of the Great Mountain.

"I'm so relieved to see that you're doing well here," Willa said, placing her hand flat on the tree's craggy brown trunk.

Beneath the layers of bark, she felt the flow of nutrients coming up from the ground through the tree's roots, which were living off the ash and decay of the ruined past and reaching farther out, down the slope of the Great Mountain, into the living forest and all its inhabitants. She sensed the minute vibration of water from ancient streams below the ground, flowing up toward the leaves. And she touched the sunlight that the tree had been gathering throughout the day as it breathed the air into the world. For her—like her mother and grandmother before her—touching the tree was like putting her hand on the slow, gentle river of time.

As she gazed out across the mountains, the magic of the river began to flow through her. Her eyes blurred. Her head went dizzy with colors and motion. She took a long, deep breath, and then she was gliding like a hawk through the sky over an endless land of rolling green mountains.

She saw Luthien and the other wolves running along their paths. As she swooped down through a thick cloud of mist, she spotted Charka and the great white bear on the shore of the hidden lake. Beyond the ravens, and down into the rocky gulch, she glided past Gillen and the other Faeran arguing with one another, nothing holding them together but memories of a riven past.

When she flew across the mountainous land to the towns beyond, she gasped at the sight of her father being thrown into a stone-walled room with iron bars, his body crumpled, weak, and starving on the grimy stone floor. A man with a scarred face and ragged brown hair was spitting at him, kicking him. Her father's head was bleeding, but his eyes were open and he was gazing through a barred window into the sky as if he was looking for her, for his daughter, for *Willa*. She reached out to him, tried to touch him with her trembling hands. Her heart ached to free him, to help him, but in the next moment her vision turned to something else.

She saw Hialeah standing in front of the men and women of the town, speaking to them, trying to persuade them, fighting for her cause.

In the next beat of her heart, Willa soared back through the sky to the far side of the Great Mountain's highest ridges and down into the Qualla Boundary, the homeland of the Cherokee. She saw her brother, Iska, standing shoulder to shoulder with his Cherokee cousins as they gazed out in shock at the devastating sight of the loggers cutting down the forests in which their people had lived for hundreds of years.

And then the current turned once again, and she came back over the Great Mountain into her own part of the world. There, deep in the forest, she saw the long, gray creatures slithering across the ground, sucking the life from everything they came in contact with.

Farther on, she saw Jim McClaren and the men of the Elkmont crew with their axes and machines, felling more of the ancient trees. The pain of it surged through her body, and she cried out, but just as quickly as she had come, the current shifted and she saw another image—the farmers and craftsmen and other humans that lived in the valley of Cades Cove, tending to their fields and their animals, working and playing together through their lives. And there, just a short distance away, standing alone in a field of yellow, was the wheat-haired girl she had seen days before.

When the vision finally ended, Willa stumbled backward and nearly collapsed. She took in a violent, jerking gulp of air, as if she had just come out of the water after being under for far too long. She pulled in deep, full breaths as she tried to comprehend all that she had seen.

Why had the Great Mountain and the Little Tree shown her all these things? What was the world trying to tell her?

Willa didn't know what the gray creatures were, but she did know this: the forest was dying. The magic of the world was fading. The trees were falling. The animals were fleeing. And there was nothing she could do about any of it. She had come to this place tonight looking for answers. But there were none.

The whole of the world was broken and she could not fix it.

Not with love. Not with friendship or peace or understanding.

And those were the only things she had to give.

There were no Faeran or humans to whom she could go for help, only the tree by which she stood.

"What am I going to do, my friend?" she asked the Little Tree in despair.

How could she fight all this? The human machines were just far too powerful and the forces far too great. She was not a warrior. She did not kill or hurt or threaten. Neither could she run from this enemy. She could not blend or hide. How could someone like her defend what she loved?

"Does it even matter what I do?" she asked the Little Tree, lifting her hands in exasperation. "Do my decisions make any difference to my life or anyone else's? You've shown me all this, but where can I go? What can I do to help the breaking world?"

She gazed around at the barren emptiness of the gray, ash-covered ruins. Was this it? Was this the end? She and her clan were the last of the Faeran people, and among her clan, she was the last of the woodwitches, the only one who had any remnants of the forest and the Great Mountain still within her, the only one who had been trained in the old ways. Is this what the death of the world looked like? Was all this what the Great Mountain was trying to tell her?

She looked over to where the ruins were being engulfed by the encroaching edge of Dark Hollow. She could see the blue glowing fireflies, the sleeping luna moths, and all the other creatures—a strange, undead world.

Was that the future?

Was that the death that was coming?

Or was it a glimpse of the past?

She felt an incredibly distant memory lurking in the back

of her mind, so faint that she wasn't even sure it was there. A few notes of an old song. She couldn't bring the notes forward enough to actually sing them or piece the song together. It was more like she sensed a hole in her memory where something used to be, and now she needed to fill it.

And then she began to hear more of the notes in her mind, and finally she began to hum them, soft and uncertain at first, and then with more knowing, and the slow, warm pleasure of remembering. It felt like water trickling into a small stream at first, but once the water found its way, the stream became a river. Finally, she found the full melody of the song and began to sing. It became more and more clear in her heart and her voice, and the power of it ran through her.

It was an ancient song that her grandmother had taught her, the song of growing that the woodwitches had used to bring the branches and vines of the forest to life and then weave them one into the other, the woodbine and the oak, the laurel and the creeper, twisting and turning, up and up into glorious living walls, green and alive.

The clouds above her head began to open up to the glistening black brilliance of the clear midnight sky.

And as she sang, Willa rose to her feet and began to dance upon the ruins, spinning slowly around on the flat surface of the scorched old stone, her arms stretched out, her head tilted back, and the light of the heavens falling like raindrops onto her face. Spinning, spinning, spinning in the light of the stars and the planets and the moon, she felt the magic of Dark Hollow and the Little Tree and the Great Mountain itself coursing through her.

Soon she began to hear other voices joining in. She saw the ghosts of her loved ones—misty gray figures that looked like they had been pulled from the clouds overhead—singing and dancing around her. Her mother, her grandmother, and her great-grandmother from long ago were there. She spotted the ghost of her father, and the padaran, and her old jaetter rival, Gredic. Then the other jaetters, and the guards, and all the Faeran people of old were gathering in the great hall. They were all watching her, and dancing with her, and singing the ancient song of their people.

It felt so strange that everyone was there now—not just the Faeran who had cared for her, but those who had hurt her. Not just the Faeran she had loved, but the ones she had hated. All of them had shown her the way.

For a few moments as she danced, it felt as if she could almost do it. She could weave the walls of a new lair. But she knew that it required the harmonizing voices of multiple woodwitches—real, living woodwitches, not just the Hollow's ghosts of times past. A lone woodwitch could not sing the song of growing as it was meant to be sung. *There is no I, only we.*

Finally, after a long time, Willa slowed. She stopped spinning and she stopped singing. And then she stood quiet and still in the deepest, loneliest silence she had ever known.

She sat down at the base of the Little Tree.

And there she stayed, just thinking.

After a while, she lay flat on her back and looked up through the limbs of the tree. As the stars moved ever so slowly across the sky, flickering in and out between the leaves, she gently fell asleep, and in her sleep, she dreamed—not of the deep green forests that she so dearly loved or the Faeran lairs of old. In her dream, she saw only one thing.

Waving fields of wheat.

When she woke the next morning, she knew.

She knew where she must go.

And she knew who she must find.

Driven by what she had learned from her journey to Dark Hollow and the Little Tree, Willa headed down the mountain toward Cades Cove.

When she smelled the faint scent of smoke rising from the stone chimneys of the log cabins and clapboard homes, she found a spot in a tall tree on the slope where she hoped to be able to look down into the valley of the humans.

The warmth and light brought by the rising sun felt so different on her face than the dark, cool place she had put behind her. But the branches of the tree she was in were so thick that they were blocking her view.

"Ehla da duin," she said as she touched the boughs, and they swept gently aside.

Now she could see much of the valley stretched out in front of her. Some of the humans were leaving their homes and going off to work in the fields, or walking down the road to reach their jobs with the logging crews. Others were staying near their homes, working in their vegetable gardens, milking their cows, and tending to their sheep.

Willa scanned one way and then another, looking for any sign of the wheat-haired girl. In her dream, the girl had been in or near Cades Cove, but at the moment, she was nowhere to be seen.

She did spot one little girl, no more than seven years old, running out the back door of her house with a woven basket to collect chicken eggs. But the chickens hadn't laid the eggs in the chicken coop, where they were supposed to. They had laid them at the rock-lined wall, in the horse barn, under the shed, and many other places. The little girl seemed to know all the spots to check, and she ran from one to the other, quickly filling her basket, and then returned to her momma waiting for her in the kitchen doorway.

A short distance away, Willa noticed a father teaching his son how to fix a broken wagon wheel. It reminded Willa of the way her grandmother had taught her the ways of the forest.

For all that she was seeing, there was still no sign of the wheat-haired girl.

Willa climbed down from the tree and began to walk along the perimeter of the valley. She came to an area where several dark-skinned humans were working shoulder to shoulder with white-skinned humans in a cornfield. She wondered how strange it must feel to have the same skin color all the time, to be born a single shade—black or white or brown—and not be able to change it.

Farther on, she saw several families loading beeswax, blackberries, and more products of the forest into their wagons to be taken off to Knoxville and Gatlinburg and the other towns that her father had told her about.

During one of their long talks while sitting by the river, Nathaniel had told her about a great war that had ravaged the humans forty years before. His kin, and many of the other mountain families, had been Southerners, but they had also been something called "Unionists," which meant they were against slavery and against withdrawing from the country. He said that the Unionists living in these mountains were attacked mercilessly by Confederate soldiers and marauders during the war. From the killings, disease, and destruction—and the devastating poverty that followed—the community of Cades Cove had gone from seven hundred people down to two hundred fifty. It had taken forty years for Cades Cove to grow back to its previous numbers. In some ways, the story reminded Willa of her Faeran clan, which had dwindled to fewer than a hundred now. And she knew from Hialeah and Iska that the Cherokee living in the Qualla Boundary were struggling as well. It seemed as if only the new humans, with their giant saws and their steam-powered machines, were thriving.

All through the morning, Willa observed the people of Cades Cove, looking for a glimpse of blond hair or any sign of danger. She was convinced that the girl was the key to the mystery she was trying to solve. But first, she had to find her.

Later in the afternoon, she watched a dozen families come together to help a pair of young humans raise a barn. Farther on, she saw the neighbors of an elderly man help him tend to his farm. Throughout the valley, people were selling and trading with one another, taking care of themselves, but taking care of each other as well.

When she thought about her own Faeran clan, she knew that they were never going to survive unless they somehow pulled together. But how could they? Their world was being destroyed all around them.

As she studied the humans of Cades Cove, Willa came to the conclusion that maybe—for the Faeran and the Cherokee, for the Northerners and the Southerners, for the old-time mountain families and the newcomers, even for the animals—the age of clans was over. They were all living in the same world now. The era of *separation* had passed. It seemed as if the only way *any* of them were going to survive was *together*.

As she continued her search, walking along the rim of the valley and then climbing another tree, she saw what looked like a mother and a half dozen children of various shapes and sizes running and playing in a field. She was shocked by how much noise they made when they screamed and shouted, and how they flailed their arms when they ran, as if they had all lost their minds.

Beyond the herd of small, noisy humans, she could see a tract of shoulder-high corn, and beyond that, moving gently with the wind, a waving field of wheat.

And there, walking through the tall grass, just as she had seen in her vision, was the wheat-haired girl, her long tresses blowing in the breeze.

Willa's chest seized with trepidation. She peered toward the distant figure. There she was! Right there!

Willa sniffed the air and quickly checked the area to make sure none of the snakelike creatures were on the prowl. But she didn't see or smell any sign of them.

When she looked back out into the distance, the girl was just walking alone through the field, her open fingers gliding gently over the tops of the tall, yellow grass.

Willa narrowed her eyes, trying to see every detail.

Who was this girl? What was she doing out there?

She looked so small, her white skin and blond hair blending into the wheat. It seemed as if the mother and the other children nearby didn't even see her.

And where were the girl's dark and shadowy creatures? Did she only call them forth when she needed them?

As the questions roiled through Willa's mind, it felt like her whole body was tingling.

Her father had warned her many times to stay away from Cades Cove and the other human communities, for he knew the dangers of these places to her.

And this girl in particular was extremely dangerous. She had been at the logging site where the first two men had been murdered, and she had been at the gorge when the gray creatures attacked. She had been wherever death had come. Even so, Willa longed to go and talk with her, to demand answers, to understand who she was and why she was doing these things.

Trying to stay quiet and still, Willa watched the girl from a distance. But her pulse thumped in her temples like a human's clock.

She looked down the trunk of the tree at the ground below her and then back out at the valley. She knew she shouldn't, but her mind seemed to be making its own decision without her. One way or another, she had to find out who that girl was.

Willa climbed down the tree.

When she got to the ground, she peered across the valley again. She could still see the wheat field. But the girl was gone. She had disappeared.

Had she run away? Did she duck down into the wheat to hide?

Willa scanned the horizon, looking for the girl this way and that, but she just wasn't there.

Did I imagine her? Willa wondered. *Is she some kind of ghost?*

"You've been watching me," a voice said behind her.

"And you've been watching *me*," Willa said, turning slowly to look at the girl.

She was standing just a few feet in front of Willa now, a white-skinned human with long blond hair, her pale blue eyes steady and serious. There had been a fierceness in the girl's voice, and a similar fierceness in Willa's reply.

Willa was just about to ask why the girl was using her creatures to kill people, but the girl spoke first.

"What's your name?"

"Willa. What's yours?"

"Adelaide. Where do you live?"

"In the forest, up on the Great Mountain."

Adelaide's blond eyebrows drew together. "On Clingmans Dome, you mean?"

"Yes," Willa said. "Where do *you* live?"

"Here in Cades Cove. How old are you?"

"Thirteen. How old are *you*?"

"Thirteen. You're green most of the time."

"Like the trees," Willa said. "And you're white."

"Like my mother and father," Adelaide said in return.

It was like they were fighting, back and forth, question after question, each one faster and fiercer than the last, but then Willa interrupted the pace of it and asked the question she'd really come to ask.

"Why did you attack the men in the gorge?" Willa demanded.

The girl stopped abruptly, startled. "Attack the men?" she said, her voice straining. "I didn't attack the men. Why are you saying that?"

"I saw you with those creatures," Willa said. "You were running with them, running *toward* the men in the gorge. And you were spying on us, following us . . ."

"I have nothing to do with those horrible, slimy beasts!" the girl said, nearly snarling at her. "I have no idea what they were or where they came from."

Willa's nostrils flared as she closed her mouth and exhaled. She tried to remember every detail of where she had seen the girl and what she had done, but before she could gather her thoughts, the girl continued.

"The first time I saw you was by the ravine with the mother bear and the little cub—" the girl started to say.

"You didn't just *see* me," Willa interrupted her. "You *helped* me, didn't you?" Though why, Willa still didn't understand.

"I tried," Adelaide said, nodding. "You would've helped me, too."

Willa frowned. What kind of comment was that from a mortal enemy? Here she was attacking this girl, accusing her of wrangling fiendish beasts and murdering humans, and she says something like that!

"I saw you charge toward the men in the gorge," Willa said, trying to stay focused on her accusations. "I saw you! You were controlling the creatures!"

"I wasn't!" Adelaide said, raising her voice.

"Then what were you doing?"

"I was trying to scare them away," Adelaide said.

Willa pressed her lips together in frustration. This made no sense. If this girl wasn't the key to everything, if she didn't know what those creatures were, then Willa was no closer to helping her father. "Why in the world would you try to do *anything* with those creatures?" Willa persisted. "Why were you even there?"

"Why were *you* there?" Adelaide asked in return. "Where did you learn to blend into your surroundings like that when you were with the mother bear?" She seemed far more interested in asking her own questions than answering Willa's.

"My mother and grandmother taught me," Willa said quickly. "Now answer my question. Why were you there?"

"I couldn't even believe it the first time I saw you do it," Adelaide said. "I've been looking for you in the trees and the bushes ever since."

"*You've* been looking for *me*?"

"Of course," Adelaide said.

Willa had no idea what Adelaide meant when she said that. But despite everything, despite her frustration and her disappointment, she was beginning to like this girl, her frankness, the way she talked and asked questions. And the girl seemed to have an uncanny lack of fear or uncertainty about her.

Down in the valley, a screen door slammed shut. Adelaide flinched. She looked toward the distant sound. Then she turned back at Willa. "I have to go."

"Why?" Willa said. Suddenly she felt strangely disappointed that the girl had to leave.

"Do you want to visit me again?" Adelaide asked with hopefulness in her voice.

"I have many more questions to ask you," Willa said.

"And I have many more to ask you," Adelaide said.

"I can't go into Cades Cove," Willa said, "but you could come into the forest with me."

"I would like that," Adelaide said, smiling and nodding. "I'm not a bad person, you'll see."

"Tomorrow morning," Willa said. "I'll be here waiting for you."

"I'll meet you here," Adelaide agreed, and then she turned and ran, her long blond hair flowing behind her.

Willa watched from the forest as Adelaide headed toward the houses. As Adelaide got more and more distant, Willa whispered, "Turn around one last time. . . ."

A heartbeat later, Adelaide slowed, and then she turned and

raised her hand in a gentle wave of good-bye up toward Willa, as if she knew she would be watching her.

A warm sensation of pleasure poured through Willa's body. In a human gesture she had never used, she raised her own hand and waved in return.

Adelaide continued toward a white clapboard house nestled between the wheat field, the dirt road, and the edge of the forest. As she entered the area behind the house, a man limped out toward her.

When they met, he did not embrace her or put his arm around her. He stood firmly in front of her, blocking her entrance into the house. It was too distant for Willa to make out the actual words that he said, but Adelaide stayed put, her shoulders slumped and her head down. And then, when the man was done speaking to her, Adelaide trudged glumly inside.

As Willa watched, she slowly realized something.

She recognized the yard.

She recognized the house.

And she recognized the man.

She knew why he was limping.

It took her several seconds to comprehend what it meant.

That night, Willa climbed into one of the large oak trees in the forest, crawled out onto a branch, and slept, missing Charka's warm body curled up beside her.

All through the night, she dreamed of her father and sister, the loggers chopping at the trees, and the girl with golden hair.

When she woke the next morning, a spear of worry jolted her. What if the girl didn't come back to her? Willa hurried over to the spot where they had agreed to meet, her breathing tight and nervous.

As the sun peaked over the mountain and filled the valley of Cades Cove with light, she watched the back of the house from a distance. She just tried to keep breathing as she waited.

Finally, the screen door nudged open and the girl slipped out. She crept across the yard and ran up the slope toward Willa.

"I'm so relieved you're here," Adelaide said when she arrived, panting as she spoke. "I thought maybe I'd dreamed it all."

Willa smiled. "Me too."

"Where did you sleep?" Adelaide asked.

"In this tree," Willa said, touching her hand to the trunk.

"Really? Isn't that dangerous?"

"Humans can't see me when I'm sleeping in a tree," Willa explained.

"I mean, won't you fall out?"

"The tree holds me."

"What do you mean? How?"

"Usually, the branches do it on their own, but if for some reason they don't, then I ask them to."

"You ask them . . . ? That's amazing."

As they were talking, Willa looked down into the valley and toward the house.

"You're wondering about my father," Adelaide said, seeming to read her thoughts.

"He's the foreman of the loggers," Willa said.

"Yes," Adelaide said. "And even so, you brought him home. Thank you."

"Why were you out there, watching us?" Willa asked. "And after everything that happened to your father, why did you stay hidden?"

"When I finish with my chores, I follow my father to the cutting sites."

"But why? Why would you want to go to those terrible places?" Willa asked.

"My father is very strict," Adelaide said. "He doesn't let me go into the forest alone. He's scared I'll get eaten by a wolf. He hates wolves. But I want to see new things. Especially animals."

"Like bears maybe . . ." Willa said.

"Yes!" Adelaide said excitedly. "Like the little bear cub in the ravine. I was so worried about what was going to happen to him, and then I saw you go down to help him."

"Wouldn't your father get angry if he knew you followed him? He's right that the cutting sites are very dangerous. Wouldn't you get in trouble?"

"Oh yes, big, big trouble," Adelaide said, nodding vigorously. "He'd be extremely angry and lock me in the shed for a week to teach me a lesson."

Willa tried to read Adelaide's face, but it didn't seem like the girl was joking. Nathaniel would never do anything like that, but maybe Jim McClaren would.

"And you were following your father that day when the men went through the gorge . . ." Willa said. "You saw the creatures attack them. . . ."

"I've never been so scared in my life," Adelaide said, her voice tightening.

"Me neither," Willa said, shivering as she remembered the hissing beasts ripping the men to the ground.

"I ran to help my father," Adelaide said, "but he fell over the ledge before I could get to him. I didn't know what to do. Luckily, you were there."

Willa thought back to her long trek through the woods

with the limping McClaren. "I could have used another pair of hands. . . ."

"I watched for a while, to make sure he was okay with you, and then I ran home to get help," she said. "What were those things, anyway?"

"I don't know what those creatures were," Willa said, "but I think I might know where they came from. It's a place I call Dark Hollow. There seem to be many strange things there."

Adelaide stared at her, taking in this new information. "But what is it? What is Dark Hollow?"

"I don't know exactly," Willa said, shaking her head, "but I need to find out. I need to figure out what those creatures are and if they had anything to do with the deaths of the two loggers at the logging site."

"To help your father . . ." Adelaide said.

Willa was surprised that the girl understood so much of what had gone on. She must have been close by most of the time, watching and listening to her and McClaren.

"That's right. But for other reasons, too," Willa said. "Those creatures are killing everything in their path."

"I'll help you," Adelaide said suddenly, stepping toward her.

"What do you mean?"

"We'll work on it together. We'll save your father, like you saved mine."

Willa looked at her. She sensed that Adelaide didn't truly comprehend what she was offering to be part of.

"It's going to be dangerous," Willa warned her.

"I know," she said. "I saw what happened to the men in the gorge. But we have to keep it from happening again, right? We don't have a choice."

Willa looked at Adelaide in amazement. There was something about the girl that gave her hope.

As they were talking, Willa kept wanting to ask what it was like to be the daughter of a tree-killer. But something held her back. What if Adelaide started asking *her* those kind of questions? *How does it feel to be the niece of the murderous tyrant of the Faeran people? How does it feel to be the cause of your own people's destruction?*

Adelaide had been kind to her, especially in her offer to help, and Willa tried to do the same. "What about *your* father?" she asked. "Is his leg healing all right?"

"I can tell it hurts him, but he tries not to show it," Adelaide said. "That's how he is—never likes people to see him sick or hurt or scared or anything like that. He told my mother that he fought off a pack of wolves to get home."

Willa realized she had seen Adelaide's father when he was both hurt and scared.

"No, we didn't fight them off," she said. "We asked them to leave us alone, and they did."

"You mean *you* asked them," Adelaide said. "Just like you ask the trees. My father doesn't speak to wolves—he shoots them. I've seen him do it. And I've been watching him long enough to know that he has lied lots of times, to my mother, to his men . . . and to me."

"I'm sorry," Willa said, hearing the sadness in her voice.

"It's all right," Adelaide said, putting on a brave face as she glanced up at Willa and then looked away quickly. "Let's go to the logging site."

"Why there?" Willa asked.

Adelaide raised her eyes and held her gaze. "Because we have a mystery to solve, and that's the scene of the crime. Maybe there's clues of some sort. We'll figure out what happened."

Willa nodded, liking this girl more and more. "Follow me," she said, touching her arm. "We're going to be traveling fast, so stay close!"

As Willa tore through the forest, she expected Adelaide to fall behind, but the girl remained right there, running along beside her.

"Keep going!" Adelaide called out, bursting with a smile. Her skin was so white, it was almost like she was glowing. And her blue eyes sparkled as they took everything in, as if the world was there only for her to see.

They trekked up the slope of the valley, and then cut across a shallow col between two rounded summits. From there, they traveled steeply downhill into a shaded cove between two spurs of the Great Mountain, and then up again on the other side. When they reached the top of the next ridge, they could see the mountains rolled out in front of them, disappearing into a blue haze in the distance and turning into the sky. The earth was never straight or flat or the same in these mountains, but sloped and twisty, and filled with the broken rocks of ancient times.

"We're almost there," Willa said as they made their way

through a stand of pine trees and came to the ravine where she had rescued Charka.

She and Adelaide scaled their way down to the gushing stream at the bottom, waded across the tumbling water, and then climbed up the far wall, helping each other along the way.

When they finally reached the other side, they stood in silence, shoulder to shoulder, and gazed out across devastation. All the trees were gone. The men and machines had left nothing behind but bare mud and severed stumps. Willa swallowed down the bile that came up her throat.

"I hate what they're doing," Adelaide said in a low, gravelly voice.

"The two loggers were killed somewhere near this site," Willa said.

"The Elkmont crew's base camp was over there, on the other side of the cutting field," Adelaide said, beckoning Willa to follow her. "Come on."

They found where the loggers had stored their equipment, corralled their mules, set up their tents, built their railroad tracks, and done all the other things they normally did when they took over an area. But she and Adelaide discovered little else. They searched for signs of a physical struggle, torn clothing, or even empty bullet casings, but the land was so trampled and destroyed that they couldn't find any clues at all.

"It seems like any other logging site," Adelaide said, the corner of her mouth raised in discouragement.

Willa was just about to agree, but as they were talking, she saw something in the distance that didn't make sense to her.

"What's wrong?" Adelaide said, clearly startled by the sudden change in her expression.

"Look," Willa said, gesturing across the killing field toward the far edge of the forest.

Willa couldn't make out exactly what it was. It looked like a dark cloud coming out of the trees.

"Is that a swarm of birds?" Adelaide asked.

As the shape got closer, it became clear that it was a long, flowing current of butterflies, like a river in the sky. The winged beauties were shiny black with flashes of iridescent blue and patterns of yellow dots. There were thousands upon thousands of them, fluttering across the cutting field.

Smiling and laughing, Adelaide said, "Look at them, Willa! Just look at them! They're magnificent!"

Willa gazed in wonder. It was indeed a truly beautiful sight.

But then the stream of butterflies suddenly shifted direction.

Willa's eyes narrowed as she watched them.

It didn't appear to be a random movement. The butterflies seemed to have turned deliberately . . . toward them.

"They're coming to see us!" Adelaide said excitedly.

Willa's heart began to pound.

"Look at them!" Adelaide said. "They're amazing."

But Willa shook her head and reached for Adelaide's hand to pull her closer. "Something's not right. . . ."

The dark stream of butterflies was still coming straight toward them.

Perspiration flashed across Willa's skin and her muscles tightened.

Unable to stand it any longer, she leaped forward and shouted, *"Dee an-tra dee-say-ich!" Do not come this way!*

"What is it? What's wrong?" Adelaide asked, grabbing Willa's arm in fear. "What's happening?"

But the butterflies did not change course. They were getting closer and closer, their sheer numbers beginning to blot out the sun with a wall of darkness.

"Dee an-tra dee-say-ich!" Willa shouted again as loud as she could, snarling toward the cloud, but still the butterflies did not turn.

"Willa, please . . ." Adelaide said, tugging at her.

"Dee-sa!" Willa screamed at the cloud. *Stop!*

But the black-winged creatures did not obey, and Willa knew that it wasn't just because some insects weren't always the most cooperative of friends.

"These aren't normal butterflies," she said. "They're from Dark Hollow."

Her mind and her body were rapidly filling with nothing but instinct. She glanced toward the closest trees in the distance.

"We've got to run, Adelaide," she said, pulling her friend toward the forest as the first of the butterflies began to flutter around them. "Whatever you do, don't let them touch you!"

Willa and Adelaide sprinted across the killing field, past one stump after another, the black cloud of butterflies just behind them. The moment they reached the edge of the forest, Willa tackled Adelaide to the ground and shouted *"Florena!"*

She held Adelaide down as the grasses and vines grew rapidly over their bodies, blanketing their arms and legs and torsos with green. The light around them went gray, like an eclipse was covering the sun, as thousands of butterflies descended upon them.

"I've got you," Willa said, wrapping her arms around her friend.

Adelaide gasped as the grass spread over their faces and everything went dark. "I'm scared, Willa!"

"Hold on . . ." Willa whispered. "Just breathe, steady and slow. . . ."

As she held her, Willa could feel Adelaide's heart beating as fast as a frightened sparrow's.

"Steady and slow . . ." Willa whispered, trying to pour her stillness into Adelaide the way a tree pours the water of its roots into a neighboring tree that needs its help.

From inside the cocoon the plants had created around her and Adelaide, Willa could not see the butterflies, but as the insects came closer, the air became noticeably colder.

When she finally felt the cold pass, Willa waited for a few moments and then slowly pulled back some of the grass and peeked out.

There appeared to be nothing but normal forest around them.

"What do you see?" Adelaide whispered.

"I think it's safe," Willa said, gently moving the grass and vines aside.

But just as they got to their feet, Adelaide clutched her arm and pointed. "There!"

As Willa pivoted, she saw three black shapes in the distance charging toward them. And they weren't clouds of butterflies. But they weren't human, Faeran, or any kind of natural animal, either. She knew it was impossible, but the creatures coming toward them seemed to be burning with black flame. The beasts were massive in size, with thick, trunk-like bodies, hunched over and lurching as they moved, their black-smoldering upper limbs seeming to drag behind them, and the rush of cracking sticks filling the air.

Willa had no idea what the creatures were, and in this

moment, she didn't want to find out. She grabbed Adelaide's hand and bolted in the opposite direction.

The earth rumbled as the beasts hurtled toward them.

Willa's sprinting feet beat against the ground. Her heart pounded. Every muscle in her body felt as if it were bursting with the lightning of pure fear.

Adelaide stayed right with her, matching her strides.

Willa glanced back as they ran. Despite the huge size of the creatures, they moved with incredible speed. They were getting closer and closer. The thrashing sound of breaking branches was growing into a great storm all around them. The smell of rotting decay choked the air. And the cold hit them like a wall.

Willa frantically scanned for a place for her and Adelaide to hide, but one of the beasts was already right on top of them. The earth was shaking beneath Willa's feet. A great, sucking wind pulled the air from her lungs. A black wave of darkness engulfed her.

The memory of the men in the gorge flashed into her mind—the cold, and the crippling, agonizing pain they had endured.

It was coming.

She knew she was going to die.

And then, suddenly and inexplicably, the beast shifted direction.

It ripped past her like a terrifically strong gust of ice-cold wind, leaving a tumult of twisting air behind it.

As Willa turned in astonishment, she saw all three of the

beasts barreling off into the forest, moving away from her and Adelaide at rapid speed.

Willa stumbled to an exhausted stop, and Adelaide stopped with her, the two of them gasping for breath, stunned by what had just happened.

As the dark beasts disappeared into the distance, the crackling storm of breaking sticks faded, the odor of decay diminished, and the trembling ground went still.

"They passed us by . . ." Willa said, her voice shaking.

"What did you do?" Adelaide asked, gazing in the direction the creatures had gone.

"Nothing," Willa said, as confused as she was.

"I thought for sure they were going to kill us," Adelaide said.

"That one was coming right for us, but at the last second, it actually turned away. It purposely avoided us."

"It was like they were on some sort of mission," Adelaide said. "Those things were huge! Did you see how big they were?"

"And it got very cold when they came at us, just like the snakelike creatures. . . ."

"So you think they were from Dark Hollow . . ." Adelaide said.

"They must have been."

"But what does all this mean? What are these things?"

"I don't know," Willa admitted, shaking her head. She had no idea what the creatures were or why they were coming.

Adelaide looked around them warily, peering through the trees in all directions as if she was expecting another creature of Dark Hollow to charge at them at any second.

"I don't know what's going on, Willa," Adelaide said uncertainly, "but I think we should get out of here."

Willa nodded, knowing she was right. "Come on," she said, touching her friend's shoulder. "I know a place that I'm sure you're going to like."

31

As they walked through the forest, Adelaide looked over at her.

Willa realized how much faith her friend had put in her, to come up into the mountains with her, to follow her without question, and to keep following her even as the sun began to set.

By the time they reached the spot Willa had wanted to show her friend, the forest had gone dark around them except for shafts of moonlight coming down through the leaves.

"This way . . ." Willa said, taking Adelaide's hand, ducking down, and leading her through a wall of entangled underbrush.

They came to a small, secluded glen deep in the forest, a quiet, graceful place where the earth dipped gently down into a shallow, bowl-shaped meadow, with flowers and ferns growing in abundance, and the branches of the surrounding trees providing a ceiling of green above.

"This little glen is one of my favorite spots in the world," Willa said softly.

"It's beautiful . . ." Adelaide said as she gazed around them. "Just perfect. . . ."

"Let's sit here," Willa said, suggesting a spot on the rim of the glen so that they were looking down into it.

As they sat beside each other in the cool night air, Willa felt the warmth of Adelaide's shoulder against hers and heard the sound of her breathing. Willa had been here many times. She had pondered here, imagined here, and fallen asleep here. Adelaide was the first and only person she had ever shown it to.

Adelaide did not ask her why she had brought her to this spot. She seemed to understand that there was a purpose to it.

"If we're very lucky," Willa said quietly, "in a few minutes, something will begin to happen in the center of the meadow. . . ."

"There!" Adelaide gasped, pointing toward several dots of yellowish-green light glowing in the darkness in front of them.

"It looks like our friends have arrived . . ." Willa whispered.

"They're fireflies!" Adelaide said excitedly.

A few more of them lit up, and then many more. Soon the glen was filled with thousands of blinking, glowing green fireflies. These weren't the weird, out-of-place fireflies of Dark Hollow, but the kind of natural fireflies that Willa had known all her life.

"They're really pretty!" Adelaide said, grasping Willa's hand as they watched the show of light.

"There's something more to come . . ." Willa whispered.

"What's going to happen?" Adelaide asked, her voice quieter than the beat of a moth's wing.

"Watch . . ." Willa whispered.

At that moment, the glittering display of fireflies went dark. Suddenly she and Adelaide were staring at nothing but a wall of blackness. Every firefly in the glen and the surrounding forest had turned off its light at the exact same moment.

"Whoa!" Adelaide said. "What happened? Where'd they all go?"

"Just watch . . ." Willa whispered.

All at once, every firefly glowed to life and started blinking, filling the glen and the surrounding forest with a dazzling, awe-inspiring display of sparkling light. Hovering above the ferns and in the flowers and up into the trees, they were *everywhere.*

"That's amazing!" Adelaide said.

And just as she spoke, the light of the fireflies disappeared and they were plunged into darkness once again.

Adelaide gasped. "What's happening? What are they doing?"

Willa counted, "One, two, three, four, five, six, seven, eight." And on the count of eight, all the fireflies started flashing again. They blinked and glowed and sparkled for eight beats of her heart, as if reveling in the glory of their ability to pierce the darkness. And then they all went off for eight more beats.

When the fireflies came on, they were each flashing in their own way, but at the same time they were connected, synchronized, all working together, like one giant organism of glimmering light.

"I've seen fireflies down in Cades Cove, but nothing like this . . ." Adelaide said, her voice trembling with wonder.

"I've counted twenty different kinds of fireflies in these mountains so far," Willa said. "There are various kinds of green ones, white ones, yellow ones, and blue ones. Some large, some small. Some of them blink fast and others slow. Where your father's crew has been logging near the Elkmont Camp, there is a greenish-yellow synchronous firefly that only comes out for a few nights in the early summer each year. Sometimes I see blue ghost fireflies, tiny little creatures that glow with a constant, steady blue light as they hover close to the ground."

"I like that name, 'blue ghost fireflies,'" Adelaide said. "What are these fireflies here called?" she asked, gesturing toward the meadow.

"I've only seen them in this one glen, among this particular kind of fern. I think they might be the last of their kind. But I don't know if they even have a name, or if anyone else has ever seen them other than you and me."

"That's amazing," Adelaide said. "We're watching a rare display of the famous Adelaide-Willa Firefly."

Willa laughed and nodded. "That sounds just about right."

"I really appreciate you showing me this."

"You're welcome," Willa said, smiling in the darkness.

But then Adelaide's voice became more serious. "If the loggers trample these ferns or those black creatures come here . . ."

"Then the magic of these fireflies will be lost. The people of the future will never even know they existed."

"My father says that magic isn't real," Adelaide said, not as a challenge, but with sadness and resignation.

"Is that what you believe?"

"I don't know. I can't remember."

Willa looked at Adelaide. What did she mean by that?

"But what about you?" Adelaide asked. "What do *you* believe?"

"The fireflies lighting the darkness, the wolves howling at night, and a tree that lives for three hundred years. It's all magic, isn't it?"

Adelaide smiled, seeming to like her answer. "I think *you're* magic, Willa."

"I'm just a person," Willa said softly, "just like you."

"I saw you with your father and sister. Do you have other family, too?"

"My younger brother, Iska, has gone to live with his cousins for a while, and I had another brother, named Inali, who passed away."

"I'm so sorry," Adelaide said. She paused and there was quiet between them for a moment. And then she asked gently, "What about before that? What about your mother?"

"I had another family years ago, but they all passed away."

"I'm so sorry," Adelaide said. "I know that must be very sad."

"I guess I'm like these fireflies here," Willa said. "The last of my kind."

"Maybe they sense that," Adelaide said.

"What about your home and your family?" Willa asked.

"You know my father, and I have a mother and four brothers

and six sisters. We're all very different, but we eat our meals together and we do our chores. I hate splitting the kindling and hoeing weeds, but I like feeding the goats and the dogs, and taking care of the chickens."

"And you like walking through the fields of wheat," Willa said.

Adelaide's eyes sparkled a little bit in the moonlight as she nodded. "Yes, I love going out into the fields. It's very peaceful."

As Adelaide spoke, it struck Willa how different their lives were, and yet how similar she felt to her friend at this moment.

Just quiet now, they sat on the edge of the glen and watched the fireflies long into the night, both of them too content to move.

Willa knew that Adelaide's mother would be worrying about her. And McClaren would get angry at Adelaide again, probably worse this time. But the thought of parting from her friend filled Willa's heart with more sadness than she could bear.

As the display of the fireflies slowly diminished, with fewer and fewer lighting up until there was nothing but the cloak of night once more, Adelaide huddled close to her, a warm presence in the coolness of the mountain air.

Willa thought it was strange that even after the fireflies had gone dark, it still felt magical just to stay here for a while.

Finally, she turned and looked out into the darkness in the direction from which they had come. Willa had never feared the forest at night, but at this moment, deep down inside, she felt something seeping into her body. Not a sense of immediate threat, but the feeling that the dangers of the world were slowly surrounding them and would soon destroy everything they loved.

There were dark forces spreading through the forest. And it seemed like these new dangers could fall upon them anywhere and at any time. She didn't want to say it out loud, but she knew she had to get Adelaide home.

32

As the moonlit valley of Cades Cove came into view, a wave of dread passed through Willa. Not because of the chaos of the world, but for one simple reason. She didn't want to say good-bye to her new friend.

Adelaide slowed to a stop and turned toward her, a somber expression on her face. "I hate leaving you out here in the woods all alone, Willa," she said softly.

"I'll be all right," Willa assured her, and then she looked at Adelaide's house in the distance. "It's you I'm worried about. I hope you don't get in trouble for coming home so late."

"I'll be all right, too," Adelaide said, echoing her in words and tone. And then, in a startling burst of movement, Adelaide threw her arms around Willa and pulled her close. "I don't know what my father is going to do when I get home, but whatever it is, spending time with you was worth it." She pulled out of the embrace and looked at Willa with fierce determination. "I'll come back up here as soon as I can."

Willa knew she had to stay focused on helping Nathaniel and Hialeah. She couldn't afford to delay by making friends or following the whims of her heart. But something deep inside her was telling her that she'd have a better chance of succeeding with Adelaide than without her.

"I'll meet you here as soon as you can get away," Willa said.

Adelaide squeezed her one last time, and then let her go and ran.

Standing at the edge of the trees, Willa watched Adelaide rush down the slope toward home. Just as she opened the back door, she turned and looked up toward Willa. Adelaide paused a moment, and then slipped quietly into the house.

The moment she was gone, Willa felt it. She felt it hard. A lump in her throat. A sense of silence, of stillness. A sense of *emptiness*. By going into that house—*into that human place*—it was as if Adelaide's soul had been covered up and then disappeared.

Willa's heart beat ten, twenty, thirty times, her mind just waiting and watching, praying that Adelaide was all right.

But there was a heaviness in Willa's chest and it wasn't going away.

Finally, she left the cover of the trees and went down into the valley. Staying low and quiet, she crept toward the house.

As she reached the backyard, a startling barrage of noise erupted from inside—yelling and shouting, and glass shattering against a wall. Willa's chest seized with anguish. Through the candlelit windows, she saw the silhouettes of figures moving back and forth.

"Do you realize how late it is?" Adelaide's father shouted. "Where have you been? Your mother has been frantic!"

If Adelaide replied to her father, she spoke so softly that Willa couldn't make it out. All Willa could hear was the whimpering of Adelaide's brothers and sisters huddled in the back room of the house.

"You don't see the others doing these things!" Adelaide's father shouted. "They're good sons and daughters. They do their chores, they come home when they're supposed to. This is no time for your foolish, disobedient games, Adelaide. I've got men dying on the job, Cherokee blocking the logging roads, and some mountain girl stirring things up in Gatlinburg! I don't want to come home to find your mother in tears because she can't find you!"

Willa's heart lurched when she heard Jim McClaren's words. Was he talking about Hialeah? And what about Nathaniel? Desperate to hear more, she skulked through the backyard until she reached the rear wall of the house, her heart beating so hard that it felt like it was going to burst.

"I'm sorry, Father, I really am," Adelaide said. "I didn't mean to cause any trouble."

Willa heard what she thought must be Adelaide's mother's voice as well, the three of them arguing, their voices getting louder and louder. Suddenly Jim McClaren shouted, "You've got to stop with these stories, Adelaide! Stop this lying!"

"I'm telling the truth!" Adelaide fought back. "I'm trying to help you! Don't go back out there, Father. It's too dangerous!"

"When I left here, I told you to stay around the house, but you disobeyed me!" her father continued. "And now you come in here and tell me not to go to work? I won't stand for it!"

Willa heard the sounds of McClaren stomping across the room as Adelaide scrambled away from him, screaming, "Father, no! Please!"

The back door burst open. Willa leaped in startled surprise. Jim McClaren came striding out of the house. He had Adelaide by the arm and was pulling her, forcibly, across the backyard. Adelaide kicked and screamed, trying to yank herself free, her hair flying, but he was much larger and stronger. When he reached a small shed at the edge of the yard, he thrust her inside, slammed the door, and locked it with an iron padlock.

"This is for your own good!" he shouted into the shed. "One way or another, you're going to learn to obey me!"

Jim McClaren tramped back into the house, slammed the door shut, and shoved the bolt into place with a loud *clank*.

Left in the sudden stillness of the night, Willa gazed at the silent, dead-walled shed a few feet away, her heart breaking as she waited, listening for any kind of sound from within, a word, a whimper, even a breath.

When Willa saw the candles in the house go out for the night and she heard the last murmurs of Adelaide's brothers and sisters before they fell asleep, Willa crept over to the shed in the backyard and crumpled down against the door.

"Adelaide . . ." she whispered through the cracks between the boards.

There was no answer.

"Adelaide, it's me. . . ."

Willa took a long breath and let it out, waiting.

"It's me, it's Willa. . . ."

"He didn't hurt me," Adelaide whispered.

"I'm so sorry about everything," Willa said softly.

"Please don't be sorry," Adelaide said. "I knew I was going to get in trouble. My father is just trying to protect me. He's trying to keep us all safe."

Willa looked at the iron padlock on the door. "Do you want me to try to get you out?"

"No," Adelaide said. "This is where I belong,"

Feeling as if her heart was drowning, Willa put her shoulder and forehead against the door. She heard Adelaide do the same on the other side.

Willa tried to push her fingers in between the slats of the door, but the gaps were too narrow and she couldn't get them all the way through. Adelaide pressed hers into the gap from the other side. And in the middle, their fingertips touched. Adelaide's fingers felt warm and soft, and Willa could tell that they were trembling.

That night, Willa didn't sleep in a house or a lair or a tree. She slept on the ground, leaning against the door of the shed. And Adelaide leaned against the other side, the two of them touching the tips of their fingers through the slats.

Feeling that single, small touch, Willa slept better that night than she had in a long time.

The next morning, when the back door of the house opened, Willa startled awake. She scurried away from the building, lay flat, and blended into the grass and dirt.

A human woman with pale white wrinkled skin and long blond hair came out of the house and walked toward the shed. She used an iron key to release the padlock and then slowly pushed open the door.

"Honey, are you awake?" she asked in a gentle, tentative voice.

As Adelaide stepped out of the shed, she held up a hand to block the sunlight from her eyes.

"You should know by now that you have to do what your father says," her mother said with a sigh, handing her a biscuit and a glass of water.

"Yes, Momma," Adelaide said, glumly.

"He's going through a lot at work. He doesn't need to be worrying about you, too."

"I know. I'm sorry," said Adelaide. "I'll be more careful."

"And no more stories about dark spirits haunting the forest. Telling a man like your father that he can't go to work is like telling him to keel over and die. You should know better—that's just the way he is. He wants to do a good job for the company."

"No more stories," Adelaide agreed, her head hanging low. "But Father *did* see some of the beasts I was talking about, the snakelike things. He knows at least that part was true."

"Whatever those things were—some kind of rabid animals, I suppose—he'll take care of it. He always does."

Willa scowled at the woman's theory, and she was sure that Adelaide felt the same way.

"What about his leg?" Adelaide asked. "Is it healed enough?"

"It's better now, with the splint. He's just going to have to suffer through it. He can't take off work now."

"Why not?" Adelaide asked.

"Mr. Sutton is making big changes at the company. He's expanding the mill, adding more trains to the lines, and bringing in more logging crews. Your father's hours are going to be even longer—he already went off to the site."

As Willa heard these words, her heart sank. The forest, her father—they were running out of time.

"But that's enough questions out of you," Adelaide's mother said finally. "Now go do your chores. After that, you're free."

"I will. Thank you, Momma," Adelaide said, and ran toward the chicken coop.

As Adelaide's mother returned to the house, Willa slinked back up into the forest and waited.

She watched Adelaide run from chore to chore, gathering the chicken eggs and taking them into the kitchen, feeding and milking the goats, mucking out the pig stall, and a dozen other tasks that Willa didn't understand.

Finally, Adelaide washed her hands and face in the water basin by the back door, dried them with a rag, and came running up the mountain slope like a captured deer that had been set free.

As they came together near the tree that had become their meeting place, Adelaide embraced her.

"I'm glad you're here," Adelaide said with a sigh.

"I'm sorry about what happened."

"I'm okay." There was nothing careless or flippant about the way she said it. Willa sensed that Adelaide knew she shouldn't have stayed away from home so long. "But we need to forget about all that," she went on. "We've got to help your father."

Willa could see the determination in Adelaide's eyes. She wasn't going to give up.

"I've been thinking more and more about those shadowy black creatures we saw yesterday," Willa said. "Did you get a good close look at them?"

"It was hard to make them out," Adelaide said. "It was like

they weren't completely there, or they were made out of smoke or something."

"And it got very cold when they came . . ." Willa said.

"It reminds me of the stories the old-timers tell around the campfire to scare the children," Adelaide said.

Willa looked at her. "What do you mean? What stories?"

"You know, those scary stories people tell about some poor guy getting murdered in some horrible way, with an ax or something, and the victim's ghost comes back from the dead to haunt the man who murdered him."

"But those . . . The creatures . . . What we saw couldn't have been humans. . . ."

"Maybe humans aren't the only things that become ghosts . . ." Adelaide said uncertainly.

The quills on the back of Willa's neck slowly stood on end as she thought about what her friend had said. And then a particularly dark, unpleasant thought crept into her mind.

"Maybe not. . . . I think the snakelike beasts or the ones we saw last night attacked the two men that my father was accused of killing."

"And we *know for sure* they attacked the men in the gorge," Adelaide said.

Willa nodded, remembering the horrific sight of those men being torn to the ground. "My mind keeps going back to the way that creature moved toward us last night," she said, "and then went *past* us."

"Your blending must have fooled it," Adelaide said.

"Possibly," Willa said. "But it was charging directly at us and then, at the last second, it turned away. It didn't miss us by accident or because it couldn't see us. It purposefully avoided us."

"But why would it do that?" Adelaide asked.

Willa looked at her and nodded. "I think that's the key to everything. . . ."

"Come on, let's walk," Willa said, leading Adelaide into the forest. "When you said that maybe dead humans aren't the only ones who have ghosts, it got me thinking."

"But the creatures that attacked the men in the gorge didn't look like any kind of ghost I've ever heard of," Adelaide said.

"I didn't see eyes on them, did you?" asked Willa.

"No eyes, no mouth, nothing like that," Adelaide said.

"Did they even have heads?"

Adelaide glanced down as she tried to recall. "It was hard to make it out, but I think their ends were actually flat."

"Like they'd been cut off. . . ."

"Cut off?" Adelaide said in surprise. "What do you mean?"

"Maybe they weren't snakes at all."

"All right, but what then?"

"They were long and gray, wet and slimy, and they had severed ends. . . ."

"Worms?" Adelaide asked.

"Maybe we're thinking about it all wrong. Maybe they weren't snakes or worms or any kind of animal. Maybe they were . . . maybe they were *roots*."

"I don't understand," Adelaide said.

"Maybe their ends had been cut with axes."

"What about the really large creatures we saw last night?" Adelaide said. "If you think about it, they were like trunks with their broken limbs dragging on the ground. Did you hear the sound they made when they moved? It was like breaking branches."

"I heard it," Willa said, nodding.

"And I smelled rotting wood . . ." Adelaide said.

"I don't think they're the ghosts of humans or Faeran," Willa said. "I think the creatures of Dark Hollow are the ghosts of murdered trees."

"The spirits of trees that have been cut down!" Adelaide said in amazement. "My father doesn't want to hear about things like this, but that's exactly what they are—their ghosts!"

"So that means . . ." Willa said, trying to piece it all together, "Dark Hollow is the graveyard of the forest's unsettled souls."

Adelaide looked at her. "Just like you said, that's the key to it all. . . ."

"That's right," Willa said. "They're not after you and me."

"They're after the loggers!" Adelaide said, grabbing her arm.

The forest still held many mysteries, but Willa knew for sure that the great hemlock by the river and the other trees had been *alive.* They had possessed living spirits. How many trees had the loggers cut down? And where did the spirits of those great trees go after their bodies crashed to the forest floor? They were roaming the earth until their murder was avenged, just like the ghosts in Adelaide's stories.

"But why now?" Adelaide said. "Where did Dark Hollow come from?"

"Sit here a moment," Willa said, bringing them to a stop and lowering herself slowly to the ground beside the trunk of a large tulip tree.

Willa's thoughts went back to something that had happened more than a year before. She had been trapped in one of the lower corridors of the old Faeran lair while trying to help Hialeah, Iska, and the other imprisoned children escape from the padaran's guards. There were no living plants or animals around for her to call on for help. Out of desperation, she had resorted to the darkest power her grandmother had taught her, a power that was never to be used except in the most desperate of circumstances. *And she had used it.* She had put her hands on the dried woven-stick walls of the lair and resurrected the dead, unleashing those writhing undead sticks on the Faeran guards.

What had come of those spirits? Had they burrowed into the ground? Could they have festered and spread like black mold, feeding on the rot of the burned-out lair?

"I'm the one who did this . . ." Willa said in a horrified

whisper, as much to herself as to Adelaide. "In raising those sticks from the dead, I planted the seeds for Dark Hollow to grow."

"What sticks? What are you talking about? You didn't do this, Willa!" Adelaide said sharply, almost in anger. "You're not responsible for those vile creatures!"

As Adelaide spoke, Willa's mind went deeper and deeper into the world around her. She knew it wasn't just her resurrection of the dead sticks that had caused all this. The loggers—their destruction of the forest, the killing of the great hemlock tree by the river . . . that's what was feeding it. The more trees the humans murdered, the more Dark Hollow grew, oozing from the earth, spreading its black tentacles out into the forest, sucking the life out of any tree-cutting humans it came in contact with, like black roots reaching down the slope of the Great Mountain. How long before it reached Cades Cove?

Adelaide shook Willa by the shoulders, breaking her out of her darkened thoughts. "Willa, what's happening to you?"

"The ghosts of Dark Hollow aren't going to stop," Willa said in a flat voice. "They're going to kill the loggers."

"But what about my father?" Adelaide said. "And the other men in the Elkmont crew? We've got to warn them!"

"You already tried to warn your father to stay out of the forest," Willa said. "But he didn't listen."

"We've got to keep trying!" Adelaide said. "We've got to do something!"

As Willa sat in the forest next to the tree and next to her

human friend, she came to a vast and terrifying realization. The spirits of Dark Hollow could be the answer she'd been looking for. They could eliminate the loggers and stop the slaughter of the trees. That was exactly what she had always wanted. It was what she and Nathaniel and Hialeah and Iska had been fighting for.

Willa knew she didn't have the physical power or weapons to protect the forest by herself. She was not a warrior. But from the very beginning, she had wanted to defeat this evil. She had wanted to protect the trees. Maybe this was exactly what the forest needed to do to protect itself. Maybe she hadn't just accidentally released the unsettled spirits of the undead world—she had *enabled* them, given them power.

Adelaide grasped at her, begging her. "What are you thinking about right now, Willa? What are we going to do?"

"I don't know," Willa said, but the truth was, she knew exactly what she was thinking about. It was just too awful to say out loud.

All she had to do was do nothing. All she had to do was let the ghosts of Dark Hollow do what they had come for.

"Willa, please!" Adelaide pressed her.

"I'm just trying to figure it all out," Willa said, her eyes glazed as she looked off into the forest.

"We need to go to the logging site right away," Adelaide said. "To warn my father and the others."

Willa looked at her, taken aback by the idea.

Jim McClaren was a tree-killer. He was exactly the kind of human she wanted to stop from destroying the forest. And he was exactly the kind of human that the spirits of Dark Hollow would take down.

But when she looked at Adelaide and saw the expression in her eyes, Willa remembered that he was more than just a killer of trees. He was a human being. And he was Adelaide's father. And Willa knew that Adelaide couldn't help how she was feeling. It wasn't a choice for her. It was just *in her*. She loved her father and wanted to protect him. Didn't Willa feel the same way about Nathaniel?

"I need your help, Willa," Adelaide pleaded, her voice trembling.

Through all this, as Willa sat looking at her friend, she couldn't help but keep going back to the alternative—*not* helping, *not* warning Jim McClaren, and letting the spirits of Dark Hollow do what they were lingering on earth to do. What about *that* decision?

She tried to imagine what would happen if she chose the path to go with Adelaide or chose a different path. She tried to make it a choice, a *decision*. But the truth was, she knew she wasn't going to abandon Adelaide. She wasn't going to let her go to the logging site alone. In the end, she could only follow the path of her heart.

As she rose up to her feet, she pulled Adelaide with her.

"Come on," said Willa. "I know a shortcut." And she led the way.

They moved quickly through the forest, mile after mile. Willa could tell by Adelaide's fast, determined walking that her mind was on nothing but her father.

As they got closer to the logging site, Willa braced herself to hear the now familiar cracking thuds of axes chopping into the trunks of trees. But an altogether different kind of sound came floating toward them through the forest:

The sound of humans screaming.

A chill went up Willa's spine as she reflexively crouched to the forest floor and blended into the undergrowth.

But Adelaide cried out, "It's the loggers!" and ran toward the screams.

Willa dashed after her, her heart racing. She grabbed Adelaide's arm and tried to pull her back. But as the two of them came out of the underbrush, a full view of the logging site opened up in front of them.

Dozens of loggers had been working away with their axes and saws, but now there was nothing but shouting-and-running chaos. A horde of dark smoldering creatures was tearing through them, moving from one group of loggers to the next. It appeared as if at least a dozen ghosts of Dark Hollow were running rampant, pulling shrieking, flailing men to the ground. She could see the long snakelike creatures, and the huge trunklike beasts, but there were many other dark shapes attacking the men as well that her brain just couldn't make sense of. They were everywhere.

"Willa!" Adelaide gasped, pointing at the shadowy revenant of a massive bear that was charging straight toward them. Willa yanked Adelaide out of the creature's path. A rolling wave of coldness poured over them. And a great gust of wind swooshed past them as the roaring beast slammed into a logger just a few feet away. The man crumpled, his skin turning gray as his body slumped to the ground.

Willa stumbled back, pulling Adelaide with her. A black phantasm of a fox darted past, grazing her calf with a searing slash of burning cold. A huge, plunging mountain buffalo as black as charcoal crashed through the undergrowth and smashed into a group of fleeing loggers. An immense elk with long black burning horns speared a man against a tree and engulfed him in black flames. They were the spirits of Dark Hollow, past and the present, every one them as dead and deadly as the next.

Just down the mountain slope from her and Adelaide, four loggers on a cutting platform had been pulling a steel saw through the trunk of a large oak tree.

"Look out!" Adelaide shouted to the men, leaping as she pointed toward the shape of a smoking black wolf running toward them. The startled men turned and saw the attacking creature. Abandoning their equipment, they leaped from the platform in panic. Three of them hit the ground, got to their feet, and fled. But the fourth landed too hard. Willa heard a *crick!* as a bone in his leg broke. He cried out in pain and collapsed, shrieking frantically as he tried to crawl away from the snarling black creature.

Adelaide lurched forward, trying to run toward the loggers, but Willa grabbed her by the arm. "Stop, Adelaide! No! If the spirits touch you, you'll die!"

A short distance away, a group of wranglers in wide-brimmed leather hats and long, muddy coats was whipping a team of mules that was pulling a large log down a skidding ramp toward the railroad track. As the men saw the creatures coming toward them, some of them tried to flee, slipping in the mud on the steep slope. Another attempted to defend himself with his ax. But it was all useless against the dead. The ghosts of Dark Hollow pulled down one man after another. As the smell of the creatures hit the flaring nostrils of the frightened mules, the animals whinnied in panic and thrashed in their harnesses, desperate to escape.

Looking out into the pandemonium, Willa saw at least ten of the ghosts attacking the humans all across the logging site.

"Do you see what's happening?" Willa shouted at Adelaide. "You can't get anywhere near those things!"

"There! There he is!" Adelaide shouted as she pointed toward her father in the center of the chaos, struggling to stay on his panicking horse. As McClaren gripped its reins, the animal stomped its hooves and threw its head wildly back and forth, neighing a high-pitched squeal, its eyes white with terror.

"We've got to help him!" Adelaide shouted, trying to yank herself away and run toward him.

"Adelaide, no!" Willa shouted back at her, holding her tight.

And then Adelaide turned and spoke right into her face. "You've got to help these men, Willa," she said, pointing toward the logging crews. "That's my father down there! My *father*! Please! You've got to help them!"

Willa's temples pounded in her head as her eyes darted from one cataclysm of violence to the next, the men running and screaming everywhere she looked. Adelaide wanted her to somehow *save* these men. But how? What could she even do against the ghosts of Dark Hollow?

It felt as if everything she'd been through over the last year—the forest dying, the animals fleeing—was coming down to this one moment. If she just pulled back and let the ghosts of Dark Hollow do what they came to do, the loggers would be stopped. Her entire world would be saved!

Or she could try to help the humans in some way. But why in the name of all that was good would she save loggers? They were the destroyers, the killers of trees!

She already knew the answer. When the sheriff and those

other men had come to arrest her father, her father could have shot and killed them, but he had chosen not to fight. And when she was by the ravine, she had leaped at the chance to save the bear cub. A year ago, she had been *honored* to help Luthien, the leader of the wolves. And she had risked her life to help the imprisoned human children escape from the padaran's prison. She didn't kill animals, and she didn't kill people. She *helped* them. She *cared* for them. She fought for life, not death. These men had real lives. They had real children. She despised the fact that the loggers were killing trees, but they were living, breathing human beings. She had no idea how, but she had to save them.

Willa grabbed Adelaide by the shoulders and shook her. "No matter what you see, do not move from here!"

Adelaide pleaded with her. "I won't, I swear. I'll do whatever you say—just help them!"

Leaving her friend behind, Willa turned and raced down the hill toward the dying men.

Willa's feet pounded across the dirt, her chest heaving for air as she ran toward the closest group of loggers. They were frantically scrambling up the slope of the mountain, fleeing a pack of black-smoldering wolves that was charging after them. To Willa's astonishment, she actually recognized some of the individual wolves. They were the long-passed members of Luthien's pack that had been starved, poisoned, and shot by the humans. Dark Hollow had transformed them into black, snarling, vicious beasts bent on attack, their once beautiful amber eyes blazing with nothing but black fire.

Willa pulled in a deep breath and then ran right toward them. She was determined to block their path so that the men behind her could escape.

The loggers climbing the slope were shouting to one another and looking back over their shoulders, their eyes filled with terror. When one of the men stumbled and fell, his friends grabbed hold of him and pulled him along with them.

"Here they come!" one of the men yelled as the wave of black wolves got closer.

Willa hurled her body in front of the wolves, demanding, *"Dee-sa!"*

But the wolves didn't stop. They charged straight at her. A wall of cold hit her, and she choked on the stench of decay. Everything went black. She threw up her arms to protect herself out of reflex, even though she knew it wouldn't matter. She was going to die.

But then the blue sky opened up in front of her and the rushing sound swept past her.

Screams erupted behind her as she turned. The jaws of the black spirits clamped onto the slowest runner of the group and pulled him down.

Willa rushed forward, her muscles bursting with power. She dashed one way and then the other, desperately trying to get in front of the wolves, but they moved too quickly. They were all around her, leaping past her, sprinting, charging, biting at the men. Three of them chomped onto another logger with their black-burning teeth and drained him of life. The ghost-wolves took down one man after another, right in front of her, all around her, until every last man in the group she had tried to save was lost. A pit lodged in Willa's stomach as she gazed out across the mayhem, other groups of men screaming and running, dozens of spirits of all different kinds leaping and attacking.

She had made the choice to help the loggers, but no matter

what she did, it was useless. The ghosts of Dark Hollow were far too fast, and they didn't listen to her Faeran words.

Lowering her head in determination, Willa ran toward the center of the battle. Even if she could do nothing else, she had to protect Adelaide's father.

She dodged two of the murderous beasts and then darted through a group of fleeing men. The neighing of a frantic horse caught her attention, and she turned.

Surrounded by the bedlam of the battle, Jim McClaren's horse thrashed one way and then another, its eyes wild with fear.

"Whoa! Whoa! Easy now!" McClaren shouted as he pulled back on his horse's reins, struggling to get it under control. The pivoting steed banged its shoulder against the side of a tree, then lunged forward, nearly throwing him out of the saddle.

"Willa, behind you!" Adelaide screamed from the slope above her. Willa turned just in time to see the enormous black shape of a bear barreling rapidly toward Adelaide's father.

Willa stumbled back, startled by the size of it. The black-smoldering bear roared as it charged. A wave of cold buffeted through the forest. Adelaide's father was seconds from death.

As the bear charged, the horse reared up onto its hind legs, fiercely striking its hooves in the air, trying to fight off the towering black spirit by sheer will. But the instant the horse's hooves touched the ghost of Dark Hollow, the horse's brown hide turned stark gray. Its back legs buckled. And then its head and its long, massive body collapsed to the ground. Jim McClaren was thrown from the saddle. His body crashed against the trunk of a large tree. And then he crumpled down onto its roots.

As the massive shadowy apparition moved toward him, Willa threw herself in front of it, blocking its path. Then she lurched forward and pressed her hands to the tree, infusing it with her own life and energy. Tightening her grip, she pushed her will into the trunk and out to its branches, screaming the Faeran commands. The branches swung down to the ground, twisting and writhing like the great tentacles of an unnatural beast, right into the path of the charging bear. The two collided with an explosion of darkness. Broken branches and a wave of black smoke burst in all directions.

Two of the black burning elk charged toward her and Jim McClaren from the right, lowering their massive horns as they came. And the ghost of what had once been a mountain buffalo thundered at them from the left. Behind her, Jim McClaren struggled to get himself to his feet, but he was bent over, holding his ribs, unable to defend himself from the coming attack.

Still gripping the trunk, she commanded the upper branches to reach out to the other trees around it. She felt the essence of the trees throbbing through her body. And she felt her own life slipping into them, pouring out to them, touching the darkened spirits all around. The living trees around her went dark as death poured into life. And the ghosts of Dark Hollow went bright green as life poured into death.

With her touch and her words and her mind, she reached out to more and more of the trees, to all the trees of the forest around her, commanding them to fight the ghosts, to battle death with life.

The ache of it pulsed through her body. Her neck bent down under the weight of it, her hands still grasping the trunk of the tree through which her energy was flowing.

"Thrash and move!" she commanded the trees around her. *"Twist and turn! We must fight this death together!"*

Oak and walnut, silver bell and birch, linked one to another, branch to branch, leaf to leaf. A tall beech tree that had been living moments before crashed to the ground and exploded into dark gray ash. A maple tree burst into black flame. At the same time, all around her, the ghosts of Dark Hollow were disintegrating into piles of green leaves.

Willa crumpled down. She could no longer lift her head. She could no longer move her arms and legs. She was trunk and root. She was the water flowing underground.

She had reached so deeply into the trees that she had become one of them, touching them all, commanding them to fight, to drive themselves into the ghosts of Dark Hollow, to tear them asunder and fill them with their own life.

With *her* life.

She felt the pulse of water through her.

She felt the sunlight on her.

She felt the sway of the wind in her limbs.

She breathed in the air and breathed it out, and she felt it changing within her.

She felt her roots in the wet ground.

She felt the nutrients flowing through her.

She felt her leaves in the sky.

And she felt the other trees around her, their limbs touching her, holding her, their roots intertwining with hers.

She had become the world.

Ever so slowly, she began to feel the muffled movement of her heart, blood pulsing through her veins like sap through the limbs of a tree.

She began to feel the warmth of sunlight on her skin and the coolness of the soil around her permeating her Faeran body.

She smelled the scent of earth and plants. And she felt moistness on her cheek and her neck, her fingers and her arms.

And then she slowly opened her eyes.

She was lying on the ground, her cheek against the earth, her arms out, her fingers stuck in the dirt like roots. Vines had intertwined with her hair. Her head and shoulders were carpeted with the same leafy creepers and other plants that had grown rapidly over the rest of her body.

As she slowly lifted her head, she felt something softly tear away from her face and other parts of her body. The fine tendrils of plants that had attached themselves with tiny suction cups to her cheek and neck and hands were pulling free. It was through these tendrils that the trees and the other plants of the forest had connected to her. And it was through these tendrils that she had reached the vast web of interconnected life that linked one plant to another.

Her grandmother had taught her about it in many ways, and Willa had experienced it herself for many years, but she realized now more than ever that the individual trees of the forest did not stand alone. They touched one another, supported and sent nourishment to one another, warned one another of coming danger, and helped raise one another's young. Among the trees of a forest, there was no I, only we.

Finally, lifting her head, Willa was able to look out and see what had happened to the world.

Hundreds of trees around her were black, as if a fire had raged through the forest. Many of the dead trees remained standing, their trunks scorched, their branches bare, nothing but skeletons of what they had once been. Some of the others had crashed to the forest floor and lay broken across the ground like the blackened bones of ancient beasts. And all that remained of the tree that had been closest to her, the one she'd actually touched with her bare hands, was a heap of dark gray ash. She hadn't just damaged it. She had destroyed it *entirely.*

Her eyes clouded. A wave of nausea passed through her. And she pulled in a sudden, jerking breath.

She had made a choice that had *killed* these trees. The shock of it felt like a boulder lying on her chest.

But she saw, too, as she looked out, that in various places among the dead trees, there were brand-new living plants as well. Wherever one of the ghosts of Dark Hollow had been—whether it had been a wolf, a bear, or one of the slithering, snakelike roots—there was now a wild clump of green vegetation. In other spots, whole new trees had sprung forth.

Green into black and black into green.

Willa realized with astonishment that she had actually done it.

She had destroyed the ghosts of Dark Hollow.

She had filled them with life.

As the sunlight touched her green skin, she felt as if she wasn't inhaling and exhaling like she normally did. She didn't know how it was possible, but it felt as if, somehow, the air she was breathing was coming from *within* her.

Willa heard something coming in her direction. She turned to see Adelaide running down the slope of the mountain toward her.

"Willa!" she cried, dropping to her knees beside her, tears pouring down her cheeks. "I thought you were dead!"

Human speech sounded so strange to Willa, so out of place, like the clanking of metal.

When she answered, she thought her lips would be dry, but she found that they were moist with the taste of plants.

"I wasn't dead," she said softly to Adelaide, "just . . . *changed*." It surprised her that her voice was not the rough, creaking croak she'd expected it to be after what had happened, but as soft and smooth as the bend of a willow. "I'm all right now."

"But what happened to you?" Adelaide asked. "Why were you stuck into the ground like that with those plants?"

Willa stared down, trying to think of a way to explain it.

"My grandmother told me that a long time ago the most skilled of the Faeran woodwitches became so connected to the forest that they could actually *turn into* a tree, and then later return to their Faeran form. I think that the more I reach into the bodies and souls of the trees, the more the trees reach into me, like they're trying to take me back, trying to reclaim me as part of the forest."

"Don't let them do that anymore!" Adelaide said fiercely. "I don't want to lose you!"

"I don't want to be lost," Willa said, gripping her hand.

But the truth was, with every passing day she became less and less certain about the path she was taking. She looked around at the dead trees. "I killed them . . ." she said, her voice quivering.

"But you saved all these men, Willa," Adelaide said. "And you saved my father!"

Willa turned and saw the gray, withered carcass of the dead horse lying in the dirt. And a little farther on, there was a man on the ground, his whole body shaking.

Willa watched as Jim McClaren slowly picked himself up and looked around at the death and destruction that surrounded him. The bodies of the men who had been killed lay across the ground. But many more of the loggers were gathering themselves and coming together to help one another.

A sickening feeling churned through Willa's stomach.

What have I done? she thought, turning away and rubbing her face with her hands.

What have I done? The thought just kept pounding through her mind as Adelaide put her hand on her shoulder.

What have I done?

"Father, are you hurt?" Adelaide said as she moved toward him. "I'm so glad you're all right!" She tried to embrace him, but he held her at arm's length.

"What are you doing here, Adelaide?" he asked, his face scowling in confusion. Then he turned and looked at Willa. "And what are you doing with *her*?"

Willa's stomach tightened and she stared back at him, but she did not speak.

The human looked straight at her. "In God's name, say something, girl," he said to Willa. "What were those things? What's happening?"

"I told you before, you're killing the forest," Willa said. "Those were its ghosts." She glanced at Adelaide, wanting to have one last image of her in her mind. And then, before

Adelaide or anyone else could stop her, she turned and walked into the woods. Within three steps, she had disappeared.

She didn't want to see Adelaide reuniting with her father. She didn't want to see the loggers helping one another. She didn't want to see any of it. What she had done caused her nothing but shame.

She walked through the stand of dead, blackened trees, reaching out and touching some of them as she passed, her skin and her hair turning as black as coal. "I'm sorry, my friends," she said, tears welling in her eyes as she began to sob.

"Willa, come back!" she heard Adelaide calling out in the distance behind her, but soon the beat of her own heart drowned out the sound.

When Willa finally reached the green trees of the living forest, she kept going.

Leaving the humans far behind her, she walked alone for a long time. She wanted quiet, and to be surrounded by nothing but lush, living plants. If they would have her, she wanted to be among the trees she *hadn't* killed.

Finally, she stopped and sat at the trunk of a three-hundred-year-old tulip tree. Touching her palms to its base, she felt the water in the earth deep below her funneling into its roots, pumping up through the column of its trunk, and flowing to the sunlit leaves swaying in the breeze far above her.

She had always been close to trees, always *known* them, but something had happened when she'd called on the forest to destroy the ghosts of Dark Hollow. The plants had attached to her, and she to them. Something had changed. She didn't know how it was possible, but they were *in* her now, and she was in them. She had never felt so attuned to the throbbing pulse of their lives as she did at this moment, which made the aching pain of what she had done to them all the worse. She felt sick to her stomach.

She gazed at the trees all around her and listened to the songs of the birds above. What was going to happen to these living trees now? How long would it be before the humans she had just saved came and cut them down? How many trees would be lost before the animals began to leave? How many animals would die before the forest ceased to be?

And Willa kept thinking about her father, trapped in a dark cell among a swarm of humans far away. The only good man she had ever known had been locked up by all the others. How was she ever going to help him? What could she possibly do for him? She had solved the mystery of who or what had killed the loggers, but now what? She hadn't saved Nathaniel. Instead, she had saved the evil men who had caused his imprisonment!

As she sat at the base of the tulip tree, Willa heard the quiet crunch of leaves behind her. She turned to see Adelaide walking toward her, her blond hair falling gently onto her shoulders and her pale white face filled with sadness. But how? How had Adelaide tracked her all this way? How was she able to find her or even *see* her here beside the tree? Had their lives grown so intertwined that even the leaves of the forest could not hide her from her friend?

Without saying a word, Adelaide lowered herself to the ground, curled her body up next to Willa's, and wrapped her arms around her.

For a long time Adelaide just held her, seeming to understand what she was going through.

"Thank you, Willa," Adelaide finally whispered. "From the bottom of my heart, thank you."

Willa did not reply at first, for there was too much of a storm inside her to speak, but then she said, very quietly, "You should not thank me. I have done the most terrible thing."

"No," Adelaide said, clutching her as if to shake the thought out of her. "What you did was *not* terrible. I told you, you saved those men."

"Exactly," Willa said, staring at the ground. "I saved the murderers of trees. If I had simply walked away, the ghosts would have killed them, and the destruction of the forest would stop."

"You saved my father," Adelaide said, squeezing her tightly. "That's what you've done."

"Yes, but I could have saved the entire forest instead," Willa said, her voice ragged with discouragement. "It was a terrible mistake."

"I told you, it *wasn't* a mistake!" Adelaide insisted.

Too heartbroken to argue, Willa brought her knees up to her chest and wrapped her arms around them. All she wanted was to feel her father's embrace, to hear his voice. The vines and leafy plants of the forest floor grew rapidly, covering much of her body, as if to protect her from the pain of the world that surrounded her.

"Willa, no, please don't leave me . . ." Adelaide whispered softly, gently pulling the plants away from her. "And please don't be sad about this. What can I do to help you?"

"Nothing," Willa said glumly. "It's too late. I can't save my father and I can't save the forest."

"I'm not talking about the forest," Adelaide said, stroking Willa's cheek where the vines had taken hold of the moisture of her tears and were growing around her eyes. "I'm talking about *you*. What can we do?"

"It's over," Willa said. "There is nothing more to do."

"Don't give up," Adelaide said. "Please. . . ."

"I'm not giving up."

"It sounds like you are. Let's go see the fireflies in the meadow tonight," Adelaide said, trying to distract her, trying to make her feel better in any way she could. "Or we could go to Cades Cove, to—"

"You shouldn't be here with me," Willa interrupted, her eyes flaring up at her friend. "Go be with your father."

Adelaide stared at her, her blond brows drawn together. "No," she said fiercely. "I told him I was going to find you and I wouldn't come home until I did. He got very angry, but I ran. I don't want to be with *him*, Willa. I want to be with *you*."

"And I don't want to be with anyone," Willa said. "Just leave me alone. Go home."

"No!" Adelaide said again, tearing the leaves and vines away from her. "The forest can't have you! I'm not going to let you go!"

"I don't think you understand what I've done," Willa said.

"I *do* understand, I do!" Adelaide said. "I think *you're* the one who doesn't understand. You saved someone's life. How can that be wrong?"

"Of course it was wrong," Willa said.

"But isn't protecting life what you're always doing? Do you think the ghosts of Dark Hollow were life? They were *death,* Willa, and you know it. And you stopped them. Haven't you always tried to protect the natural world from harm?"

Humans aren't the natural world! she wanted to scream, but she didn't.

She knew it wasn't true.

They were *all* connected. Like the wolves and the deer. The families that lived in the mountains, the farmers in Cades Cove, the Cherokee, the Faeran, the animals, the trees, even the loggers with their machines—they were all part of the same world now. And their branches were intertwining whether she wanted them to or not.

Willa thought about what Adelaide was saying. Was there less value in some of those lives? Would it be right for her to let some of them die and not others?

But the truth was, because of the decisions she had made, Jim McClaren and his men had *lived*, and they were going to keep logging. They'd remove any obstacle in their path. Like her father. There was no way out of this, no way to stop what was going to happen.

Just then, a glimmer lit up her mind.

She thought about her Faeran people and the lair that had burned the year before, all the Faeran lifetimes that had been lived there over the years, and all the plants that had been woven into those walls.

Nothing but ashes now. And Dark Hollow growing beside it . . . within it . . . from it . . .

Willa began to wonder about the interconnections, not just between the people, animals, and trees living in these mountains at this moment, but between the past, present, and future. Maybe the only way out of all this was *time*, to somehow use time to her advantage. The decisions her grandmother had made long ago had caused things to happen this very moment she was living through now. And the decisions Willa was making would cause things to happen in the future. And so it was, for every Faeran and every human. Maybe she'd been thinking about the world too simply. It wasn't just interconnected—it was a *mesh* of interconnections across time, as thick as the soil was deep. And Dark Hollow was the way through it.

The ashes, she thought again.

"Willa, stop!" Adelaide shouted, shaking her by the shoulders to break her out of the trance she had fallen into. She tore frantically at the plants crawling over Willa's body. "You're growing yourself in too deep, Willa! We need to get you out of here. Tell me where we can go!"

Willa finally turned and looked at her. "We need to go to Dark Hollow, to the ashes, to the Little Tree . . ." Willa said. "To *time*."

Adelaide stared at her, unable to understand what she was saying.

"We need to go up the mountain, to the old lair," Willa said.

"All right, we'll go. Just show me the way," Adelaide said, pulling Willa to her feet.

As Willa stood, she pulled the strands of vines, creepers, and other plants away from her body and gently set them aside. They hadn't been trying to hurt or imprison her. They'd been trying to comfort and nurture her, to bring her back to them. "I'll join you someday, my friends," she told them. "But not yet."

With Adelaide's shoulder beneath her arm, helping her with every step, Willa began to climb the Great Mountain toward the ashes of her people's past.

As they made their way through the forest, up the slope of the Great Mountain, Adelaide said, "The plants seemed to be out of control back there, growing around you like that."

"They were trying to reclaim me as one of their own," Willa said.

"Well, you're not one of them," Adelaide said emphatically. "You're one of *us*. So don't forget that."

Willa smiled at her friend's fierceness, and the way she said *one of us*.

"I'm all right now," Willa said.

"So tell me about where we're going," Adelaide said as they climbed the slope of the mountain. "What's up there?"

"At some point in the future, when your father and the other men recover from what happened, they're going to go back to logging. We need to figure out a way to stop them."

"Yes, but how?" Adelaide said.

"Right now, you and I don't have the power to stop them. The problem seems impossible to solve."

"And what's changed?"

"I remembered time."

"I don't understand."

"It's easy to lose hope and think that a problem can never be solved, but I've got an idea. I should have seen it before. Everything is constantly growing and changing and dying. Things haven't always been the way they are now. And they won't always be this way in the future. People learn and change. And the world changes around them. You and I can't win this battle *now*. But maybe we can win it in the future, before it's too late. I think my grandmother saw all of this. And now I need to see it, too."

"What do you mean, 'win it in the future'? What did your grandmother see?"

"The flow of time, from the past, to the present, to the future."

"But we can't go to the future," Adelaide said.

"No," Willa said. "But we can use it to our advantage."

"But why are we going up onto Clingmans Dome? What's up there?"

"Dark Hollow's there, and my old lair and a little tree," Willa said. "My link to the past."

As they climbed the slope of the mountain, a white mist drifted through the forest, coating their skin with cool droplets of moisture, and a ceiling of gray clouds hovered over the tops of the trees.

A few hours later, Willa carefully navigated around the deepest parts of Dark Hollow and made her way toward the site of her old lair. Since the last time she was here, the oozing slime mold and weird black growths of Dark Hollow had engulfed much of what had once been the home of her people.

She and Adelaide walked across the scorched stone, through the ash and desolation, until they reached the single, giant tree growing out of the center of the ruins. The tree reached so high that it pierced the low-hanging clouds, and a golden halo of hazy sunlight was filtering down through the tops of its green, leafy branches.

"I thought you said it was a *little* tree," Adelaide said, gazing up at it in awe. "It's huge!"

"It was a bit smaller when I was growing up," Willa said with a smile, pleased that her friend liked it.

"So this is where you came from . . ." Adelaide said as she looked around at the burned, blackened stone and piles of ash.

"This entire area was a lair with walls of woven branches," Willa explained as they walked through. "There were tunnels and rooms, and places to live for all the Faeran."

"And then there was a fire . . ." Adelaide said.

"Yes," said Willa. "The entire lair burned down and everyone had to flee."

"I'm so sorry," Adelaide said. "That must have been awful." When Adelaide's hand gently touched Willa's arm, it felt like energy was flowing into her body.

As they continued on, Willa said, "This is where the great hall was." She swept her hand upward and across to indicate the scale of it. "It had a soaring high ceiling with a large hole at the top so that it was open to the sky."

Adelaide smiled as she tilted her head up toward the sun peeking through the clouds. "I can imagine birds circling up there."

Willa glanced at her in surprise. "Yes, that's right. There *were* birds up there. Come on, I want to show you something else."

She led Adelaide across the surface of the rock and down into a cave tunnel large enough for them to walk through. The stone walls had been smoothed by the flow of an ancient river.

"Where are we going?" Adelaide's voice was tinged with uncertainty.

"It's all right," Willa said, leading her through the darkness. The tunnel split one way and then another. She remembered it well.

Finally, they came to a section of tunnel where sunlight filtered down through openings in the ceiling that had been burrowed by water. And in that light, they could see what Willa had come for.

The wall was covered with thousands of handprints that flowed along the length of the tunnel like a river. The first prints were faded, barely visible, hundreds of years old. But as she and Adelaide walked along, the prints became more and more clear, bolder, richer in color, brown and blue and yellow and red.

"What is this place?" Adelaide asked, gazing at the handprints in wonder.

"This is the River of Souls," Willa explained. "This wall represents the history of our people. Each set of handprints was placed here by Faeran twins of the past. I wanted to come to the old lair to see the Little Tree, but also to see this. This is the wave of time, to remind us that we are not alone, that time has always been flowing and always will be. We are part of an ancient people who have been living for many years, and their decisions have been part of what has brought us to where we are today. And *our* decisions will be part of what shapes our descendants into what they become. There is no I, only we. Across all time."

"It's amazing . . ." Adelaide whispered, keeping her voice low, as if the ghosts of the ancient Faeran people might be disturbed if she spoke too loudly. "Did your grandmother teach you all this?"

"Yes," Willa said. One of the last of the woodwitches and guardians of the old ways, her grandmother had been surrounded by enemies who were consumed with a way of thinking that she knew would lead to the demise of her people. Willa realized now that her grandmother's only hope, in the end, had been what she had taught her granddaughter. Her only hope, in the end, was the future. Willa wanted to explain all this to Adelaide, but she could see that her friend was staring at all the handprints, just trying to take it all in.

"It's beautiful," Adelaide muttered. She seemed to be almost mesmerized by what she was seeing.

"Sit here with me," Willa said gently, guiding her to a spot at the end of the River of Souls. Willa pointed to the last two handprints, which were red in color and very small.

"My grandmother brought me here with my twin sister,

Alliw, when we were five years old," Willa said. "She asked us to dip our hands into a bowl of paint she had made from berries. And then we pressed our palms right here, one beside the other, the left and the right, the Willa and Alliw, just like a thousand twins had done before us."

Trying to keep her breathing steady and strong, Willa put her left hand over the print she had made on the wall eight years before.

To her surprise, Adelaide slowly leaned forward and put her right hand on the print next to hers. Willa thought Adelaide was trying to show that she was on her side, that she was her friend, and that although they were human and Faeran, they were sisters in a way.

Their hands were positioned opposite to one another, their thumbs almost touching, as if a single girl was pressing her two hands to the wall. Because of the way the light was falling through the holes in the ceiling, Willa's hand was cast in shadow, but Adelaide's hand was bright.

Left and right, dark and light, Faeran and human, green skin and white . . . Everything should have been different about their hands. But the more Willa looked, the more she marveled at what she was seeing. Other than the color, their hands were identical in size and shape, down to the wrinkles on their fingers.

Willa's heart began to pound in her chest.

How could this be? How could their hands be so similar?

She slowly turned her head and looked at Adelaide.

Adelaide stared back at her, her eyes wide, as amazed as she was. And then Adelaide gazed all around at the walls of the cave and the long flow of the River of Souls. Willa watched as a trace of fear crept into Adelaide's face.

"Willa . . ." Adelaide whispered, her voice trembling with astonishment. "I think I've been here before."

43

"When?" Willa asked. "How is that possible?"

"I don't know," Adelaide said, gazing around at the painted stone walls of the tunnel.

"Tell me about your family, your parents. Where did they come from?"

"My mother told me that she and my father were born in Cades Cove," Adelaide said. "They grew up together, went to the same school, and got married. Afterward, they discovered they weren't able to have children."

"But what about you and your brothers and sisters?" Willa asked.

"For the last seven years, my mother and father have been taking in orphaned children and raising them as their own," Adelaide explained. "I know you think my father is a bad man, but he really isn't, Willa. He's worked hard to provide food and a home to all his children, no matter where they come from. He's harsh sometimes, but that's because he cares for us, worries about us."

Willa listened to Adelaide's story intently. "And how did you come into the family?"

"I was so young that I don't remember it, but I'll tell you the story that my momma told me. One day she was out working in the wheat fields when she heard sniffling and crying. She searched for a long time, unable to see anyone, but she kept hearing the sounds. Finally, she found a tiny girl wandering alone, her hair so close to the color of the wheat she was practically invisible. The girl was dirty, exhausted, and hungry, so Momma brought her home and began to care for her. She and her husband asked all around to see if anyone was missing a child, but no one knew where the strange lost girl had come from."

"And that girl was you . . ." Willa said, touching Adelaide's arm.

"I was the first child my mother and father took in. But after that, they began adopting other boys and girls who had lost their parents. I was only five or six years old when I came to them, so I don't remember very much from that time, except . . ."

Adelaide's voice dwindled off.

"Except what?" Willa urged her.

"Even though I was surrounded by people, including children my own age, I felt terribly, terribly lonely, like my heart was going to break in two. I clung to my new mother and father. I remember thinking, 'I want to fit in. I want to look like them. I want them to love me. . . .' "

"Your blond hair and blue eyes . . . like your mother's . . ." Willa said in amazement. "Your white skin, and the way you talk . . . You blended yourself into a human!"

"I *am* human," Adelaide said, looking at her quizzically.

"I don't think you understand," Willa said.

"I *am* human, Willa," Adelaide said again, more emphatically this time. "It's just that I was lonely, until . . ."

Adelaide paused.

"What is it?" Willa said. "Until what?"

"Until I met you," Adelaide said.

"I'm going to tell you something, and I want you to listen very carefully," Willa said, her voice trembling. "My mother and father believed in the old ways of the Faeran, which the leader of our clan was trying to destroy. They spoke the old language and taught the old traditions to others. When I was six years old, my parents and sister were attacked by the padaran's guards and killed. This left me and my grandmother as the last remaining members of our family."

Willa stopped talking there and waited.

Adelaide was staring down at the ground. Willa couldn't see her face, so she couldn't tell what she was feeling, until she saw the tears dripping into her lap.

Willa lifted Adelaide's chin and looked into her eyes. As she slowly reached out and touched Adelaide's blond hair, it began to darken until it was the same brown as hers at that moment. And as she gently ran the backs of her fingers down Adelaide's cheek, the skin changed from white to green. Adelaide's eyes shifted from blue to emerald. Her nose, her cheeks, her lips . . . within a few moments it was as if Willa were looking into a pool of water and seeing herself.

"I know the loneliness you're talking about, Adelaide," she said softly, barely able to utter the words. "For I have felt it, too. You're my sister. . . . You're my Alliw. . . ."

Willa leaned forward and put her arms around her sister, and her sister slowly put her arms around her. They each tucked their head into the shoulder of the other, and for a moment they were one, like two bumblebees curled up in the bud of a flower keeping each other warm on a cool autumn night.

They stayed that way, beside the River of Souls, interlocked in each other's arms. To Willa, it felt as if she had been on a long, difficult journey by herself and now she had finally come home to the one she loved.

When the sunlight began to fade, Willa said quietly, "Come on, we need to go."

As they made their way out of the tunnel, Adelaide said, "I don't understand how I ended up where I did."

"You and our mother and father had gone out into the forest to forage for healing plants for our grandmother, who was sick. I stayed behind with her. As our parents were walking back to the lair, the padaran's guards attacked and killed them with their spears. I was told that you were with them at the time and that you had also been killed."

"But I guess I wasn't."

"I think there are two possibilities," Willa said. "The simplest is that when the guards attacked, our parents threw you into the ferns and told you to run, to blend, to escape any way you could."

"And when I ran away, I must have gone down the mountain a very long way. . . ."

"You were fleeing in terror. Maybe the guards chased you, I don't know, but by the time you reached Cades Cove, you must have been lost and scared and confused. You'd probably been wandering alone for days."

"And then my momma found me and started taking care of me."

"It all makes sense," Willa said. "You wanted to fit in. You blended for so long that you forgot that you were even doing it. It just became who you were. In your mind, you became a human."

Adelaide was quiet as they walked, trying to take it all in. But then she asked, "What was your other possibility?"

"This was a time when the padaran was killing all the Faeran who believed in the old ways, especially the woodwitches. Our grandmother hated the padaran. She believed that you and I were the last hope for the future of the Faeran people."

"But how does that explain what happened to me?"

"It's possible that when our parents were killed, you didn't run away on your own. Our grandmother might have carried you down to Cades Cove and given you to the human woman, who couldn't have children of her own."

"But why would she separate twins?" Adelaide said in dismay. "It's so cruel!"

"What seems terribly wrong now might have been her only choice at the time. Do you see? We try to choose the best path, but our choice might only make sense in the time and place we're in. She might have thought that by separating us—one of us among the Faeran and the other among the humans—we had a better chance to survive and become what she wanted us to become."

"Which was what?"

"We are the ones who carry the old ways inside us, who were meant to defeat the padaran and save the Faeran people."

"If that's what she did, it was a strange and cruel plan," Adelaide said.

"Grandmother once told me that certain kinds of frogs lay their eggs in two or three different ponds just in case one of them dries up or is invaded by predators. I didn't realize it at the time, but maybe we're the tadpoles in that story. She was hiding us away from the padaran. Or maybe she was looking out even further, to a time when humans and Faeran would come together. As a Faeran who had been raised by humans, you could become a bridge between our two people."

Adelaide looked at her. "And you, as a Faeran who was raised as a woodwitch, would become the keeper of the old ways. One way or another, she wanted her family to survive. "

Willa nodded. "Or maybe it's not one or another. Maybe it's both, combined, working together."

"The past, the present, and the future . . ." Adelaide said.

"Exactly," Willa said. "Alone, and faced with an enemy too powerful for her to defeat, she used time to her advantage."

As she and Adelaide came up onto the surface, the moon was rising over the rounded peak of the Great Mountain.

When Willa paused, Adelaide stopped beside her, and the two of them stood and looked up at the moon and the stars above.

Standing shoulder to shoulder with her sister, Willa felt a new kind of power coursing through her body and her soul.

"What do we do now?" Adelaide asked softly.

"We stay together," Willa said. "And we find a way to fix the broken world."

Willa followed the path at the edge of the stream, Adelaide walking just ahead of her.

"Now shift from stone to bark, all brown and craggy," Willa said as they passed the trunk of a large tree that was growing out of the rocky ground. "That's beautiful . . . good . . ." Willa encouraged her sister. "The green tree snake, the screech owl, and many other animals of the forest use camouflage to their advantage, but we are more like the lizard anole, with the ability to actively change our color to blend into what's around us."

"It feels so strange to keep changing . . ." Adelaide said as they ducked through a tunnel of mountain laurel and she blended into the waxy green leaves.

"Beautifully done, sister. Just keep practicing—you're getting better," Willa said.

Adelaide had been blending into human society as a

white-skinned, blond-haired girl for so long, she'd forgotten the colors of the forest. But Willa could see that her Faeran skills were coming back to her quickly. Adelaide was full of questions and readily absorbed everything Willa taught her. It seemed as if she wasn't learning it for the first time but *remembering* it.

Tutoring her sister in the old Faeran ways kindled a warm sense of pleasure in Willa's heart, a sense of purpose and satisfaction, like what she was doing was important and good. She realized she was teaching Adelaide in the same way her grandmother had taught her, the same lessons and words and tone of voice. It was the flowing current of their people.

As they made their way along the edge of the stream, the trickling sound of the water filled her ears and the cool mist floating off the little ripples touched her cheeks.

"Now pause by that mossy rock, still your heart, and disappear." Willa watched as Adelaide turned a grayish-green color.

"You need to know the word *ulna*," Willa said, "the Faeran word for *tree*, and the phrase *dunum far*, which means *my friends*."

"Dunum far," Adelaide repeated.

"When you address the plants and animals of the forest, you must come to them with friendship, with love, and gentleness, but above all things, you must come to them with respect. They are part of you, and you are a part of them."

They stepped over small rivulets that ran beneath their feet and trekked past waterfalls that splashed down upon the rocks. The green-shaded world of the forest was alive with lichen, and ferns, and flowing water.

"Now kneel here," Willa said, showing Adelaide a cluster of white trillium flowers growing near the stream. "Cup your hand around the plant and use your Faeran words to ask it to lift its leaves."

She and Adelaide practiced over and over again, until her sister could raise a leaf and bend a branch, until her old friends the trees began to recognize Alliw's voice again.

All through the day, hour after hour, they walked and trained. The more words Willa taught her, the faster Adelaide seemed to learn, the way a colony of moss grows slowly at first but then flourishes rapidly as more and more of the tiny plants join in. Willa knew that her sister hadn't heard the words in a long time, but they came back to her quickly and she pronounced them well.

Late in the afternoon, when Willa saw that Adelaide was getting tired, she invited her to climb into the Little Tree with her to rest.

Adelaide, who was used to the long, flatness of a human bed, clung uncertainly to the branches.

"Ask them to help us," Willa said.

Adelaide placed her open palms on the bark and used the Faeran words Willa had taught her to focus her mind. As the branches began to gather around them, the two sisters curled up together like a pair of squirrels in a soft, cozy nest of leaves.

"This is nice . . ." Adelaide sighed.

"Ella desophin." Willa repeated the words softly in the Faeran language, Adelaide's last lesson before they fell into a warm and gentle sleep.

Willa had spent too much time alone, too many days and nights without her sister, but on this afternoon, snuggled in a tree, she fell quickly and deeply asleep, dreaming of a woodland song.

When she woke, her sister's eyes were open and looking back at her. Willa felt renewed in a way she had never felt before, as if the power of her sister was inside her now, and her own power was inside her sister.

Night was falling, and a full moon had risen in the eastern sky, casting a pale silver light across the ruins of the old lair. The air was still and quiet. As they climbed down from the tree, Willa's thoughts once again turned to what she had done, how she had destroyed the ghosts that had been attacking the humans.

She led Adelaide toward the iridescent gloom at the edge of the ruins where it met with the glistening black trees of Dark Hollow.

"Where are you taking me?" Adelaide asked with a tremor of fear in her voice.

"I want to show you something," Willa said, pulling her forward by the hand.

When they reached the edge, they saw what looked like a soft glowing light.

"What is that?" Adelaide whispered.

Willa took a few more steps forward until what they were seeing became more clear. Dark, crooked trees stood before them, their branches twisted and interlocked with one another, thick and deep. The hollow's floor was covered with a mesh of tree roots. And across the ground, thousands of tiny soft points were pulsating with light.

"Is it magic?" Adelaide asked.

"There are glowworms, insect larvae, nestled in the soil."

"They're growing . . ." Adelaide said in amazement. And it was true. The light was slowly spreading across the ground toward them. And Willa could see that the roots of the trees were moving as well, slowly slithering forward. The roots of Dark Hollow were engulfing the edge of the ruins.

Willa's heart began to beat more powerfully.

"Now the earth is moving," Adelaide said, her voice tight and uncertain.

"Don't be afraid," Willa said quietly. "They're not going to hurt us."

As she stared down at the bases of the trees, Willa began to understand something. She had always known it in some way, but had never quite grasped it as fully as she did at this moment.

"The roots . . ." she said again, talking to herself, as the idea came into her mind.

She had seen the severed base of the great hemlock tree by the river and she had felt the water flowing through the roots of the tulip tree. But up to this point in her life she had taken roots for granted, focusing instead on what was in front of her eyes: a tree's trunk and branches and leaves. She realized now that the roots below the earth were as large and powerful, and in their own way as beautiful, as the visible part of a tree. The roots were what kept it standing and how it drew its strength from the soil. But the soil wasn't just dirt. The layers of earth beneath her feet had built up over time. They were the disintegrated remains of the lives and deaths, the choices and fates, of thousands of living creatures that had come before. And in that soil were all the necessary nutrients for growth.

As Willa looked deeper into the trees, she began to realize even more fully that Dark Hollow was a glimmering, glowing eruption of the past.

She turned and gazed across the empty, moonlit ruins toward the Little Tree, standing tall and magnificent in the distance.

"I think it's time," Willa said.

"Time to leave?" Adelaide said quickly. "I think you're right."

"No."

"You're shaking, Willa . . ." Adelaide said. "What's wrong? You're scaring me."

"Nothing's wrong," she said. "I can see it now. For the first time in my life, it feels as if all the world's streams are coming together and the river is flowing strong. I can sense its power and strength. The trees, the animals, the rivers, my father, the Faeran people . . . they're all connected. Do you see it? Do you feel it, Adelaide?"

"What are you talking about, Willa? You said the Faeran clan isn't going to survive another winter."

"It won't," Willa said. "Unless we do something."

"But what?"

"The words I've been teaching you aren't just words," Willa

said. "They're the words to an ancient song. And you and I aren't just sisters. We're *woodwitches.*"

Willa paused.

And then she said, "I think it's time for us to put our powers to the test."

Willa crossed through the moonlight to the center of the ruins and put her hand on the trunk of the Little Tree. "I'm going to need your help, my friend," she said in the old language.

And then she and Adelaide went to the edge of the ruins, where the scorched rock and the gray, powdery ash met the living trees and other plants of the forest.

"We'd love to have your assistance," she said to a small pine, touching it gently with her hand. "Can you lend us a twig or two?" she asked a clump of mountain laurel. "We're definitely going to need you," she said to a large old maple tree.

And as she walked, speaking to and touching the plants, she showed Adelaide how to do the same.

Soon Adelaide was strolling among the ferns, whispering the

Faeran words, touching the tops of the fronds with her palms the same way she had touched the wheat in the field.

The two of them worked through the night, until the soft blue glow of the coming sunrise seeped into the sky above the mountain. When they had gone all around the outside of the ruins, communicating with the forest plants, they finally came back to the edge of Dark Hollow.

Willa knelt at the base of an old, blackened Dark Hollow tree. "Join me," she told Adelaide.

"What are we doing?" Adelaide said, her voice quivering.

"Don't be afraid," Willa said. "Many times I've used the leaves and branches of a tree to shroud me, to hold me, or help me across a stream. But now, we're going to use the roots, the past. Beneath the earth, this tree's roots are touching the soil, the fungus, and the other trees and plants around it. And those in turn are touching the plants around them. They're talking to one another in a language so quiet, so slow, and so ancient that only woodwitches like you and I can comprehend it."

"Show me what to do," Adelaide said, nodding.

"Put your open hands on the roots like this," she said. "Clear your mind of everything but this moment, this tree, this glowing place."

Listening intently to every word, Adelaide slowly nodded.

As the sun rose and cast its golden light across the ruins and the surrounding forest, Willa began to sing, letting the feeling and words flow through her. As she remembered singing this ancient song of growing with her grandmother so long ago, the roots of the tree began to throb beneath her hands. The leaves and vines and moss on the forest floor crawled across the rocky ground of the ruins.

Adelaide started to sing with her, soft and tentative at first, like the frond of a new fern opening for the first time. More and more of the plants around them grew out into the open area of the ruins, their leafy tendrils creeping across the ground.

"It's working . . ." Adelaide whispered in astonishment.

As they sang, Willa delved into the living flow of the vines and the other plants, one connecting to the other beneath the earth, woodbine to laurel, laurel to fern. Seedlings and saplings and sprouts and shoots. Grasses and ferns and mosses.

"Now the trees," Willa whispered to Adelaide. "Keep singing. . . ."

Still holding on to the roots of the Dark Hollow tree, Willa continued to sing. She felt herself plunging into the soil, crashing deeper and deeper through the earth. She touched the roots of the other trees, and acorns and pine cones and chestnuts, the winged samaras of the maple trees, the prickly burs, and the long pods of seeds. New roots began to grow, one from the other, and saplings broke through the earth.

"Willa . . ." Adelaide whispered breathlessly as green, living trees shot into the air, newborn and free, spreading their leaves to the soaking sun.

"Keep singing . . ." Willa whispered.

Soon, a great bounty of trees and other plants were growing into the once-barren place, drawing upon the energy of the sunlight above and the nutrients of the ash below. And then Willa saw something that took her breath away.

"What's happening?" Adelaide asked when she saw the expression on her face.

Willa didn't know how it was possible, but as the trees grew before their eyes, she recognized them.

"I *know* these trees," she whispered to Adelaide.

As the two of them continued to sing the song of growing and the newborn trees reached for the sky, Willa's mind went back to years before, when her grandmother had told her the story of Faeran life and death. When a member of the Faeran clan enjoyed a long and fruitful life, was deeply loved, and finally passed away, their body disintegrated into the soil of the forest, and there remained their *seed-soul*, sometimes for a year, or a decade, or a century. And then one day, from the seed-soul, a new tree would grow, and it would glow with the soul of the Faeran who had been loved.

As Willa sang, she saw that it was the seed-soul trees of her loved ones that were growing around her—her mother, her father, her grandfathers, and the rest of her long-lost Faeran clan. They were the forest now. And they were all joining their voices with hers and her sister's.

When she finally heard the voice of her grandmother singing with her, Willa began to sob. All the loved ones of her past were here.

Beside her, Adelaide was also crying and sniffling and wiping her nose, for she, too, recognized that she was finally reuniting with her Faeran mother and father from long ago.

Willa clasped her sister's hand and they rose to their feet.

The two of them spun gently through the trees as they sang, hand in hand, dancing through the forest of their family.

Willa knelt at the base of her grandmother's seed-soul tree in the center of the others and asked Adelaide to do the same.

"Now we must begin to weave," Willa said, pressing her hand to the roots. "Keep singing the song, just as we have been, and I will show you the way."

As Adelaide sang the main melody, Willa began to sing in harmony with her, weaving her voice in and around her sister's. The leaves and branches of the growing plants began to intertwine with one another, climbing higher and higher.

With her voice and her mind, and her sister's love flowing through her heart, Willa shaped a new lair, building corridors and dens, many with openings for sunlight to come filtering down to nurture the plants and inhabitants alike.

Harmonizing their voices, the twins spiraled their notes one inside the other, creating a great hall with towering walls of woven plants, flowers, and vines all growing together, and openings to the sky far above. In the tops of the new trees, warblers and vireos and other birds flitted about, living jewels of green and gold glistening in the sunlight. And in the center of the Cathedral of Birds, the seed-soul tree of her grandmother towered high, her trunk acting as a living column and her upper branches spread across the ceiling so wide that they seemed to be touching everything around them.

The place that Willa had come to know as Dark Hollow was gone now, consumed and transformed by this new, living lair, a lair grown bright and green from the soil and darkness of the past.

And as Willa glanced outside, she saw that the trees surrounding the lair would provide nuts, berries, and fruit for the Faeran to eat. The plants on the ground and in the streams would offer shoots and leaves, nutrients and medicine—the sun and earth coming together to nourish her people.

Finally, when she looked upon the finished lair all around her, tears of happiness and pride welled up in Willa's eyes. She put her hand on the trunk of the center tree and said, "Just like you taught me, Grandmother."

"It's wonderful, Willa!" Adelaide said excitedly as she wandered through the great hall and stared openmouthed at its shimmering green beauty.

"We truly did it," Willa said in amazement, wiping the tears from her eyes.

"Now we just need a name for it!" Adelaide said.

What name should this new place have, Willa wondered, this shrouded haven in the forest? A name that combined the past and the future.

"What about . . . something like . . . Green Hollow?" Willa said tentatively.

Adelaide smiled and nodded. "It's perfect! I love it!" She opened her arms wide and twirled around. "Welcome to Green Hollow!"

Standing in the center of the Cathedral of Birds, with the lush green plants all around her, the rays of golden sunlight streaming down, and the birds flying high above, Willa gazed out of the opening in the wall toward the top of the Great Mountain.

"You did your part, and now we've done ours," she said to the mountain. *"There is no I, only we."*

As she and Adelaide traveled down the slope of the mountain, Willa felt the vibrance and beauty of Green Hollow still tingling in her body. She and her sister had grown the most beautiful lair she had ever seen, the kind that her grandmother had told her about years before.

But as they descended, a sickening feeling began to churn in her stomach. She knew that she and Adelaide had to find Gillen and the other Faeran, but with every step she took, the dread got worse.

Willa suspected that her tale of a magical new lair high up in the mountains would mean nothing to them. They were like creatures living beneath rocks who scowl at talk of the sun.

The only thing that kept her going was her memories of the stories her grandmother had told her all her life, stories of what the Faeran had once been, a good and gentle people closely intertwined with the world around them.

We are the voice of the trees, Willa, and the words of the wolves, her grandmother had said more than once. *We are the living soul of the forest.*

This was the Faeran people she wanted to believe in, not the starving, desperate creatures they were now, but the ones they could become.

"We're getting close," Willa said to Adelaide as they made their way into the gulch where she had last seen the Faeran clan.

"There they are," Adelaide whispered, pointing toward dark figures huddled in the shadows beneath an overhang of rock.

As her eyes adjusted to the darkness, Willa was relieved to see Sacram and Marcas. And she was pleased to note that the oak wilt on their faces and arms had diminished. Sacram's skin was no longer slimy and gray but darkish green like her own, and there were healthy streaks along his neck and face. His brother, Marcas, had always been strong, but the muscles on his arms looked tauter than she had ever seen them.

Willa didn't think her sister even realized it was happening, but as Adelaide gazed at the two Faeran boys, her skin began to change to the same darkish green and gray as theirs.

When Willa heard someone moving through the underbrush behind her and Adelaide, she turned. Gillen was charging toward her. Willa flinched and raised her hands to ward her off. "I know you don't want me here, Gillen, but I have news—"

"They're getting better!" Gillen interrupted her. "Sacram,

Marcas, and the others. The oak wilt is receding! Look at my arms!" Gillen proceeded to show Willa her bare skin, which was clear of any disease.

Willa took a breath, relieved to see her old friend in good spirits.

"There's something I need to tell you about," Gillen said. "We've been seeing a human wandering around the forest, looking for something."

"A human? Which human?" Willa asked, her heart skipping a beat. "Was it McClaren? What did he look like?"

"It was a female," Gillen said. "Young and tall, with a straight way of walking, and long black hair. She was carrying a fire-stick. She seemed to know the trails, like she'd been up on the mountain before, and she was searching."

"Long black hair . . ." Willa said. "Was she Cherokee?"

"I'm not sure," Gillen said. "But I thought you should know. If the humans are coming up the mountain this far, you need to be careful."

Gillen was right. Humans seldom came this far. But Willa had a feeling she knew exactly who this one was, and her heart swelled just thinking about it.

"You said you had news," Gillen said.

Willa paused. There was so much to tell her that she didn't even know where to start.

But there was one thing she needed to do first.

"I came to introduce you to someone . . ." Willa said. As she lifted her hand and turned, Adelaide materialized out of the forest, a perfect transformation from leaves into a visible, green-skinned Faeran.

"Who's this?" Gillen said, stepping back in surprise as she looked Adelaide up and down.

"This is Alliw," Willa said, smiling.

Gillen exhaled a sharp breath through her nose. "You're saying this is your sister? This is Alliw?"

"That's right," Willa said, keeping her voice calm and steady.

"I remember clearly the night they told us that Alliw and your parents died," Gillen said. "The whole lair was talking about it."

"Alliw escaped the padaran's guards and has been in hiding ever since."

"Alone? How is that possible?" Gillen said, her voice laced with disbelief. She put hard eyes on Adelaide, looking her up and down again, but did not speak to her.

"Are you really Alliw?" Sacram asked as he walked toward them. "You're Willa's sister?"

"I am," Adelaide said. "I was born in the same lair as you and the others."

"I remember you," Sacram said, nodding. "You and I used to play together, and Marcas, too, and Willa, the four of us."

"But what happened to you?" Marcas asked. "Why haven't you been with the clan?"

The idea of a Faeran living alone, separated from the clan, was incomprehensible to them.

"I was so young I don't remember it, but I think I ran in

terror when the padaran's guards killed my parents," Adelaide said softly to Marcas. She looked at Sacram and Gillen as well. "I had to blend into the world around me to hide, to survive."

Gillen stared at her. "You *willingly* broke your twin-bond with your sister? That's not even possible."

"It wasn't *willingly*," Adelaide snarled back at her. "I was *separated* from my sister. I was six years old! There was nothing *willing* about it."

"Tell me wh—" Gillen began.

"Stop," Willa said forcefully, stepping between them. "Gillen, this is my sister, Alliw. That's the end of it."

"I don't mean to cause any harm, Gillen," Adelaide said gently.

Gillen lifted her eyes and looked at her, this time holding her gaze. "I've just never heard of such a thing, two twins getting separated. I can't even imagine my life without Nellig."

"I know how strange all this must seem," Willa said, looking around at Gillen, the boys, and the other Faeran who were now gathering around. "But I don't want to fight. I have news that's more important than any one of us."

"What are you talking about?" Marcas asked, stepping forward. "What's happened?"

"Alliw and I have built a new lair for our people," Willa said.

No one spoke for several seconds. The words she had just said were so impossible that they must have thought they'd misheard her.

Finally, after the long pause, Gillen said, "What did you say?"

"Alliw and I have built a new lair for our people." Willa repeated word for word so there could be no misunderstanding.

"Why would you say something like that to us?" Gillen asked, a harshness in her tone like a person who's been wounded by a particularly cutting insult.

"I'm telling the truth," Willa said. "We built a new lair."

"Why did you come back here?" Gillen asked.

"Listen to me," Willa said. "What I'm saying is true, Gillen. It's large enough for everyone. It will provide warmth and shelter, and the surrounding forest will provide food for the winter."

"How is that possible?" Gillen asked.

"I told you," Willa said. "Alliw is my sister."

"That means she's a woodwitch like Willa!" someone in the gathering crowd said. Dozens of Faeran faces were staring at them now.

"That's right," Willa said. "She's a woodwitch like me, like our mother and grandmother, and their mothers and grandmothers before them. We used the song of growing to weave a new lair out of the living plants just like the woodwitches of old. You know that's how the original lair was built many years ago."

"I don't know anything," Gillen spat, "except the here and now."

"Then hear this," Willa said, stepping forward and looking around at all the others. "We call the lair Green Hollow. It will provide everyone here with everything you need."

"If this is true, then where is it?" one of the Faeran near the front of the crowd asked.

"We grew the plants out of the ashes of the old lair," Alliw said.

This news seemed to frighten the Faeran.

"Then the place is cursed," Marcas said.

"It *isn't* cursed, Marcas," Willa said. "The old lair is where all of us came from, and it's what we'll *grow* from. Green Hollow is yours, all of yours, to make it whatever you want it to be."

Willa stepped closer to Gillen so they could talk more quietly together. "The clan won't follow me, but they will follow you. You're their leader, Gillen. Take them to Green Hollow. Once you do that, and you earn their trust, they'll begin to listen to you. Please. Grow toward the sunlight, not the darkness."

As Willa spoke to Gillen, Sacram approached Adelaide. "Have you seen this new lair Willa's talking about? Have you seen it with your own eyes?"

Adelaide smiled and nodded. "I haven't just seen it, I helped grow it. I swear to you on the memories that you and I have playing as children. Green Hollow is there, just as Willa has described it. It's a beautiful lair, with walls of living vines and flowers and birds up in the sky."

"You were able to sing the song of growing?" Gillen asked Willa in a whisper.

"Just like my mother and grandmother taught me."

"But even if I believe you, how will I ever convince the others?" Gillen said, her voice shaking.

"I believe them," Sacram declared, nodding. "I believe everything they're saying."

"So do I," Marcas said.

"But the older ones won't," Gillen whispered to Willa. "They won't want to go. And it will be a difficult journey for some of them to get up there."

"You must lead them, Gillen," Willa said. "They'll follow you."

"And you think this new lair will protect us through the winter?" Gillen asked.

"I *know* it will," Willa said.

"I know it will, too," Adelaide agreed.

Gillen looked at Adelaide, and then Sacram and Marcas, and then back at Willa.

"All right," she said finally. "I'll get our people there somehow, and we'll begin again."

Willa embraced her before she could step away. Gillen kept her arms stiff by her sides at first, but slowly her resistance faded and she hugged Willa in return. It was as if only in that moment had she finally begun to truly believe what Willa was telling her. It was going to change everything.

"Don't be frightened, Gillen," Willa said, still holding her. "Give them hope. Show them the way to a new life. You're the only one who can."

"What about you?" Gillen asked, stepping away from her and looking at her. "Aren't you coming with us?"

"I wish I could," Willa said. "But there's more for me to do."

"Do you really think it's her?" Adelaide asked excitedly as they walked through the forest the next morning.

"I don't know," Willa said. "But she knew the direction I was headed, so it's possible that she's up here looking for me."

They had been searching the human paths, but despite what Gillen had told them about seeing a human girl, Willa and Adelaide encountered no one and found no signs that anyone had passed through the area.

As the sun rose slowly past the top of the Great Mountain, Willa showed Adelaide how to forage for berries, shoots, and other food. When they'd eaten their fill, they rested awhile curled up in the hollow of an old tree. Willa didn't realize how tired she was until she felt the warmth of Adelaide's shoulder beneath her cheek.

After they woke a few hours later, they continued on,

crisscrossing through the forest. As they worked their way through a shaded grove of giant tulip trees, Willa spotted something just ahead.

"What is it?" Adelaide asked, as Willa moved quickly toward it.

She knelt beside a small plant and studied it. "Take a look at this, Adelaide," Willa said. "Do you see here? This fern was bent by something passing by."

Marking this spot in her mind, Willa stood and scanned the area in all directions. She walked one way for a dozen steps, and then doubled back and walked the other, north and south and east and west. And then she found what looked like a slight depression in the moss.

Tracing the mark with her fingertips, Willa said, "A foot might have touched here."

Extending a line in her mind between the bent fern and the depression in the moss, Willa narrowed her next search to two directions. She tried one way, and when she didn't find anything, she doubled back and tried the other.

A slight bit of discoloration on a tree caught her attention. "Look here," she said as she showed Adelaide where a small flake of bark, no larger than a fingernail, had fallen to the forest floor. "A hand may have touched here. . . ."

A little farther ahead, Willa came to two large magnolia bushes. "I think someone may have walked between these earlier this morning. . . ."

"How in the world do you know that?" Adelaide asked.

Willa pointed to several fine, silvery strands of spiderweb

with one end attached to the magnolia but the other floating in the breeze. They were so thin, they were difficult to even make out. "Do you see them?"

"Yes," Adelaide said, studying the strand. "But what does it mean?"

"These were the long tethers of a spiderweb that stretched across this path," Willa said. "Now look directly across to the strands on this other bush. They're floating in midair as well, but the web itself is gone. Spiders usually weave their webs at night, often just before dawn, so I think someone must have come through here within the last few hours. If the web had been down near the ground, it could have been an animal that disturbed it, but up this high, I think had to be a human. Nothing walks taller than a human."

The bend of a fern, a nick on a tree, a strand of torn web—they followed the clues through the forest.

When Adelaide found a broken branch at about the height of a human knee, Willa smiled and nodded. "Good find. Now trace the line of travel to the next one."

And sure enough, a little farther on, Adelaide was delighted when she discovered the unmistakable outline of a booted foot in the wet dirt. It wasn't just a depression in the moss or a snapped twig, but an actual footprint.

Working together, with their eyes scouring the ground and the surrounding vegetation, they followed the signs through a stand of oak, pine, and hickory trees, until Adelaide stopped and whispered, "Willa, look . . ."

Willa lifted her head and saw the tall, lean figure of a human girl standing in the distance on an outcropping of rock. She was holding a long rifle in her right hand and wearing a leather satchel over her shoulder as she looked out across the rolling green canopy of the forested mountains.

"It's her!" Willa said, a flood of happiness rushing through her body. "It's Hialeah!"

"You go talk to her first, and then I'll join you," Adelaide said.

"All right," Willa said, nodding. "Just hold back a little bit until I have a chance to tell her about you."

Willa smiled as she watched Adelaide blend into the vegetation and disappear.

"How's this for pulling back?" Adelaide said, clearly pleased with her new Faeran skills.

"It seems I'm a good teacher," Willa said, still smiling.

"Or I'm a good student!" Adelaide said, laughing a little. "Now go before she gets away."

Just as Adelaide said these words, Hialeah pulled back from the view of the mountains and ducked into the forest.

Willa ran after her, excited to finally see her sister again.

"Hialeah . . ." she said breathlessly as she came up behind her.

But as soon as Hialeah turned, Willa knew from the expression on her face that something terrible had happened.

49

Hialeah rushed forward and pulled her close. "Oh, Willa . . ." she said, her voice filled with both sadness and relief. Willa had never seen her sister so upset. Her voice was strained, her body shaking.

As Willa held her, she could feel all the pain and struggle her sister had been through since they'd last seen each other. "What's wrong, what's happened?" Willa asked. "Where's Father?"

"I've been trying to help him, Willa . . ." Hialeah said, her voice cracking. "The authorities locked him in a jail cell in Gatlinburg. They've formally charged him with the murder of the two loggers."

"But there's—"

"There's a witness who swears he saw Father kill them," Hialeah said. "They plan to execute him, Willa. They're going to hang him!"

"Hang him . . ." Willa gasped. It felt like her heart was sinking into a heavy black ooze. How could the humans treat a man as good and noble as her father in such a vile, unfair way?

As Hialeah stepped back from their embrace, Willa saw that her face looked weathered and her normally shiny black hair was dull and matted. "I've been visiting him as much as I can, taking him food and water," she said. "And I've been gathering the other mountain families."

"Can they help?" Willa said, clinging to any hope she could.

"So much has happened, Willa."

"Tell me," Willa said, anxious for any news.

"Before he was arrested, Father had been trying to convince the other mountain families to join in a resistance against the Sutton Lumber Company," Hialeah said. "Remember when the sheriff and loggers came to the house and asked him where he was the day of the murders? Father said he was working in the orchard."

"But there was river mud on his boots . . ." Willa said.

"That's right," Hialeah said, nodding. "It turns out that he'd been meeting secretly with the mountain families and their allies from town. That's where he was when the murders occurred, but it's become so dangerous to go against the logging company that he couldn't reveal the names of the people he'd been meeting with. The loggers and even the authorities will do *anything* to keep the business going. Father is their most vocal opponent. And now they've got him."

"They're going to cut him down like a tree . . ." Willa said in dismay. It felt like her world was crumbling in on her.

"Even from jail, he's still trying to stop the loggers," Hialeah said. "I've become his eyes and ears, his voice and messenger. He told me to take the train to Knoxville and Asheville to talk to his allies there. They've all been coming, Willa, gathering in Gatlinburg, rallying to his cause—to him, and what they're doing to him, but also to stop the logging, too. The two causes have become one and the same to many people."

"But what about this witness who says he saw Father kill those men?"

"Most of the people in town are in favor of the logging, especially the business owners and the men who have jobs with the company. There's one logger in particular—he's the key witness in the case. His name is Luther Higgs."

"The one with the scar on his face who came to the house when they arrested Father . . ." Willa said. "His brother was one of the men who was murdered."

"Luther has always hated Father. They've known each other since they were in school together years ago. Now Luther swears that he saw Father kill his brother and the other logger at the Elkmont Camp."

"He's lying," Willa said.

"Everyone on Father's side has been desperately searching for evidence that will help prove his innocence, but right now, all the authorities have is two dead men and Luther's claim. We need to find the real murderer. But it's like whoever killed those men has evaporated into thin air. I keep thinking that maybe Luther himself killed them, even his own brother, and then concocted this whole story to protect himself. I just don't trust that conniving little man."

Willa thought back to the way Luther had acted when he came to the house with the sheriff to arrest her father. He'd been filled with anger, but he'd also seemed nervous and cowardly, like the last thing he wanted to do was to actually face his enemy in a real fight.

"The sheriff is coming up to the Elkmont Camp to gather evidence for the case against Father," Hialeah said. "He's demanded that Luther show him the exact spot where the murders took place."

"So Luther is going to be with him?" Willa said, looking at her in surprise.

"I've come ahead, but they should be arriving at Elkmont tonight," Hialeah said.

"Then that's our chance," Willa said, feeling a surge of excitement.

"Our chance?" Hialeah said. "Did you find something, Willa? Do you know what really happened to those men?"

A thousand thoughts and images cascaded through Willa's mind. *Had* she found something? She didn't even know where to begin in explaining it all. Dark, shadowy beasts lurking in the night, snakelike roots slithering through the forest, a black cloud of deadly butterflies . . . She'd seen the ghosts of Dark Hollow with her own eyes and even she doubted what she remembered.

"I'm afraid no one's going to believe what I have to say," Willa muttered. But even as she said the words, an idea began to form in her mind. Maybe she didn't have to convince *everyone* that the ghosts of Dark Hollow had been real. She just had to convince one particular man.

"If the three of us work together . . ." she mumbled to herself, starting to think out loud.

"The three of us?" Hialeah said with a quizzical look.

Just then, a twig snapped, and Hialeah turned toward the sound. A leafy green area of the forest transformed into the haunting image of a blond-haired, blue-eyed girl. And as the girl walked toward Hialeah, the girl's skin and features shifted into a dark green spotted creature of the forest who looked identical to her sister.

Hialeah's eyes widened as she pulled in a long breath filled with awe.

As the sun set behind the mountains and darkness fell, the moon and stars disappeared behind a cloak of clouds, leaving nothing but a murky black world below.

The only light was the small, flickering campfire, with the two human men huddled around it, as if the faint glow of their meager fire could somehow protect them from the black immensity of the ancient forest that towered around them.

Willa crawled slowly through the darkness, her heart thumping harder the closer she got to the men. She'd taken on the color of the forest floor to remain invisible, but that didn't stop the small stones on the ground from digging painfully into her palms and knees. *Just get what you came for, Willa,* she told herself, using her old mantra from back when she was a night-thieving jaetter working for the padaran. *Just get what you came for.*

The two men were sitting on logs near the campfire, gazing into the orange, dancing flames, their backs to the darkness. And it was in that darkness that Willa crept, so close now that she felt the heat of the fire.

The sharp odor of gunpowder touched her nostrils, and Willa noticed the sheriff's rifle leaning against the log beside him, and the pistol in a holster on his belt. The sheriff, a heavy-set man, was sitting in a slumped position, his elbows on his knees, as he stared into the fire, his eyes glazed. He sometimes rubbed his white mustache and beard absentmindedly as he took in long, heavy breaths. It appeared that the day's journey to reach the Elkmont cutting site had exhausted him.

Luther Higgs sat across from him, his long, scraggly gray-brown hair falling down his back like rotting vines. He held a double-barreled shotgun across his lap, gripping it in both hands, and he wore a long, wicked steel knife in a sheath at the back of his hip, where he could quickly whip it out and put it to use.

Willa crawled even closer. When she reached the edge of the campfire's glow, she was immediately behind Luther Higgs's back, so near that she could smell the repugnant stench of his chewing tobacco when he spat it out of his mouth.

This was the man she'd come for.

She slowly looked back at Adelaide a few body lengths behind her. Her sister had blended her previously pale white skin into the color of pure darkness. Adelaide's expression was nervous and uncertain but filled with anticipation as she waited for Willa's signal.

Willa turned her head in the other direction and saw Hialeah a short distance behind them, well hidden in a clump of young trees.

The three of them were thieves in the night—creeping, crawling, slipping unseen and unheard through the shadows. For years Willa had been taught to hide, to disappear, but tonight, she had another purpose entirely.

Hialeah nodded to her, and mouthed the word *Ready*.

Willa nodded in return, met Adelaide's eyes one last time, and then turned back to Luther Higgs.

She came up just behind him, close enough to make out the rough weave of his shirt.

"Now that we're finally here . . ." the sheriff said to Luther. The sound of his voice was so loud that it made Willa flinch. "Come morning light, I'm gonna want you to show me the murder scene."

"I'll take you up to the general vicinity where it all happened," Luther said as he poked embers with a stick.

"I'll want to see the exact spot," the sheriff said.

"I reckon there ain't gonna be much to see anymore."

"Leave that to me," the sheriff grumbled. "What about the bodies, the burial sites?"

"You've already asked me that a hundred times, Sheriff," Luther said.

"And I'm asking you again," the sheriff said, his voice deadly serious in its tone.

"I already told you, there ain't no burial sites."

"Why not?"

"I'll take you up there tomorrow," Luther replied.

"You didn't answer my question," the sheriff said.

As the two humans were talking, Willa snuck up behind Luther. Staying low to the ground, she reached up and lifted the bottom of his shirt. Her temples were pounding. Her fidgety legs were telling her to run, flee, escape. But she could not run. Not now. Not *ever* until her father was free. With her other hand, she raised her small companion and slowly set him on Luther's back.

As soon as the deed was done, Willa scurried away, ducked behind a bush, and blended.

The spider began crawling on Luther's back, its eight furry legs creeping along his bare skin, right up his spine. Suddenly, the man leaped to his feet, screaming, flailing his arms and legs, furiously pulling at his shirttail. "Aah!" he shouted as he danced wildly around the fire.

"What the— You gone crazy, Luther?" the sheriff demanded. "What in blazes are you doing?"

Peeking from her hiding spot, Willa was relieved to see the large black spider drop safely into the leaves and skitter away. *Thank you, my friend,* she thought. *You did that perfectly!*

"There was somethin' crawlin' up my back—a spider or something!" Luther said.

The sheriff groaned. "You scared of little spiders now, Luther?"

"The dang awful thing was crawlin' straight up my back like it was goin' for my neck!" Luther shouted at him.

Willa whistled like a screech owl, and a dozen actual screech owls trilled a haunting, high-pitched sound in return.

"What's that?" Luther asked, looking up into the trees.

"They're just owls," the sheriff said, clearly trying to stay calm.

Adelaide, who had snuck up behind Luther, hissed a series of long *sssikk-sssikk-sssikk* sounds, like the haunted roots of Dark Hollow.

Luther whirled around, his face white with shock as he peered out into the darkness that surrounded them. "Do you hear that?"

The sheriff heaved himself to his feet. "I heard it. What was that?"

Sssikk-sssikk-sssikk!

"Oh my god, they're coming!" Luther cried, staring in the direction of the sound.

While the men were distracted, Hialeah ran into the circle of light, threw a wet blanket over the campfire, and dashed away into the woods.

"Footsteps!" the startled sheriff said as he pivoted.

But there was nothing to be seen in the darkness of a smothered fire. The long wet hissing sound continued.

"Oh my god, not them things!" Luther cried, his hair flying as he turned one way and then the other.

Hialeah charged toward him, scraping a long branch through the rocks and leaves to make an eerie slithering, snapping sound. Luther screamed in panic.

"What's happening, Luther?" the sheriff asked, peering into the night.

Willa howled like a wolf, and two dozen wolves howled in return at close range all around them.

"It's wolves!" the sheriff shouted, fear catching in his voice. "Get your gun up, man!"

Lunging through the darkness, Hialeah slammed a branch into the back of Luther's legs, knocking him to the ground.

"No, no, no, not again!" Luther screamed as he scrambled frantically to stand. "Them ain't no wolves, Sheriff! Our guns aren't gonna make any difference!"

"What do you mean, 'not again'?" the sheriff demanded. "Of course they're wolves! Aim your gun!"

Willa touched the tree beside her and asked it to sway its branches above the men, raining sticks and spiders upon them.

"They're coming, Sheriff!" Luther shouted.

But soon, all the branches of the trees around them were thrashing.

"It's just a storm!" the sheriff said. "Get your wits about you, man. We've got our guns. We've got our knives. We can defend ourselves from a pack of wolves. Now come on!"

"They're here! They're here! Run!" Luther screamed as he turned tail and sprinted into the forest, leaving the sheriff to fend for himself.

And it was at that moment that Willa realized exactly how Luther's brother and the other logger had come to their gruesome end. They hadn't just been pulled down by the ghosts of Dark Hollow. They'd died with the terrified shrieks of the fleeing Luther Higgs ringing in their ears.

Luther ran through the darkness, tripped over a tree root, and fell to the ground, where he curled up into a cowering ball.

"*Ee-a-gat!*" Willa said to the forest.

Suddenly, the wolves stopped howling. The trees ceased thrashing. The owls went quiet. And the three sisters gathered together in the shadows to watch what happened next.

With a touch of her hand, Willa asked a few trees to move their branches aside. The clouds had cleared and moonlight came through the opening overhead. The sheriff made his way through the now quiet silvery forest until he found Luther curled up on the ground, shaking and mumbling to himself.

"Get up," the sheriff said gruffly, shoving Luther with his boot.

The cowering man slowly lifted his head and looked around him.

"What was that all about?" the sheriff demanded. "You've been through this before, haven't you. If those 'things' weren't wolves, then what were they?"

"I don't know, Sheriff," Luther said. "I don't know nothin'."

"Don't give me that," the sheriff said. "Did those things have something to do with the deaths of Davin Rutherton and your brother? You said you saw Steadman shoot those men. He's got the rifle skills to do it, no doubt about it. But it's been nagging me about the bodies. Where are they, Luther? Where are the bodies of those dead men?"

"How should I know!"

"You were there when they died," the sheriff said in a monotone.

"Maybe he threw them in the river!" Luther snapped. "Did you ever think of that? You've already got the murderer! You and that judge need to get on with it and hang him like everybody wants!"

"Why would he throw the bodies in the river?" the sheriff asked, not allowing Luther to change the subject.

"Do I got spell it out for you, Sheriff? He was trying to hide the evidence!"

"Did *he* throw them in the river or did *you* throw them in the river?" the sheriff asked.

"What?" Luther said, staring at the sheriff in disbelief. "Are you accusing *me* of murder now?"

The sheriff looked back toward where their campfire had been. "What about these animals you saw? The wolves or whatever they were. Maybe *they* killed the men. You were awful scared just now. . . ."

"You would've been, too, if you'd seen—" Luther cut himself off, like he'd said too much. "I told ya, I saw Steadman do it!"

"Did you confront him? You must have been angry that he had just killed your brother."

"Of course I did!" Luther shouted. "I chased him, but he was as slippery as a spring eel and I couldn't catch him."

Sheriff looked at Luther for a long time, like he was weighing things in his mind. When he finally spoke, his tone was flat and emotionless and filled with a dreadful certainty.

"If you confronted Steadman and he ran away, then he wouldn't have had time to drag the bodies to the river."

Luther stared back at the sheriff with helplessness and hate in his eyes. His lip curled in anger. He knew the sheriff had caught him dead to rights in a lie and there wasn't anything he could do about it.

"So, what did you do with the bodies, Luther?" the sheriff pressed him.

As Willa watched from the shadows, she could see the rage boiling up inside Luther, his lips pressed together, his nostrils flaring. He wanted to fight back, to shout, to throw his fists, but he knew he couldn't.

This was what she had come for. He had twisted himself up and tripped on the sticks of his own deceit.

The sheriff unclipped handcuffs from his belt and grabbed Luther's shoulder.

"Hey, what are you doing?" Luther complained, trying to pull away, but the sheriff gripped his wrists and snapped the cuffs around them.

"I think you ran, Luther," the sheriff said in disgust. "I think those rabid wolves, or whatever they were, attacked the three of you. Rutherton and your brother turned to fight, but you dropped your gun and ran like the dickens, leaving those two poor souls behind."

"You got it all wrong," Luther said.

"No," the sheriff said bluntly. "It took me a while, but I think I finally got it right now. You were ashamed that you ran and left your own brother to die, so you made up this whole cockamamie story about Nathaniel Steadman."

"It's not my fault!" Luther cried out. "It wasn't my idea! None of it was!"

"What are you talking about?" the sheriff said gruffly, shaking him by the shoulder. "What are you saying?"

"Please, Sheriff, you've got to believe me. It's not my fault! When I told the boss that Rutherton and my brother had been killed, he got this real peculiar look on his face, like, I don't know, like maybe some kind of opportunity had come his way. He told me to lie about it, to lie about it all."

"Your boss?" the sheriff said. "You mean Jim McClaren?"

"No, the *big* boss—Mr. Sutton, the owner of the lumber company. He got me in his talons and wouldn't me let go, told me to make up this whole story against Steadman or he was going to make my life miserable—throw me off the crew, get me evicted off my land, god knows what else. None of this was my idea! Sutton made me do it!"

Luther's words seemed to give the sheriff pause. The lawman stared at the ground, slowly shaking his head, clearly angry that he'd been deceived. But more than that, he just seemed sick and tired of the whole thing. When he lifted his chin, he leveled his eyes at Luther once more.

"False accusation is a serious crime, Luther, no matter who told you to do it. You can't go around accusing innocent people of crimes they didn't commit. I'm going to release Nathaniel Steadman immediately and put you in jail instead. And I'll do my darnedest to make sure you stay there for a long, long time."

As the sheriff said these words, Willa turned to her sisters. They both had huge grins on their faces. She wanted to shout their victory to the owls and the wolves and the moon above, but she knew they couldn't make a sound. When she wrapped her arms around them, it felt like waterfalls of happiness were gushing between them.

They had finally saved her father.

As the sun rose over the meadow where she and her two sisters were sleeping, Willa felt the warmth of its rays on her cheek. When she slowly opened her eyes, she saw Adelaide curled up in the ferns beside her and Hialeah a few feet away, stretched out long and straight on her back, the crook of her arm draped over her eyes. Exhausted from the night's adventures, the three of them had slept into the late hours of the morning.

Seeming to sense that someone else was awake, Hialeah slowly turned her head and looked at her.

Hialeah had sharp black eyebrows and beautiful brown eyes. And in those eyes Willa could see all that her sister was feeling—the serenity, the contentment, and the joy.

For more than a year, Hialeah had been suffering from the hardest blows that had ever hit her—the loss of her mother to attackers she could not fight, and the death of her little brother to a sickness she could not heal. Willa knew that, deep down, Hialeah had felt as if she was nothing but dust in the wind, floating helplessly, with no power over her life and no power to help the ones she loved.

But so much had changed now. Hialeah had helped her father when he was in jail, bringing him food and water, keeping him alive. She had taken his messages to the surrounding cities and spread word of the resistance. And she had found her sister on the mountain, ensnared the lying Luther Higgs, and gained their father's freedom.

Hialeah had fought, and she had won.

Willa slowly reached out her hand to Hialeah, and Hialeah slowly reached out in return. When their fingers touched in the middle, Willa felt her sister's power in those fingers.

Hialeah was no longer the dust. She was the wind.

As she and Adelaide crossed through the trees toward the house, Willa caught the faint scent of chimney smoke on the air and breathed a sigh of relief.

"They're home," she said.

As they went up the steps onto the front porch, Willa could see the amber glow of candlelight in the windows.

The moment she stepped inside, her father shouted, "Willa!" and strode toward her. He opened his arms as they came together, and he pulled her close.

She wrapped her arms around him and held him tight. He felt so tall and strong, like the trunk of a beloved tree.

This is home, Willa thought. *This is where I belong.*

"And who did you bring with you?" Nathaniel asked, stepping back from Willa as he noticed a young girl standing quietly in the doorway. "A new friend?"

Used to blending in with those around her, Adelaide had reflexively taken on her blond-haired, blue-eyed human appearance.

"She's more than a friend, Father . . ." said Willa, not sure where to begin.

"She's our Faeran sister!" Hialeah blurted out happily. Ever since they'd worked together to trick Luther into exposing his lies, Hialeah and Adelaide had been the best of friends.

Nathaniel gazed around at all three of them, a little confused.

"Show him," Willa said.

And in that moment, Adelaide shifted into the streaked-and-spotted, green-skinned Faeran appearance of her twin sister.

"Oh my lord . . ." Nathaniel said, gasping. "My heart hasn't been that shook since the first time I saw you step out of the forest, Willa. This is your long-lost sister? This is Alliw? That's wonderful! I want to hear the whole story."

It was late in the evening, long after their usual supper hour, but in celebration of all that life had given them, they prepared a special meal. Adelaide helped set the kitchen table while Hialeah put out the food. Willa fetched a small barrel of orchard cider from the fruit cellar, and her father lit the kerosene lamps all around.

When they sat down to eat, her father raised his glass, and said, "To being back together again!" and everyone raised their glasses with him. "Welcome to the family, Adelaide!"

Adelaide smiled, lifted her glass of cider, and then took a long, hearty drink.

A few days before, when the sheriff had taken Luther back

to town, Hialeah had followed to make sure that Nathaniel was released from jail, and then father and daughter traveled home together. Adelaide and Willa, meanwhile, had taken the forest route. Willa knew her new sister wouldn't able to stay long, but she was so glad to have her there.

Gazing around the table at her loved ones, all of them talking and laughing and telling their stories, Willa wished the jubilation and contentment of that evening could last forever.

"I'm grateful to be back home, I truly am," her father said, but his tone had turned somber and the lamplight flickered across his furrowed brow. "But I'm afraid our problems aren't over."

"What do you mean, Father?" Willa asked.

"Luther's accusation that I murdered those two men was a good excuse for the logging company and local authorities to get rid of me. But now that I'm free again and they know about the meetings I've been holding, they're going to look for some other way to take me down."

"But you own your land, so they can't cut here, isn't that right, Mr. Steadman?" Adelaide asked.

"It's true that we own the land we live on, like most of the mountain families. But the logging company tries to convince the local landowners to sell their property, which many are willing to do for quick and easy cash. And if landowners say no, the loggers and authorities pressure them."

"Father's not going to sell," Hialeah said confidently to Adelaide. "His family has lived here for generations."

"So the loggers can't come here, right?" Adelaide asked.

"Unfortunately, it's not that simple," Nathaniel said. He got up, pulled a tattered piece of paper from a cabinet drawer, and laid it carefully on the table. It was so worn and faded with age that the letters were nearly gone.

"This is the deed to my land," he said. "It was given to my great-great-grandfather in 1783, after he fought in the War of Independence, and handed down through the generations to me. But, as you can see, the deed is so faded that it's unreadable. It also references landmarks that no longer exist. Like many of the families in these mountains, I don't have good legal documentation for my property lines, or even that I own the property at all. So the Sutton Lumber Company can come in, claim that it's public land, and cut the trees before anyone can stop them."

"That's awful!" Adelaide said, clearly startled by the ruthlessness of the loggers, including her own father.

"But things are going to change," Hialeah said, a note of hopefulness in her voice. "Father's a hero now!"

"I wouldn't go that far," Nathaniel said, laughing.

"You two should've seen it," Hialeah said. "When they released him from jail, there was a crowd of supporters waiting for him outside. Everyone wanted to talk to him and hear what he had to say."

Willa looked at her father in surprise. He had lived in the woods all his life and had seldom concerned himself with the outside world, but now he had taken up this banner and lifted it for all to see.

"It's true that many people in Gatlinburg finally seem to be waking up to the fact that the Sutton Lumber Company is doing real damage to the forest," he said. "And Hialeah helped me reach out to people in Asheville and Knoxville as well. None of those folks would've been there if she hadn't gone to fetch them." He smiled at her gratefully.

"But you're the one who got them all to agree," Hialeah said, standing up and putting her arm around her father's waist.

"What did they all agree to?" Adelaide asked. It was the same question that was on Willa's mind.

Nathaniel leaned forward. "We're going to turn the entire Smoky Mountain region into a protected area."

Willa could hear the excitement in her father's voice and see the glint in his eyes. "But what does that mean?" she asked.

"We're going to make the Smoky Mountains a sacred place, a sanctuary," he said. "It won't be a local park or even a state park. We want it to be a *national* park, land that will be protected forever by federal law. The logging will end. Now and for all time."

Willa felt her chest swell with her father's words. If this succeeded, then everything she had hoped for would come true. The trees, the animals, even the Faeran would survive. "What can we do to help?" Willa asked excitedly.

"There are still a lot of people in Gatlinburg dead set against the idea. Some say logging is good for the economy and it represents progress. Others are angry that they would lose their jobs."

Willa glanced at Adelaide, expecting her to be worrying about her own father, maybe staring down at the floor as they were all talking. But Adelaide was looking right back at her, her eyes filled with determination, with *alliance*. She, too, had seen the devastation caused by the Sutton Lumber Company.

"The truth is," Nathaniel continued, "it's going to be difficult for many people, including us probably, in terms of the ownership of our land and the restrictions placed on us. But it's the right thing to do."

Willa nodded. "For a long time I've felt helpless and alone because I didn't have the power to fight the loggers. No one can."

"What are you saying, Willa?" Hialeah interrupted, her brows furrowing in annoyance that her sister would talk so discouragingly. "What do you mean no one can?"

"Let her finish," Nathaniel said gently.

"I'm sorry, I don't mean *no* one can," Willa said. "I mean no *one* can. I'm saying that we can't do this on our own, not even with the mountain families and the city people behind us. We need *everyone* to join in. Our brother Iska and the Cherokee are struggling against the loggers just like we are, but *they* can't fight them on their own, either." Willa turned to Adelaide. "And I bet some of the people in Cades Cove are against the logging, too."

Adelaide nodded. "They stay quiet because so many men in the Cove work for the company," she said in a small voice. "But they can see the damage it's doing to the forest."

"That's what we need," Willa said. "The mountain families, the city people, the Cherokee, the Cove folk, the Faeran, the trees, the animals, the mountains, and even the loggers. We're all connected. *All of us.* And none of us can survive alone. If we want to stop the destruction of the forest, we need everyone to work together."

Willa paused and took a deep breath, looking around at her family. "I don't know how to reach all these people out in these distant places, or how to speak to them in a language they will understand. I can't go to where they live. I can't walk on the land that is flat or live in the places where there are no trees. But you can, Father, and so can Hialeah and Iska. And Adelaide can talk to the people in Cades Cove. We need them all."

When she finally finished, her father nodded. "You're right, Willa," he said. "You're exactly right. We don't need four voices or twenty. We need thousands."

Hearing her father's words, and imagining the future he described—a future in which the forest was protected—brought a greater sense of hope to Willa than she'd felt in a long time. But then a troubling thought crept into her mind.

"How long, Father?" she asked. "How long do you think it will take to get everyone together and stop the logging?"

Her father grimaced and shook his head. "I don't know. The Sutton Lumber Company is making a fortune cutting down these trees, and they're not going to give up easily. We have to create the national park as fast as we can, before it's too late."

After the others had gone to bed, Willa went out into the cool nighttime air to think. She climbed the walnut tree in front of the house where she had slept with Charka.

Her mind was still abuzz with everything her father had told her about the humans coming together to protect the forest.

She looked up at the rounded peak of the Great Mountain, lit bright with moonlight. It loomed there, all quiet and powerful, its dark green slopes gazing out across the silent world.

"Is this your doing?" she asked.

Willa remembered the time she had climbed to the mountain's highest point. She'd been crying and lonely, grieving the loss of her grandmother. Looking out across the horizon, she'd seen nothing but mountains in all directions.

She had come to understand since that day that there were worlds beyond her own, worlds that were flat, worlds that had no trees, worlds full of roads and horses and trains. And people—lots of people. And it was these voracious worlds that were consuming the trees of her forest. Would the inhabitants of these worlds truly come together to save hers?

She looked up at the Great Mountain once more. "Is all of this your doing?" she asked again. "Are you showing me the way?"

The power of the mountain was in its size. Its age. Its silence. But the wisdom of the mountain was the life that it brought forth. For a fleeting moment, as she stared at the peak's forested slopes, it felt as if it was answering her.

And the answer was *yes*.

She heard a rustling of leaves below her. "What are you doing out here all alone?" Adelaide asked from the base of the tree.

"I'm not alone," Willa said. "Come on up here."

"This one looks easy," Adelaide said as she quickly scaled the trunk and joined her in the upper branches. *She's gotten so much better,* Willa thought with pride.

"So, you didn't like the bed in the house?" Willa asked her. "It's where my brother, Iska, sleeps when he's home."

"I've never been able to sleep too well in a normal bed," Adelaide said, snuggling with her.

"So you decided to come out to see me," Willa said.

"I know you've got something on your mind. Is it the park? What do you think? Do you believe it could really happen?"

"I believe in my father," Willa replied. "But I don't know about the rest of the humans. I *hope* it can."

"*My* father isn't going to like the idea one bit," Adelaide said.

"I'm sure he won't," Willa agreed.

Curled up together in the tree, they looked out at the mountain and felt the weight of what they knew to be true: the world was a far bigger and far more powerful place than the both of them, and there were many things beyond their control, beyond the control of even their fathers. But feeling the warmth of her sister beside her, Willa sensed that there were some things that *were* in their control, some things that they could try to change for the better.

"I've been thinking that maybe tomorrow morning, we'll go back to Cades Cove," Adelaide said.

"Yes," Willa said, knowing what she was thinking.

"We'll speak to my father."

"Do you think he'll listen to us? Do you think he'll join us?"

"No," Adelaide said. "But we've got to try."

The mist of a light rain coated Willa's cheeks and arms as she and Adelaide walked toward Cades Cove. There was a surprising coolness to the day—autumn coming—and the tiny droplets of water filled their hair. But the mist and the rain didn't bother her. It felt like nothing could bother her. She had reunited with her Faeran sister, built a lair for her people, and freed her father from jail. All the streams of her life were coming together.

"My mother and father are going to be relieved to see me," Adelaide said as the valley came into view.

When they arrived at the back door of the house, Adelaide invited her to come in, but Willa didn't trust human buildings she didn't know, especially this one.

Seeing her hesitation, Adelaide said, "I'll be right back. I just want them to know that I'm all right, and then we'll tell them about the park."

Willa watched through the screen door as Adelaide walked toward her mother in the kitchen. Adelaide had taken on her mother's appearance once more, with her pale skin and long blond hair, but now that Willa was closer, she saw that the woman's skin was wrinkled with age and her hair was going gray.

"I'm back, Momma," Adelaide said softly.

"Oh, Adelaide!" her mother cried out as she turned and embraced her, a puff of flour going up around them. "I was so worried about you!"

"I'm fine, Momma," Adelaide assured her. "I—"

"But where have you been, Adelaide?" Mrs. McClaren asked, holding her by the shoulders.

Adelaide seemed taken aback. "I talked to Father. . . . I told him I had to find my friend. . . . Didn't he tell you?"

Mrs. McClaren blinked and then looked down and wiped her floured hands on her apron. "I'm afraid I'm a mess."

"It's all right, Momma. Where's Father?" Adelaide asked, touching her shoulder. "I thought he'd be home recuperating from everything that had happened."

"Oh no, you know him—there's no rest for your father, especially now." Mrs. McClaren reached out to Adelaide and picked a bur from her hair. "You haven't been in the bushes, have you? The woods have become far too dangerous for any of us to go into."

"Where's he gone, Momma?" Adelaide asked.

"He's been sleeping at the logging camp," Mrs. McClaren said, brushing a small twig off Adelaide's shoulder. "Apparently there's talk about creating some kind of national park that will close the mountains to logging, if you can imagine such a thing. So Mr. Sutton has moved all the crews and equipment to your father's area and given him instructions to cut as much as they can before the government stops them."

Willa couldn't believe her ears. It felt like someone had punched her in the stomach. The loggers weren't just coming back, they were coming back in even greater numbers!

"B-but . . ." Adelaide stammered, as flustered as she was. "But what did Father say to them?"

"There was nothing he could say," Mrs. McClaren said. "He's no longer the foreman of the Elkmont crew."

"What?" Adelaide asked. "Mr. Sutton fired him?"

"Oh no. Mr. Sutton has put your father in charge of *all* the crews, everything the company has. It's a big responsibility, and he's increased his pay, with bonuses for him and all the men if they can meet the new cutting quotas."

"But I don't understand," Adelaide said. "After everything that's happened, didn't he tell them he couldn't do it? Didn't he quit? Where is he now?"

"Quit? Why would he quit?" Mrs. McClaren asked, looking at her curiously. "He has eleven children to feed, Adelaide. Including you."

"I know, Momma," Adelaide said impatiently. "But where?"

"Where what?"

"Where is Father cutting?" Adelaide asked, her voice rising in agitation.

"He said there had been some kind of accident where they were working. It's become too dangerous there. So he's moved all the cutting operations up onto the high slopes on the other side of the river."

Willa's heart lurched. That was her father's land.

"He's breaking his promise!" Adelaide said.

"I don't know what you think you heard, Adelaide, but you know your father would never break a promise," Mrs. McClaren said. "He's a man of his word."

As the two of them argued, Willa heard less and less of what they were saying. All she could think about was warning her father. *The loggers are coming!* For all she knew, they had already arrived, laying train tracks across her father's land, slashing down the trees that lived along the river, and hauling the carcasses down the mountain to Sutton Town.

Willa stepped into the doorway and Adelaide saw her over her mother's shoulder. "Momma, I need to go," she said.

"What? You just got here!" her mother said in confusion. "Adelaide, please, where are you going? It's dangerous out—"

"I'm sorry, Momma," Adelaide said. "I'm grateful for everything you've done for me, but now it's time for me to go." She quickly embraced her mother good-bye, and then dashed out into the rain with Willa, immediately turning the same green color as her sister.

They ran mile after mile through the forest. Willa's legs ached. Her lungs gasped for air. And her entire body was soaked. But she just kept on going, pushing herself as fast as she could. She knew only one thing for certain: her father would defend his land with his life.

55

So tired from running that she felt wobbly in her legs, Willa finally slowed to a walk and tried to catch her breath, panting as she stumbled along, the rain still pelting her and Adelaide.

"I . . . didn't . . . think . . . you'd . . . ever . . . slow . . . down," Adelaide said between heaves, wiping the water out of her face as she walked beside her.

"I think we're getting closer to where the loggers might be," Willa said. And even as she said it, something caught her eye. She stopped and looked down at the rainwater running in little brown streams across the rocky ground.

"What's wrong?" Adelaide asked.

Dread poured into Willa's body. She suddenly felt heavy, like she couldn't move. It was as if she was watching blood trickle across the rocks. The blood of the earth itself.

"The rainwater moving across the rocks in this area is normally clean and clear," Willa said. "But now it's muddy."

"What does that mean?"

Willa's eyes scanned the surrounding forest and the path they'd been following as she got her bearings on exactly where they were. Then she looked up the slope in the direction the water was coming from. If they left the path at this point and trekked straight up through the forest, farther up the mountain, they would end up at the hidden glen where she and Adelaide had seen the synchronous fireflies.

"Come on," Willa said, "we've got to go up there."

As they delved into the forest and hurried up the slope of the mountain toward the glen, Willa kept seeing more and more of the brownish-red earth streaming across the ground.

"What do you think is happening?" Adelaide asked as they climbed.

"Something has disturbed the soil," Willa said, her voice tightening.

As she and Adelaide pushed through thick vegetation and trees, her lungs pulled in faster and faster breaths. It was getting harder and harder for her to breathe.

A gust of wet, blustering wind hit Willa's face. And then they walked into a muddy clearing.

They found themselves staring in shock at a bare slope where a large swath of the forest had been utterly destroyed, all the vegetation and underbrush cleared out and every tree cut down. There was nothing left on the mountainside other than severed stumps, discarded branches, and mounds of thick, sliding mud beneath the pouring rain.

Wiping water from her eyes, Willa looked around, trying to understand exactly where they were. The extent of the destruction made it difficult to recognize what she was seeing, but the wrenching truth slowly seeped into her heart like the mud that was oozing past her ankles. This barren scar upon the land had once been the beautiful, fern-filled, hidden glen of the synchronous fireflies and its surrounding forest.

Beside her, Adelaide was coming to the same realization. Her mouth kept moving like she was going to say something, but all she could muster was a whimper that sounded like a tiny scream. "No . . ." she finally said. "No, it can't be . . ."

Willa stumbled forward, nearly losing her balance in the slippery mud. As she looked out across the devastation, her legs felt weak beneath her. Her face felt hot in the cold rain, not only with the shock and sadness of what she was seeing, but with a seething anger. McClaren had *promised* he'd never go near her father's land!

Willa watched as the mud flowed past them. Without the roots of the trees and other plants to hold it in place, the layers of soil that had taken thousands of years to accumulate were being washed away in a single rain. The dirt was flooding down the mountain, pouring into the streams, and filling the once crystal-clear rivers. She knew that the trout and other fish in those rivers were going to die, and without the fish, the otters would die. Once again, it struck her: the trees, the dirt, the insects, the rivers, the trout, the otters, the wolves, the deer . . . *they were all connected.*

"What's going to happen to the fireflies?" Adelaide asked desperately, even though it was clear she already knew the answer.

"They can't survive this," Willa said, her voice ragged.

"What are we going to do?" Adelaide asked, trying to wade through the mud out into the clearing. "They destroyed it! They destroyed it all!"

"There's nothing we can do," Willa said, reaching out and pulling her back. "The glen is gone, Adelaide. We've got to keep going."

Sliding through the mud and pouring rain back down the mountainside to the path, they ran through the forest.

Soon they came to another area that had been completely clear-cut, not a tree left standing for what seemed like miles. They had no choice but to try to go right through it to the other side.

As they slogged through the vast barren landscape of severed stumps, Willa looked back over her shoulder to where they had come from. She could no longer see the dark green line of living forest behind them. And when she peered forward she couldn't see any sign of the forest ahead, either. She felt her strength withering. She was losing hope. She had never been in a place with no trees.

"Come on, Willa," Adelaide said, holding her shoulders and pulling her along.

When they finally reached the forest, Willa found new strength and pressed on harder than ever. With the wind blowing and the thunder clapping overhead, it felt like she had to physically push through the storm.

She and Adelaide climbed up and over a ridge, and down through a forested valley. They traversed ravines and crossed rivers. Willa's legs throbbed with pain, but she knew she had to press on.

Finally, they began to ascend the long, steady slope that would take them up through a forest of ancient trees to her father's property.

They came upon a narrow slot that had been slashed through the forest with saws and axes. The earth had been covered with a thick layer of gravel. And two long steel tracks had been laid across the ground and spiked onto wooden blocks.

Bile rose up in Willa's throat as she stared down at the tracks. *This is the coming of death,* she thought.

"It looks like the base camp is that way," Adelaide said, pointing along the tracks going down the slope of the mountain.

In the distance, Willa could make out the shapes of wagons, logging equipment, tents, and wooden boxcars that had been converted into living quarters for the men. She could smell their cooking fires and their mules.

When she turned and looked up the tracks, they seemed to go on and on through the woods, in the direction of her father's property. It was like looking at a spear that was flying toward Nathaniel's heart.

A pit formed in her stomach. The logging crews of the Sutton Lumber Company weren't coming from the direction of the Elkmont Camp like she and her father had been expecting.

They were coming from the east, to the back of her father's land, toward the orchards. That meant that the loggers were much closer than she or her father had realized.

"I need to get up there to the house and tell my father," Willa said.

"Go as fast as you can," Adelaide said. "I'll run down to the camp and find my father. I'll try to stop him from doing this."

"Be careful," Willa said.

They embraced one last time.

And then, as Adelaide ran down the tracks toward her father, Willa ran up the tracks toward hers.

Rain spattered against Willa's face as she ran. The wind was blowing so hard she could barely see as she followed the railroad tracks up the mountain. Her feet splashed through the water streaming across the ground.

She couldn't help glancing over her shoulder, worried that she shouldn't have separated from Adelaide. What was McClaren going to do when his daughter confronted him about his lies and betrayal?

As Willa continued up the mountain, she kept wondering where these cold metal tracks were taking her. She couldn't shake the feeling that she was rushing headlong toward some terrible catastrophe.

She came to an area where she recognized some of the trees along the tracks. She was getting close to the back side of her father's property. When the narrow slot abruptly opened up into a much wider area, she crouched and took cover in the underbrush at the edge of the forest.

She was horrified by the scene in front of her. Even through the rain, she smelled the stench of the burning coal. Thick plumes of black smoke poured from the steam engines stationed up and down the slope of the logging site.

A train locomotive sat on the tracks a few dozen strides from where she was hiding. She'd never been this close to one of these mysterious beasts before. The massive hulk of black iron was coated in strange mechanical intricacies she didn't understand. The engine's bowels glowed with fire as soot-blackened men shoveled coal into its burning belly. The raindrops falling onto its hot metal surfaces hissed and disappeared as if the beast could kill even the rain.

Connected behind the locomotive was a long line of iron-wheeled train cars. Steam-powered boom cranes were grasping severed trees in their giant claws and heaving them upward with the sound of groaning metal and grinding gears. As the cranes dumped the logs onto the awaiting flatcars, the earth rumbled beneath Willa's feet.

Once the train was loaded with logs, the locomotive would pull them down the mountain to the sawmill in Sutton Town, where they would be cut into long, thin pieces. There she imagined the figure of Mr. Sutton himself, the great overlord of it all, standing in dominion over his vast factory of death.

Willa knew the locomotive was a man-made construction. But waiting there on the tracks, it seemed more like a living, breathing, hissing monster than a machine, and it would not be thwarted by a storm, or emotion, or the ancient song of the trees.

The horrific sight of sawed trunks, broken branches, and cut-up limbs was everywhere. As she looked out across the carnage, it seemed to stretch on and on, all up and down the mountain, with many crews and machines working at once. It was by far the largest logging operation she had ever seen.

And among the mayhem of men and machines and slaughtered trees, one figure stood out. He was riding a horse through the middle of it all, pointing at the workers and shouting orders at them.

Willa clenched her teeth. Jim McClaren wasn't back at the base camp. He was *here*, supervising his crews as they cut down tree after tree. She had seen his previous horse die, but this new one looked larger and stronger, its powerful haunches moving him easily up and down the muddy slope.

When this human had been wounded and he needed her help, she had guided him safely home. When the wolves attacked, she had protected him. When the spirits of Dark Hollow were about to take his life, she had destroyed them. And now, despite the oath he had sworn never to come to her father's land, here he was. And he had come with many more men and giant machines, all with one goal: to find the largest, oldest, most beautiful trees of the forest and cut them down as fast as he could before his time ran out.

Snarling with anger, she pulled herself back into the forest. She moved quickly through the trees, skirting the edge of the logging site. She had to get up to the house.

But suddenly a rapid burst of gunshots cracked through the air. Willa caught her breath and ducked down into the ferns. The loggers were running and shouting, hiding behind their equipment.

"Get off my land or I'm going to shoot more than warning shots!" a man shouted from somewhere farther up the mountain. Willa's chest tightened. It was Nathaniel!

A group of three guards with rifles took cover behind the locomotive in front of Willa and shot blindly up into the forest.

"We've got you outnumbered, Steadman!" one of the guards shouted. "You've got no chance! Just go home!"

A bullet smashed through the window of the locomotive's cab, raining down glass shards onto the man who had shouted the warning.

"It's going to be your head next time!" Nathaniel Steadman yelled from above. "Take your equipment and get out of here!"

But as more of the loggers grabbed weapons and took positions, Willa could see that there were far too many of them for her father to fight.

She crawled rapidly beneath the ferns and made it to the base of an oak tree, then peeked up toward her father's position.

He was lying on the ground, shielded by an outcropping of rock. Her heart ached to see him there alone against all those other men. He didn't stand a chance.

But as she studied the terrain around him more closely, she noticed the barrel of another rifle sticking out of the nearby bushes. Then she spotted the movement of someone's shoulder. She counted—one, two, three, four . . . There were more than a dozen other men and women with rifles positioned along the ridge. Many of them were her father's age and wore the same kind of slouch hat and plain clothing. Some were older. Others were just teenagers, young boys and girls who must have only recently learned how to fire their rifles. They were the mountain families, the landowners who had come to help their neighbor and protect their trees from the logging company.

"You have no legal right to be here!" her father shouted. "So turn yourselves around and get on back down to the lowlands where you belong before we start shooting more than windows!"

But despite her father's bravery, Willa could see from her position that the logging company's hired guards had no interest in legalities. As Nathaniel shouted at them, a group of men with pistols and knives was creeping their way up the slope to her father's far right. She didn't know if it was Jim McClaren or Mr. Sutton himself who had brought in all these extra men and weapons, but it was clear that the logging crews had come prepared to defend themselves. And they were encircling her father and the others from three different sides, slowly surrounding them.

The situation looked hopeless. *Pull back, Father,* she kept thinking. *Pull back! Go home!*

But then she saw something else, up on the slope to the left, between the encroaching men and her father. It was hard to make out from this distance, but she thought she could identify a girl with long black hair moving carefully from tree to tree, staying low to the ground. Hialeah? And there was someone next to her—a boy, his hair similar to hers. It was Iska! Willa's heart swelled to see him. And then Willa spotted what was behind him. Hialeah and Iska weren't alone. They had brought at least thirty or forty other Cherokee men and women that Willa could see from her vantage point, and there might have been more hidden up in the rocks. Willa pulled in a hopeful breath.

Unlike Nathaniel and the other mountain families, who had brought their rifles and shotguns, the Cherokee were not wielding guns or other weapons. They were standing shoulder to shoulder, their arms interlocked but their hands empty as they moved through the forest, forming a human wall. They were protecting her father and the forest trees with their own bodies!

Tears welled up in Willa's eyes.

You did it, Hialeah! she thought. *You did it! You are the wind!*

Just as they had talked about, Hialeah had run to the Qualla Boundary. She had talked to the Cherokee and convinced them that Nathaniel's battle was their battle, and they should all fight the loggers together.

When the lumbermen saw the Cherokee blocking their path, they raised their pistols.

"Get out of here! Get back! We're coming through!" the loggers shouted, but the Cherokee did not move.

One of the loggers shot over their heads. Another ran at them, brandishing his pistol. "You're gonna get yourselves killed if you stay here!"

But still the Cherokee stood strong.

The gang of loggers moved forward and shoved into the line of Cherokee. The men on each side grappled with one another. Willa saw two of the loggers trying to push her brother to the ground, but Iska struggled against them. Hialeah rushed toward him.

A shuffling sound startled Willa. Whispering voices. Just a few steps in front of her, a new group of men was maneuvering into position, joining those who were already hiding behind the locomotive.

"Stay low," one whispered to the others. "Get your rifles ready!"

These four men looked different from the others. They were dressed in leather skins and carrying much longer rifles, like they were marksmen of some kind. And then Willa noticed that their leader was wearing a ring of bear claws around his neck. *I know this man,* she thought, pushing a blast of air through her nose. He was one of the hunters who had shot across the ravine and killed Charka's mother.

She glanced up toward Iska and Hialeah, but all she could see through the pouring rain was the loggers trying to push their way through the Cherokee line.

The marksmen in front of her broke off from their allies and went skulking up through the cover of the trees to get a better angle of attack on the mountain families.

Willa quickly blended into the trunk of the oak tree beside her and tried to slow her rushing heart. As the men slinked past her one by one, they came so close she could smell their wet leather clothes.

The marksmen used the underbrush and the trees for cover just as she did, maneuvering up and behind the line of resistance that the mountain families had established.

Willa felt like every muscle in her body was pulling taut. Should she try to yell out and warn her father? Would he even hear her through the rain and all the other noise?

Her heart pounded in her chest. As the four creeping marksmen took up their position, she could see that her father and the mountain families had no idea they were there.

Staying low and quiet, the leader of the marksmen issued instructions to the others using hand signals. And then all four of them raised their rifles to their shoulders and aimed straight at her father.

57

As she watched the pandemonium erupting before her, Willa was frozen in shock, helpless.

And then it came to her.

She would not scream.

She would not fight.

Instead, she would show these men the future they were creating.

As strange and wicked a place Dark Hollow had been with its deadly spirits, it had taught her one thing: that the roots under the ground—the roots of the past—were as important and strong as the trunk, and the branches, and the green leaves reaching toward the sun. The past was the soil, the foundation, the nutrients. And inside it, whether it was good or evil, there lived a tremendous power. She had many times asked the branches and leaves of the trees to shroud her and care for her.

But now she would go deep into the ground, into the ancient roots of the world.

Even as she decided what she was going to do, she knew she shouldn't do it. She'd already connected herself to the trees too deeply—to turn death into life when she destroyed the ghosts, to create Green Hollow, to do all the things she had done—and if she kept doing it, there was going to come a point where she'd go so deep that she wouldn't be able to get back. But she didn't care. Her father, her sister, her brother, the mountain families, and the Cherokee were all making their stand here and now to protect the forest. And no matter what it took, she was going to stand with them.

She threw herself to her knees and thrust her hands against the earth. "I need your help, my friends!"

She drove herself down into the roots of the forest, reaching one tree after another.

"I need you to move, my friends, like you've never moved before. . . ."

As the rain poured down and the thunder and lightning crashed overhead, a squall of blowing wind came tearing through the trees. Rainwater flowed between her feet.

No, she didn't scream, she didn't fight. She simply asked the trees to pull their roots from the soil. Let the loggers see what the world would become without them.

All up and down the mountain slope, roots slithered out of the ground, pushing up through the earth and clinging to the bedrock, but leaving a thousand years of soil to fend for itself against the forces of driving rain and wind.

Willa looked toward the four guards aiming at her father. The ground beneath them collapsed. They shouted and dropped their guns, grabbing on to trees and rocks and whatever they could as the rainwater tore the earth from around them.

The entire side of the mountain gave way. Loggers all across the site started screaming "Mudslide!" They knew exactly what it was, because they had caused many before.

In the distance, one of the boom cranes teetered with an iron groan and toppled over, tumbling down the mountain, snapping cables and smashing equipment as it fell. The railroad tracks bent and crumpled under the force of the moving earth. The train cars piled one on top of the other with great, banging crashes, the mud engulfing them as they rolled down the slope.

Men were running everywhere, scrambling up to high ground, grabbing bedrock wherever they could find it.

Beneath Willa's feet, the seeping ground began to tremble and crack. The flow of rainwater came up to her shins. She clung to a rock.

A few strides in front of her, the steel train tracks began to twist and buckle with the swelling wave of mud sliding down the mountain. Rivets popped. Iron bolts snapped in two. The steaming black locomotive that had been indomitable moments before tilted to one side. The guards and coal shovelers who had been using the train for protection shouted and ran, scurrying for stable ground like frightened rats.

She found herself rooting for them and holding her breath as they pulled each other through the mud and clung to the rocks. "Run!" she yelled, half in anger at them and half in fear that they would be hurt. She hadn't intended to kill these men, only to destroy their tools of death. *"Run!"*

The steel of the tracks shrieked as it bent, and the locomotive finally toppled over and went tumbling down the slope, pulling the long line of train cars with it in a landslide of mud and machines. Willa leaped out of the way and hugged the trunk of the oak tree that had attached its roots to the bedrock below.

The train cars crashed into the steam cranes farther down, causing yet another mass of mud and machines to roll down the mountain.

Gasping for breath, Willa looked up at the rocky outcropping where her father had been.

"Everybody get to high ground!" Nathaniel was shouting to the mountain families and Cherokee as they pulled back from their position on the rocks. Willa could see them on the other side of the mudslide, fleeing up the mountain toward safety.

"Run, Hialeah! Stay on rock!" Willa's father shouted. "Iska, look behind you!"

Iska hadn't realized it, but there was a Cherokee woman caught in the mudslide behind him. When he heard his father's shout, he turned back and pulled her clear of the mud, and then the two of them scrambled for high ground.

But as Hialeah, Iska, and the others got to safety, Nathaniel stayed behind, holding on to the outcropping, his feet slipping and sliding in the roiling mud as he looked out across the chaos.

Willa's heart lurched. "You need to run, too, Father! Hurry!" she shouted. But through the rain and wind and screaming men, she knew he couldn't hear her. She also knew the ground wouldn't hold much longer. Not even the rocks. "Run, Father!"

Willa peered in the direction he was looking.

In the distance, she spotted Jim McClaren on his horse, his face stark white with shock as he watched the destruction of his logging site, all his men running and screaming as the trains and cranes and all his other machines tumbled down the mountain.

The giant brown wall of mud came hurtling toward him. He yanked the reins of his horse to flee. He was just about to spur the animal into a gallop and escape, when he saw something that made him immediately pull back the reins.

Willa was confused. Why was he stopping? She glanced up toward her father on the high ground. Nathaniel wasn't looking at McClaren anymore. He was staring at what was behind McClaren, the reason he had stopped right in the path of an oncoming mudslide.

When she turned to look, Willa gasped. To her shock, Adelaide was standing on the slope, a short distance below her father. Just as she had always done, she had followed him. But now she stood paralyzed with fear as she watched a mountain of mud coming down on top of them.

McClaren immediately drove his horse toward her, desperate to reach her. Willa was sure he had no idea why she was there, but nothing mattered to him except saving his daughter.

"Adelaide!" he screamed as the mud came pouring through and hit the horse's legs. McClaren struggled valiantly to stay in his saddle and save his daughter, but his horse was swept right out from under him.

Swimming through shoulder-deep mud, McClaren grabbed on to a large branch sticking out of the torrent. "Just hold on, Adelaide! I can reach you!" he shouted. But even as he said the words, everything around him, including the branch he was clinging to, slid down the mountain and he was swept away.

Willa watched in horror as the wall of mud plummeted straight toward Adelaide. From this great distance, there was nothing Willa could do to save her.

Nathaniel dropped his rifle and leaped from the rocks. Willa shrieked at the sight of him falling through the sky. He hit the ground in front of the landslide and sprinted to Adelaide. He dove toward her and wrapped his body around her just as the wall of mud and debris poured over them. Willa cried out as they disappeared into the moving earth.

Abandoning the safety of the oak tree that had protected her, Willa charged forward, slogging through the thick sludge. "Adelaide!" she screamed. "Father!"

She swept her arms through the debris, frantically searching for any sign of them.

"Father! Where are you?" she shouted. "Adelaide!"

Willa scoured the rocks and mud and broken branches in despair. Her father and Adelaide appeared to have been entirely engulfed. She felt the hope draining from her body.

"Don't give up, Willa!" Hialeah shouted as she came running down the mountain toward her. Her sister hadn't fled to the high ground with the others. She'd stayed to help her father and Willa.

"We've got to keep searching for them," Hialeah said as they came together, clutching each other's mud-drenched bodies.

Feeling a second surge of strength, Willa led the way down the ruined, earthen slope. She and her sister crawled through the mud and sticks, climbing and searching, sometimes on their hands and knees, other times scrambling among the boulders.

But there was no sign of them.

Far below, the steam-driven boom cranes, the hissing locomotives, and the flatcars lay in heaps of tumbled iron. The long steel tracks that had been torn from the side of the mountain lay like muddy, broken sticks.

Looking at the destruction she had caused, Willa felt numb. She had stopped the logging and destroyed the Sutton Lumber Company. But none of that mattered now. She felt the weight of her lost father and sister settling through her body, anchoring her to the earth.

She fell to her knees in despair.

As she looked down, pieces of vine and tendrils of leaves that had been torn asunder by the landslide and were now lodged in the mud began to grow across her hands and up her arms, the shredded leaves becoming whole and green before her eyes. She didn't know if the little plants were desperately looking for her help or trying to console her, but they were renewing themselves around her.

The world had become so still.

The thunder and lightning had passed.

Even the rain had stopped.

Adelaide and Nathaniel were gone.

There was no blood.

There were no bodies.

They were just gone.

Willa looked over at Hialeah, and Hialeah looked at her.

The earth had swallowed them whole.

It seemed so long ago to her now. But days before, when Willa came upon the mother bear looking down into the ravine, should she have saved the cub?

After the band of loggers were attacked, should she have guided Jim McClaren back to his home?

When she was distraught with loneliness, should she have returned to Cades Cove to find the wheat-haired girl?

Should she have destroyed the ghosts of Dark Hollow to save the lives of the loggers?

She had made her choices.

All of them.

And now the results lay before her in a mountain slope of mud. The wreckage of the logging equipment at the bottom looked like a pile of broken metal beasts lying one on top of the other.

All the loggers had fled back toward their camp.

She and Hialeah stood alone on the side of the mountain. Willa didn't know what to say. She didn't know what to do. Her father and sister were gone.

"There!" Hialeah shouted, pointing toward a mound of mud and trees that had collected at the bottom of a ledge.

Willa gasped when she finally saw what her sister had spotted in the broken branches and other debris: a man's pale white hand sticking out of the mud.

"We've got to dig for him!" Hialeah shouted.

Willa and Hialeah got down on their knees and started clawing through the dirt with their bare hands.

"He won't be able to breathe!" Hialeah shouted as they burrowed.

But then they both abruptly stopped.

Willa stared down in shock.

The hand wasn't attached to an arm.

It was attached to what appeared to be a large ball of sticks.

"Keep digging!" Hialeah said as they frantically scraped the mud away.

Willa could see that the sticks that formed the ball were woven tightly together and they weren't brown and dead like those in her old lair. They were green and alive, which meant they had grown just moments before.

"What is this thing?" Hialeah asked with dismay.

Willa put her hands on the ball of woven sticks and said, "Please release him, my friends," in the Faeran language.

The sticks unraveled and came apart. Inside, they saw the

bare, pale white shoulder blade of a man, his shirt ripped from his body.

As they pulled more of the sticks away, they uncovered his back. He was curled into a ball, the bumps of his vertebrae running down his spine in a long, arcing curve.

They kept digging until they reached his head and his arms, which were pulled inward like he was a baby being born.

"It's him, it's Father!" Hialeah said, working faster and faster. "He's got to breathe! We have to get him out!"

Nathaniel's body was badly bruised in multiple places, and there was a bloody wound to his head and his back. Willa carefully removed the mud from inside his mouth and nostrils.

"I can't tell if he's breathing!" Hialeah cried as she desperately wiped the dirt from his face.

His eyes were closed and he wasn't moving.

All the muscles of his body were tightly wound, as if he had wrapped himself around something that he desperately wanted to protect.

After they pulled more of the sticks and mud away from him, the curled-up shape of the man collapsed onto the ground. His arms fell open, and his body lay limp.

They finally saw what he had tried to shield from harm: a small, pale-skinned girl with blond hair.

"Adelaide!" Willa cried out, disentangling her from her protector's limbs.

Knowing it was their only chance, Adelaide had used her Faeran powers to grow the ball of sticks around her and Nathaniel, to encase them in a cocoon just as Willa had done when she and Adelaide were attacked by the black butterflies of Dark Hollow.

When Adelaide gulped for air and sucked in a long, loud breath, Willa clutched her in her arms. "You're alive!"

At first, Adelaide seemed too weak or too stunned to speak. She just gazed around at the bleak devastation. But then her eyes landed on Willa's father. And that's when the words finally came.

"Your . . . father . . . saved me . . ." Adelaide cried, gasping for air between her sobs. "But I . . . couldn't . . . save him. . . ."

Willa knelt over her father's body and examined him, trying to keep her breathing and hands steady. She could see that a fractured bone was sticking out of his shin. Bones in his left arm and hand also looked broken. A large black-and-purple bruise clouded his back where a rock had struck him. There were many smaller cuts and contusions all over his body. But the worst of all was the wound to his head, which was still dripping blood down his face. Seeing her father like this made Willa want to break down and weep, but she pulled in a long, deep breath through her nose and told herself to stay strong.

She leaned forward and put her ear to his bare chest, listening for a heartbeat.

"I think he's breathing," she said to her sisters, "but it's very faint."

"We need to get him to a doctor," Hialeah said, her voice trembling.

"The closest one will be in Gatlinburg or Cades Cove," Adelaide said.

"They're both too far away," Hialeah said.

"Willa, can you do anything for him?" Adelaide asked. "Can you help him?"

Willa mentally sifted through all the different healing plants and ointments her grandmother had taught her about. She could find herbs to slow bleeding, fight a fever, or reduce swelling. But she knew of no plant that could bring him back to consciousness or repair the damage he had suffered when rocks and branches crashed into his head and chest.

"I might be able to give us some time," she said. "But I can't cure these wounds."

"There's got to be something we can do," Hialeah said.

"Let's see if we can carry him," Adelaide suggested.

Hialeah grabbed his head and shoulders. Willa took his legs. And Adelaide supported the middle of his body. The three of them lifted him and tried to carry him through the forest. After a short distance they were exhausted, and they collapsed back down to the ground.

"We can't just give up," Hialeah said, wiping her eyes with the back of her hand.

"Adelaide, do you remember the way to Green Hollow?" Willa asked. "Can you get up there?"

"Yes, I can make it," Adelaide said, nodding.

"I'll slow the bleeding and treat his wounds the best I can, but we need more help. I want you to run as fast as you can to Gillen and tell her what's happened. The clan won't listen to me, but they might listen to you and Gillen together. Make sure you blend into your Faeran form. And get Sacram and Marcas on your side first. They know you. They'll be willing to help. Then maybe the others will follow."

"What should I say to them?" Adelaide asked.

"Tell them we destroyed the machines of the humans. But in time, more loggers will come. You, my father, and Hialeah are the links between the mountain families, the Cherokee, Cades Cove, Gatlinburg, and everyone else who cares about these mountains. Tell Gillen that if the Faeran want to live, they need to help us save this man."

"I'll tell them," Adelaide said.

"I don't know how far Hialeah and I will be able to carry him on our own, but you and the Faeran will need to find us wherever we are. I will ask the forest to help, so look to the trees, and especially the ravens, to guide you."

"Got it," Adelaide said firmly. But then she stopped. Her eyes softened and she went quiet. "Before I go, there's one more thing I need to know, Willa. . . ." Adelaide looked down the mountain toward the logging camp.

"Yes, I saw him," Willa said. "Your father ran into the face of great danger to try to save you. But the mud came and swept him and his horse away. I don't know if he made it. . . ."

Adelaide pressed her lips tightly together, and slowly nodded as she looked at the ground.

"No matter what happened," Willa went on in a softer voice, "and regardless of everything he did, I do know that your father loved you, Adelaide."

Adelaide swallowed hard as she listened to Willa's words. And then she spoke so softly that it was almost impossible to hear her. "I know he does."

Willa watched in silence as her sister looked down the slope into the distance. "If he's . . . If he's still alive . . . they'll take care of him in the logging camp." Adelaide paused and then said it again, as if to assure herself. "They'll take care of him."

Finally, she turned away. She looked at Nathaniel, lying wounded on the ground. And then she lifted her eyes to Willa. "I'll bring our kin as fast as I can."

With that, Adelaide gave Willa and Hialeah one last embrace, then ran up the slope of the mountain and disappeared into the forest.

Hialeah pulled a knife from her belt and began cutting large sections of fabric from her skirt. As she worked, she said, "I saw Iska and the others climbing the rocks on the upper side of the mudslide. So they're safe. If you find me some sticks, I can use them as poles to make a stretcher from this fabric. Then it'll be easier for us to drag Father wherever we need to go."

Willa found two long, straight sticks in the debris.

"I guess we're not going home," Hialeah said as they fastened the stretcher together.

"Not yet," Willa said.

"Where are we going to take him?"

"To a place that's impossible to find."

Willa stumbled, her legs weak and trembling beneath her, her muscles aching with every step. Her hands burned with pain, her skin tearing and bleeding where she was gripping one of the wooden sticks of the stretcher. Hialeah was pulling the other, gasping for breath as they dragged their wounded father up the mountain.

Willa knew that if Hialeah hadn't been there, urging her on, step after step, mile after mile, she would have collapsed from exhaustion and given up long before. But Hialeah was fierce of heart. She just kept going, higher and higher up the mountain, the two of them heaving and dragging and lifting their father.

They made it about halfway before Willa's legs gave out entirely and she could go no farther. It wasn't a matter of choice or decision. She just wasn't big enough or strong enough to drag her father so far, no matter how much she needed to. She and Hialeah lay on the ground in exhaustion, unable to continue.

When a flock of ravens came flying in, circling among the branches of the trees above them, calling and croaking in triumph, an immense sense of relief poured into Willa's body.

She turned to see a group of Faeran walking toward her and Hialeah through the forest.

Gillen and Adelaide were side by side, leading Marcas, Sacram, and at least thirty other able-bodied Faeran.

Adelaide had done it! They had come.

"Alliw said you needed our help." There was a tinge of clan pride in Gillen's voice.

Glancing over at Adelaide for direction, Sacram immediately moved forward and lifted Willa to her feet. Marcas grabbed one of the sticks of the stretcher, relieving a grateful Hialeah, and with Gillen on the other side, they began to pull. Two more Faeran stepped in to lift the back end off the ground.

"This way," Willa said as she led them through the forest. "We have to hurry." Her father was still unconscious, and the grayish pallor of his skin worried her.

They moved rapidly now, the members of the Green Hollow clan taking turns carrying the stretcher. They trekked deep into the hidden coves and forested ravines, making their way across the mountains much faster and farther than any one of them could have done alone.

As the Faeran carried her father, Willa saw something she had never seen before—all her kindred moving at the same speed and in the same direction, pushing and pulling and lifting, synchronized as if they were all one being.

It was a small thing, and she thought that probably no one else even noticed it—they were just working together to do what needed to be done. But her grandmother had told her stories of the Faeran clans of the past and all that they had accomplished. It gave Willa confidence that as long as they had trees around them, these young Faeran were going to survive.

When they finally reached a high, rocky ridge, Willa asked them to stop and set down her father.

From there, they all gazed out onto a vast cascade of blue mountains, one layer of ridges after another, with nothing but misty clouds in between them.

"Where are we?" Hialeah asked. "We've been traveling for hours and it just looks like more mountains."

"We're exactly where we need to be," Willa said. "You and Adelaide and I must go on alone from here."

She quickly checked on her father's condition and then looked at Gillen, Sacram, Marcas, and the other Faeran. "Thank you for your help," Willa said. "I know it's difficult to see it now, but you haven't just saved my father's life. You have also saved our people."

As she and Adelaide said good-bye to their forest kin, Willa noticed Hialeah watching the Faeran with steady eyes. Willa knew that when Hialeah lost her mother, her spirit had been clouded with bitterness for the vile Faeran creatures who had killed her. But now Hialeah was seeing something else, her world expanding into a new understanding, for the Faeran of Green Hollow had come to her father's aid when he needed it most. Hialeah was seeing before her that there were many different kinds of Faeran, just as there were many different kinds of humans—the deceitful and destructive, and the honorable and true.

"We've got to go," Willa said, and the three sisters grabbed the stretcher. They made their way down the slope and into a wall of dense white fog.

"What is this place?" Adelaide asked uncertainly as they entered the mist.

"You're taking us to the healing lake of the bears . . ." Hialeah whispered in amazement, for her mother had told her the Cherokee legend many times.

"It's our father's only hope," Willa said.

"But the story says that only bears can find their way through the fog."

Willa smiled. She lifted her chin to the sky and shouted, "Charka! It's Willa! You've got to come out! You've got to find me!"

"Charka . . ." Hialeah said softly, her voice filled with admiration. "I see what you've done, Willa. . . ."

"She's always got a plan, doesn't she?" Adelaide said.

But even as they were talking, Willa began to worry. Nothing was happening. There was no sign of her friend.

"Charka! It's Willa!" she shouted again. "Charka!"

Still nothing.

"What if he's not here or he doesn't hear us?" Adelaide asked.

Willa wasn't sure what to do. If Charka didn't come to her, there was no way to find the lake that could heal her father.

"It seems like we're just going to have to wait," Adelaide said.

"We don't have time to wait," Hialeah said, an edge of frustration in her voice.

"Charka!" Willa shouted again, growing increasingly anxious.

When she knelt beside her father to make sure he was still breathing, she could feel his heartbeat, but it had slowed, and he felt cold and clammy.

"There!" Adelaide gasped, pointing excitedly.

Willa turned to see a small black shape running toward them through the swirling mist.

Charka came charging through the fog and leaped at Willa so enthusiastically that he tackled her to the ground. The little bear groaned and whimpered in happiness to see her.

"Hello, hello, Charka!" she said as she stroked his muzzle and hugged him repeatedly.

"Well, well, if it isn't the little bear come to our rescue," Hialeah said, obviously pleased to see him and no doubt remembering the scolding she had given Willa when she brought Charka to the house.

"Lead the way, Charka," Willa told him. "We need to get to the lake right away."

They followed the cub through the fog. It was so thick, they had to put their hands out in front of them to move any distance at all without running into a tree or rock. The bear trundled steadily along and they struggled to keep up with him.

As the mist finally began to clear, the healing lake of the bears came into view. It was entirely surrounded by green, forested mountains, and waterfalls poured into its sides.

Willa had been here before, but the lake was far more beautiful than she remembered.

It was clear to her that much had happened since she had left. Uniting Charka with the ancient white bear had rekindled the guardian's waning spirit. Dozens of new bears had come to his call from far and wide, and now they were wallowing in the warm, healing water of the lake and gathered along its shore. Flocks of ducks wheeled across the sky, their glittering wings reflected in the lake's smooth golden surface.

But the white bear had spotted them from a distance and was now charging toward them, growling with anger that of all things, of all crimes, Willa had brought *humans* to the lake of the bears for the first time.

"Get back," Willa said to her sisters as she stepped forward to face the lake's protector head-on.

The massive animal stopped in front of her, rose up on his hind legs, and let out a thunderous roar.

Willa crouched to the ground, her whole body quaking, but she did not give way.

The bear showed his teeth and clacked his jaws. The spittle of his open mouth flung across her cheeks as he threw his head back and forth, bellowing at her.

With her heart pounding and her arms shaking, Willa slowly rose to her feet in front of him and began to speak. "I know that this lake is your realm and your magic, not ours," she said. "But I need your help, my friend."

The white bear growled and lunged. He swatted at the air with his giant claws, angry that she had been so foolish and disrespectful as to bring humans through the fog and to the very shore of the hidden lake.

"I know you believe that humans are not worthy of the lake's healing," she said. "Humans hunt and kill your kin. They eat your flesh. They cut down the forests in which you live. I know all this is true."

The white bear slammed down onto all fours, his ears flattened and his black lips drawn back in a snarl. He was still angry, but at least he was listening to her Faeran words.

"But whether we like it or not, the forest is changing," she said. "Human beings are part of these mountains now, like the trees and the bears and the rivers that flow into the lake. We are all connected. Our fate is tied with theirs."

As Willa spoke, the white bear looked at Hialeah standing behind her and at the wounded Nathaniel lying in the stretcher at her feet. He blew bursts of air through his snout, making it clear that he did not accept what Willa was telling him.

"It is true that if we don't stop the humans from destroying the forest, they will eventually come here and destroy this sacred place. But I beg you to understand that there are some humans who don't want to destroy. There are some humans who will fight to protect this place we love." Willa slowly pointed at

Nathaniel. "He is one of the leaders of those humans. My father is one of the trunks to which all the roots are connected. If he dies, the rest of the forest could die with him."

The white bear gazed at her for a long time, as if looking deep into her soul and examining the truth of her words.

But then his shoulders hunched and he brought his jaws together with a loud snap.

Willa lowered her head. She knew exactly what it meant.

The great bear had been watching over these mountains for five hundred years. In his experience, the humans from across the sea had brought nothing but death and destruction. He had seen so much of the past that he had lost his ability to imagine the future. As wise as the leader of the bears truly was, he could not see what she could see: that this human was worth saving. This man and his daughter, and the others like them, weren't going to destroy the forest. They were the only ones who could save it. The bear's many years of experience had blinded him in such a way that he could only see what the humans had been, not what they were going to become.

And in that moment, as she realized all of this, Willa's heart sank, for she knew the great bear's answer. It was in the way he was standing his ground in front of her and not stepping aside, and in the way he had clacked his teeth.

He was telling her, *No, you cannot bring this man into the healing lake of the bears. He is a human. Let him die.*

62

The white bear had made his decision. And as he turned away, Willa could tell that he expected it to be followed. *Immediately.*

She knew that if she tried to ignore him and quickly drag her father's body toward the lake, the white bear would become enraged and attack. And he'd command the other bears to attack as well. There was no doubt in her mind that they would kill her father, and probably the three sisters who tried to defend him.

"Grab the stretcher," Willa said. "We need to leave."

"What? Wait! No!" Hialeah said, her face erupting with confusion and anger. "We can't leave! The lake can heal him!"

"The white bear will not allow us to approach the water," Willa said, as she and Adelaide grabbed the poles of the stretcher and began pulling it away. "We must go quickly."

"What are you talking about?" Hialeah said. "Why won't he allow us to use the lake?"

"Because our father is *human*," Willa said. "Now come on. Quickly. We must leave."

As she looked down the shore of the lake, she saw the white bear glancing over his shoulder at them just as she and Adelaide were pulling the stretcher into the trees. Seeing that she was doing what he had commanded, he kept walking in the opposite direction, as if he didn't even want to smell the human beings in his vicinity.

But young Charka stayed at Willa's side, and seemed to be as sad as she was.

"We can't just leave. . . . Please, we can't . . ." Hialeah pleaded as she followed Willa and Adelaide into the woods.

Ignoring Hialeah, Willa took a few more steps, dragging her father a little farther into the forest, until the trees and undergrowth concealed all of them from the view of the bears down the shore.

"Here," Willa whispered to Adelaide, and they stopped pulling.

Willa dropped slowly to her knees beside her unconscious father. His breathing had slowed so much that she could barely feel it. His skin had turned gray and his lips were dark. She knew he was almost dead.

There was no chance to get him to a doctor in Cades Cove or Gatlinburg, and even if they could, she didn't think a doctor could save him.

Her father was going to die.

Choices, she thought. *There is one last choice left. . . .*

She knew it wasn't a choice that her father would approve

of. He was going to be very upset when he found out. But once again, it felt like there was no other choice she could make other than to follow the path of her heart.

"I'm so, so sorry, Father," she whispered, resting her forehead against his. But he couldn't help her or guide her. She knew what she must do.

She used to ask herself if her choices made any difference in the world. Should she take this path or that one? Should she save the bear cub or turn away?

She had come this far to realize one truth: we each become the choices that we make.

If we blend into the appearance of a human for long enough, we become almost human, like Adelaide. If we fight to protect something long enough, we become its guardian, like her father. The choices we make in our lives aren't just the paths we take, they are the shape we are turning ourselves into.

She let her hands slip down to the ground and she began to sing. She touched the tree she was kneeling beside, a yellow birch with roots that ran across the surface of the ground. It was Dark Hollow that had shown her the path and power of the roots. And as she closed her eyes and slipped down inside them, she realized that it was too easy. The roots were too ready for her arrival, too ready to take her in.

As she moved through the roots and sang the ancient song of the trees, she asked them to grow, to push through the earth for her one last time. Not to rise up and battle the men of iron. Or to pull themselves from the earth and show the humans what the world would be like without their protection. This time, she was doing it for an entirely different reason: *to steal.*

She had been raised by the padaran as a jaetter, a night-thief, and she had been the best in her clan. *Move without a sound. Steal without a trace.*

The roots grew rapidly beneath the ground, plunging through the dirt and sand, until they reached the edge of the lake. And from there, the roots began to draw the water into themselves.

"Yes," she whispered. "Yes, that's it. . . . Keep it coming. . . . Yes. . . ."

As the water of the lake came toward her, she could feel it, the pressure, the force, the magic of it. It began to fill her.

While Adelaide, Hialeah, and Charka gathered around and watched in confusion, she hunched over her dying father.

As the roots of the trees and the leafy vines attached themselves to her body, Willa began to sob, and in her dripping tears, the water of the lake began to fall onto her father's body.

She had cried so many times before, but she had never cried like this. The tears just kept coming, welling up inside her and flowing through her, as if there was an infinite pool of tears within her.

And they were falling onto her father.

She could feel herself slipping away, down into the soil and the roots of the trees, but she kept going. She had to let the water of the lake flow through her.

She had saved the little bear.

She had found her Faeran sister.

She had built the new Faeran lair.

Like the Great Mountain had shown her, she had done her part.

And now she would do this one last thing, or all would be lost, cut down by the men who were yet to come.

Suddenly, her father's mouth gasped open and he pulled in a long, deep breath. He wiped the dripping water from his face. He moved his legs and arms and he began to sit up, clearly confused about where he was and what had happened to him.

"Dee-sa," Willa said to the roots and the other plants. "That's enough. Stop."

She felt as if she had drowned and was waking from a long, dark sleep. She pulled herself away from her father and struggled to get to her feet.

"What is this place?" her father asked, looking around.

"It's one of the places you're going to save, Father," Willa mumbled, but her vision was too blurry to see him, and she was too weak to go to him. She stumbled a few steps away.

"What's wrong, Willa?" Adelaide said, rushing toward her and trying to keep her steady on her feet.

"Stay with my father and Hialeah," Willa tried to say to Adelaide. "They're going to need your help." But she wasn't sure the words were coming out of her.

Willa took a few more steps, with Adelaide holding her upright. "I just need to walk . . ." Willa said, but her voice was weak and hoarse.

And then she felt something happening to her legs. The soil

beneath her bare feet seemed to be moving. She sensed trembling ferns and vines around her. She tasted the moisture in the air. She could not see with her eyes or hear with her ears in the normal way, but she somehow knew a flock of ducks was coursing across the sky overhead, their wings whistling. She pictured their reflection tracing across the setting sun on the surface of the lake. As the water streamed down her cheeks, the same golden light and the reflection of the birds was there, mixed into her tears.

"Willa, tell me what's wrong," Adelaide said desperately. "What's happening to you?"

Willa crumpled to the ground. Vines and grasses grew over and around her body. The roots of the surrounding trees connected to her.

She felt her limbs touching the soil.

"I love you, Adelaide," Willa whispered.

"No, no, no!" Adelaide cried out in despair. "Don't tell me that! Stop it! Make this stop!"

Nathaniel and Hialeah came rushing over, and her father tried to hold her.

"Willa, don't leave us . . ." he said, his voice filled with pleading and astonishment.

She heard the voice of her father.

She heard the song of her crying sisters.

She felt the sunlight on her skin.

She felt the earth in her bones.

She felt her roots in the soil.

She felt the breeze swaying her limbs.

And she felt the water coursing through her and rising toward the light.

They all gazed upward.

A man.

A human girl.

A Faeran girl.

And a young black bear.

They all gazed upward at the tall and glistening tree that had grown beside the lake, its green limbs outstretched toward the golden light of the setting sun.

THE END

Acknowledgments

It took more than thirty years, but through the hard work and commitment of visionary Americans working together, the Great Smoky Mountains National Park was established in 1934. To this day, it remains one of the largest, most visited, and most beloved protected places in the world.

This book is a work of historical fiction/fantasy. But if you're interested in the time period, please research the real-life heroes who helped form the park, including Horace Kephart, George Masa, John D. Rockefeller Jr., and the citizens of North Carolina and Tennessee. I would like to thank the U.S. Department of the Interior, the Great Smoky Mountains National Park, the Great Smoky Mountains Association, and the Friends of the Smokies for their support and encouragement with *Willa of the Wood* and *Willa of Dark Hollow*. Special thanks to Steve Kemp, an expert in the Great Smoky Mountains, who helped me with many of the historical and botanical elements of the story.

For the sake of pacing, I compressed certain timelines and details. For example, in 1901, when the story takes place, industrial logging was just getting started in the region, and Elkmont Camp didn't take on that name until a bit later.

Thank you to my friends and colleagues in the Eastern Band of Cherokee, especially to Esther Taylor, the wonderful media coordinator at Cherokee High School, and Bo Taylor, a renowned Cherokee storyteller, who provided advice and consultation on both novels in the Willa series. I've included Cherokee characters in my stories of the Blue Ridge Mountains because I have the deepest respect for the Cherokee people and wish to honor them in every way I can.

I want to thank my wife, Jennifer, who helps me develop and refine my stories, and who is the much-appreciated first reader/editor of each draft I write. We met in a writing workshop twenty-six years ago, and she's been helping me become a better writer ever since. I also want to thank my three daughters—Camille, Genevieve, and Elizabeth—who have always been an important part of my writing.

Thank you to Stephanie Lurie, my awesome editor at Disney Hyperion, and to Emily Meehan, the VP/publisher extraordinaire at Disney Hyperion, and the whole Disney Hyperion team, who have always been so supportive of me as a writer.

Finally, I would like to thank my freelance editors, including Sheila Trask, Sam Severn, and Jenny Bowman. And thank you to my literary agent, Gail Hochman; my foreign agent, Marianne Merola; my publicists, Scott Fowler and Lydia Carrington; and my TV/film agents, Brooke Ehrlich and Geoffrey Sanford.

ALSO BY ROBERT BEATTY

Serafina and the Black Cloak

Serafina and the Twisted Staff

Serafina and the Splintered Heart

Serafina and the Seven Stars

Willa of the Wood